I0733807

Also by Roger Neumaier

Imprints from an Odyssey
The Cuban Girl
Alex in Deutschland
A Home in the Bitterroot
Joseph Imagines God
Poetry and Reflection
What Happened to Him
The Green House

More information about each of these books is available at https://neumaierbooks.com

The Weimar Journals

---

*A Confluence of the 1920s
and the 2020s*

By Roger Neumaier

Cover Photo by Roger Neumaier

Published in Paperback and eBook, November 2025.

Printed in the United States of America

Library of Congress Control Number: 2025923267

ISBNs: 978-1-956920-19-2 (paperback);
978-1-956920-20-8 (eBook)

*Those who do not remember the past
are condemned to relive it.*
— George Santayana

Preface

7/4/2025— Introducing Myself

Over a century ago, my grandpa served in the Kaiser's army. After the Great War ended, Grandpa returned to Berlin and married Grandma. Berlin, the capital of the Weimar Republic (the German republic that existed between 1918 and 1933), was overwhelmed with political and economic chaos. In 1922, my grandparents, along with their young son, my father, immigrated to the United States to escape all of that chaos.

Grandpa's surname was *Braun*. When the family arrived at Ellis Island, the immigration clerk wrote *Brown* on the family's immigration papers. And *Brown* it has stayed.

In Berlin, Grandpa worked as a machinist. But his dream in the new country was to own a farm. That's why the family moved to Billings, Montana. Grandpa had heard that land was cheap in Montana, that they were almost giving it away. He wanted some of it.

After arriving at Ellis Island, Grandpa put his small family onto a train, and they made the long journey across the country to Billings. For one reason or another, Grandpa never ended up buying that farm. Instead, he used his skills as a machinist to repair horseless carriages. In 1927, Grandpa opened his own automobile repair shop where he worked until the day he died.

My name is Hans Brown. Until a few years ago, my home was in Billings. But after my wife passed in 2014, I retired and moved upstate to Great Falls.

The Weimar Journals includes entries selected from my personal journals written over the past fifty years. It also includes descriptions of a series of unusual dreams, letters from the first half of the last century from my grandma's sister, Ilse, and several newspaper articles and historical notes.

There are two sections in *The Weimar Journals*. The first brief section, *Project Beginnings,* includes a few journal entries that explain how this book came to be. The second section, *Entries, Dreams, Letters, & Historical Notes,* contains my journal entries, pretty much in the order I wrote them. Interspersed among these entries are my grandma's sister's letters, my dreams, a couple of newspaper articles, and several historical notes about the Weimar Republic.

I hope you enjoy reading *The Weimar Journals* as much as I enjoyed assembling it.

Project Beginnings

7/30/1969— My First Journal Entry

My buddy Bruce transported troops into and out of some pretty severe battles along the Mekong Delta. A week ago, I saw Bruce sitting on his cot, bent over and writing in a little black book. I asked him what was up.

In his usual slow and easy southern drawl, Bruce said, "I'm making an entry into my journal, Hans. I'm describing today's medevac mission. It was pretty damn intense."

I think I just replied with a *Huh?*

He explained, "Whenever something upsets me, when it's gnawing at my gut, I write it down— describe it in my journal. That reduces my stress. I've kept a journal now for about four years. It always helps."

I asked, "Could I see what you wrote?"

Bruce chuckled and replied, "Sorry, Hans. I never share anything from my journals— not with anyone— ever. That's the secret to always feeling comfortable writing it down. I don't worry about anyone judging me— or asking stupid questions about why I wrote what I wrote. I can be totally up front about whatever's tearing me up— you know— in my gut."

Bruce closed his journal, gave me a thoughtful look, and added, "You ought to try it, Hans. You might find it works for you the same way it works for me."

I asked, "What happens when you die? Aren't people gonna read it then?"

Bruce gave a soft laugh and said, "Today, I'm dealing with the stress of piloting a Huey into a hellhole. In fifty years— after I am gone, if someone reads my journals— or even if I get blasted out of the sky tomorrow and someone reads them sooner, I won't give a damn. Won't be a problem."

The next day, after Bruce returned from the commissary, he handed me a black journal and a ballpoint pen. I opened the journal. Its pages were blank— the only writing was inside the cover where Bruce had written, *Give it a try, pal. You might like it. Writing in a journal is like having a buddy you can always count on, one who understands and will never share your secrets. Keeping a journal is like putting a scrapbook together. You can look back on it at some point in your life and read the word pictures you wrote will describe the points in your life that were once important to you.*

I thanked Bruce, told him I might give it a shot. Later that evening, I placed the black book at the bottom of my footlocker. It had been a nice gesture. However, keeping a journal wasn't my cup of tea.

This evening, I learned Bruce's Huey was shot down this morning, with no survivors. I've lost a few friends here in this crazy war. But losing Bruce— that has really hit home.

I decided to go ahead and try writing in the journal— Bruce's last suggestion to me. I pulled that little black book out of my footlocker and began to write. This is my first entry.

I will miss Bruce— more than I ever could have imagined.

Bruce, if somehow you are aware that I am giving your journal idea a try, if you can know what I am writing in it, well, thank you, pal, for your friendship. It meant a lot to me.

8/8/2016— A Neighborly Invite

In January, a couple of days after I moved into my home here in Great Falls, my next-door neighbors, Ronnie and Sandy Swenson, came over, introduced themselves, and welcomed me to the neighborhood. Along with some kind words, they brought me a home-baked apple pie. The Swensons are good people.

Since then, while working in our yards, Ronnie and I have chatted over the picket fence that separates our properties. I've learned we have a lot in common. Ronnie was raised in Great Falls and has lived here his whole life. He went into the service after high school and served in Vietnam. After his tour of duty, he came back to Great Falls and married Sandy, his high school sweetheart. A week later, Ronnie went to work for his father, who owned a Great Falls insurance brokerage. When Ronnie's dad passed away, Ronnie inherited the brokerage. A few years ago, he sold it and retired.

Ronnie invited me over for a beer today. I mentioned that it's been difficult making friends here in Great Falls. He told me that once a month, he gets together with a few of his buddies from high school. He and his friends graduated together in the class of 1967— the same year I graduated. They all played together on the Great Falls High School football team.

Ronnie asked me if I wanted to come to one of their coffee get-togethers. I could meet some of his buddies. If I were interested, I was welcome to join their group. They call themselves *The Bison Coffee Roundtable*. The group is named after their high school football team, the *Bisons*.

I didn't hesitate in accepting Ronnie's invitation. It's been pretty lonely around here.

8/15/2016— The Bison Coffee Roundtable

This morning, Ronnie and I walked over to the Electric City Coffee House. It's a nice little coffee shop on Central Avenue. The coffee and pastries are pretty good, and I appreciated being introduced to Ronnie's friends.

There are six members of the Bison Coffee Roundtable. They were all born in the same year as me— 1949. They've known one another since grade school and played together on the Great Falls High School football team. There used to be more members in the group, but a few have passed away. That may be part of why Ronnie was so welcoming to me, even though I hadn't gone to school or played football with them.

Ronnie sat at the head of the table. I was next to him. Jim, who still works part-time as a bank security officer, was on my right. Next to him was Doc Brennan, a retired doctor. I don't know Doc's first name. Everyone just calls him *Doc*. Jack sat at the end of the table opposite Ronnie. He ran a local hardware store until it closed a decade ago. Steve was on Jack's right. He is a retired construction worker. And Jerry, who retired from Montana's Highway Patrol, was across from me.

The group may have attended high school together, but after that, their lives went off in different directions. Jack went to a private Christian college in Minnesota. I don't know what he studied. Doc got both his bachelor's and medical degree from the University of Washington.

Both Jack and Doc had student deferments during the Vietnam War. All the other guys enlisted right out of high school and went to Nam. After serving, Ronnie got an associate's degree from Montana State here in Great Falls. The others didn't go to college.

The group's sports conversations were a nice change of pace for me. Everybody at the table was a Yankees, Twins, or Mariners baseball fan. The group likes to talk about the Great Falls' high school football team— the Bisons. I gathered that this year's football team is supposed to be better than last year's.

There was also a brief discussion about politics. It focused on Donald Trump. Everyone who spoke up supported Trump except for Doc.

I enjoyed hanging out with the group. As we walked home afterwards, I told Ronnie I'd like to be included in their get-togethers in the future.

Ronnie gave me a thumbs-up.

12/7/2016— Making a Friend over Coffee

I woke up to a bright and sunny morning. I decided to walk over to downtown Great Falls and treat myself to a latte and a pastry. As I stood in line at Electric City waiting to order, I heard someone call out my name. I looked over my shoulder and saw Doc, one of the guys from the Bison Coffee Roundtable. He invited me to join him at his table after I ordered my drink. A few minutes later, we were talking about how nice Great Falls is. Doc was suggesting a few things to do around the Cascade County region.

After we had spoken for about ten minutes, Doc looked at his watch and said he had to run. He told me we should get together for another cup of coffee soon— at a time when he didn't have to rush. We agreed to get together next week.

I'm pleased. I've been pretty lonely, not knowing hardly anyone around town. The only people I know well enough to have a halfway decent conversation with (other than my daughter Jeannie and her family) are a few of my neighbors and other members of the Bison Coffee Roundtable.

12/15/2016— Coffee with Doc

I got together with Doc for coffee today. It was a pleasant visit. We told each other about our backgrounds. I told him about losing Mary and moving here. I was impressed. Doc is a good listener. He asked a lot of questions about my childhood including a few questions about my grandparents. He said he was interested in them because they came from Berlin. He told me he had gone to a conference in Berlin a few years back and found the city fascinating even though he couldn't speak any German.

Doc told me I should make that trip someday. I responded that it was a good idea and maybe I would.

Doc told me about his life as well. He grew up in Great Falls. He was the quarterback on the Great Falls High School football team. He also ran the hundred-yard dash and, as a senior, went to the Montana State high school track finals. Doc said he was offered a scholarship to play football at North Dakota State. But his father was a doctor here in Great Falls and wanted Doc to also become a doctor. So, Doc ended up studying at the University of Washington, where he got his bachelor's and medical degrees before returning to Missoula, where he served his residency and met his wife. After that, he returned to Great Falls and provided family medical care to locals for almost forty years. Doc retired a year ago. He told me he missed his patients but was glad to be away from all of the bureaucracy, the paperwork, and the insurance companies.

Doc gossiped a little about other members of the Coffee Roundtable.

"This group of guys is pretty conservative," he said, "and I understand why. Most of them went off to Vietnam right after graduation, like you did. Three of our high school football pals didn't make it back from the war. And Steve, he almost lost his life after he stepped on a land mine. In the last few years, the economy has been hard on Jim and Steve. They've been on unemployment a lot. And Jerry's wife left him a couple of months before he retired."

I listened and absorbed. Doc seems like a pretty good guy. We agreed to try to get together for coffee again soon.

2/1/2017— Coffee, Doc, Journals, and Dreams

Over the years, when something meaningful happened to me, I found the time to describe it in my journal. Each time one of my black books filled up, I put it away, bought a new one, and continued my occasional journal entries. Over the last fifty-plus years, I've filled a dozen of these

black books in that way. I've written about a lot of things—
my marriage and the joy Mary and I experienced when
Jeannie was born; the death of Mom, Dad, and Mary;
problems from work; conflicts with those close to me; and
an occasional interesting dream.

Several dreams (occurring years apart) were about an
imaginary young couple in Berlin during the 1920s and
1930s. Those dreams were pretty amazing. When I woke
up after each of them, I would get out of bed and write up
the dream right away— often in the middle of the night.

Until recently, I hadn't ever mentioned those Berlin
dreams to another person. In fact, I had never shared even
one journal entry with anyone— ever. But about a week
ago, I broke my rule. I mentioned the series of dreams to
Doc. After I spoke about one of the dreams, Doc asked me
if I always remembered dream details so clearly.

I laughed and told him, "Each morning, my grandma
had me tell her about my dreams. Probably, because of her,
I got better at remembering them as I got older. Often, the
only things I could remember were vague, and I'd start to
forget what occurred in them. But Grandma would push
me to remember the dream. She told me that after I awoke
from an interesting dream, as I lay in bed, I needed to
think through every detail I had observed. She told me I
should try to recall each thing that happened in the dream
in the order it had happened. Grandma told me that if I did
this, my ability to recollect what I had observed in the
dreams would improve. She said that remembering dreams
is a good kind of discipline."

After I said that to Doc, I stopped speaking for a
moment as I reflected on how Grandma had taught me so
much— and how heavily she'd influenced my life.

I looked back at Doc and added, "I retained that discipline even after I entered the military. When I woke up after a meaningful dream, I'd go over the things I'd noticed in the order in which they happened in the dream. Once I started keeping a journal, if a dream was worth remembering, I'd just get up and write it down in my journal— even if it was the middle of the night. I probably write up one or two dreams a month. The ones I don't write up? Even if I sit in bed remembering and thinking them through— I eventually forget 'em."

I thought about it for a moment. I'd never really considered how well I remembered those dreams. I had just done what my grandma had told me to do.

I elaborated. "I still struggle to remember some dreams. But these? The ones that took place in Berlin? They stand out. When I wake up, the details are so vivid, Doc. They are much easier to recall than my other dreams— almost as if the event had just happened in front of me and I had been wide awake throughout it. And it is weird how one Berlin dream would always pick up the story from the last— with the same characters— their lives moving forward through the nineteen-twenties and thirties."

Doc gave me a look as if he was wondering whether I was bullshitting him. I think that's because Doc is a retired family physician. He had told me he'd gotten used to people making up stories— creating fantasies to explain or justify a health complaint. Doc told me he was never afraid to challenge a patient's stories in order to find out what really happened.

Anyway, Doc started giving me the third degree, peppering me with one question after another about my Berlin dreams.

"Were your dreams about people or places your grandparents had described to you? Maybe you'd read books about the twenties and thirties in Berlin and Germany? Perhaps your subconscious was reassembling details from things you had read or that your grandparents had spoken about? Are you sure you didn't see some movie that inspired this series? Maybe you thought about each dream so much afterwards that it inspired you to sort of extend what happened— embellishing details over time and imagining that they fit together into a complete story?"

I thought about his questions for a couple of minutes as I sipped on my latte.

Then I responded, "Yes. My grandparents often spoke about Berlin. But they left Germany in 1922— before any of my dreams took place. My grandma's sister, Ilse, remained in Berlin. But the dreams' clarity, Doc, the way they followed one another— coming out of the blue, separated sometimes by months and other times by years— that's what seems so weird. And as far as embellishing the dreams, I wrote each one down in my journal as soon as I woke up. They were fresh recollections when I recorded them."

I was digging my hole deeper and wider. But admitting that I had documented them in my journal— that was my big mistake.

Doc sat up erect, was silent for a minute, then asked, "Can I see those journal entries?"

"Nope, Doc." I didn't even hesitate in my response. "A buddy of mine in Nam— the guy who first turned me on to keeping a journal— he advised me back then, *never share a journal entry with anyone— ever.* I have taken that advice literally. So, sorry, Doc. I won't share them with you either."

Doc wasn't about to be denied. He spoke about how fascinated he was with dreams in general and how mine seemed especially unusual. Doc told me he wanted to learn from my dreams. He promised not to share anything he read with anyone, adding that as a medical doctor, he'd spent his whole career keeping personal secrets.

Doc worked on me for a while. When he was done stating his case, I was a little overwhelmed.

I said nothing as I gave his request some thought. I had known Doc for a while. He'd always seemed like a straight shooter— and his last point was pretty compelling. As a medical provider, Doc had been required to keep all sorts of secrets.

While I sat silently, trying to figure out how to respond, Doc stared at me.

Finally, I said, "OK, Doc. You win. I'll let you see two or three of the dream entries."

This evening, I went down to my basement, opened my trunk of memories, and pulled out a few old journals. Over the years, after I filled up a journal, I'd put that black book away and start a new one. I never read through old entries. As I looked through the journals taken from the trunk, I was surprised by how many entries each journal held.

As I read through a few of the entries, I chuckled. I could see Mr. DiPasquale's impact on my writing style. The only activity I participated in in high school was the school newspaper, and DiPasquale was our sponsor.

I remember DiPasquale telling me, "Hans, you need to write the facts. Readers want to know what happened. They don't want to know how you felt. They want to know what occurred. Always remember the mantra, Brown, not ideas about the thing, but the thing itself."

I chuckled as I remembered how often he had repeated that. But I could see in the journals that he had drilled it into me. As I went through my journal entries from decades ago, I saw his huge impact on my writing style.

Anyway, I went through the journals, page by page, looking for Berlin dream entries. When I finally found one, I realized I couldn't share it with Doc. He wouldn't have understood it. In fact, he wouldn't be able to understand any of those Berlin dream journal entries. I had written all of my Berlin dreams in the German language, and Doc has already told me he couldn't speak a word of German.

If I were going to share any of these dreams with Doc, I would have to translate them into English. I emailed Doc to let him know that the dreams had been written in German. I knew I would need to explain to him why they were in German and how I learned to speak the language.

Below is what I emailed to Doc:

How did I learn to speak German? In my Grandparents' home, only German was spoken. Grandma never had any desire to learn English.

My parents both worked. Grandma started taking care of me on weekdays when I was just a month old. Each morning, Mom would carry me across the street to my grandparents' home. I would spend the day with Grandma who only spoke German to me. As I got older, I walked over to my grandparents' home before I went to school.

Grandma always fixed my lunch bag and would send me off to school. After school, she had a piece of apple strudel and a glass of milk waiting for me.

I loved the fascinating stories Grandma would tell me about growing up with her sister Ilse in Berlin. She would put on wonderful puppet shows for me and read me Grimm's Fairy Tales— all in German. As I got older, I would tell her about my days in school— also in German. To this day, I can speak German as well as I can speak English. When I saw that I had written my dreams in German, I wasn't surprised. I just hadn't anticipated it.

A few days later, when Doc and I got together, I brought three journals that had Berlin dreams in them. I showed Doc the journals in the original German. Then I translated each dream entry aloud. After I finished the third one, I looked up. Doc had a weird look on his face. I wasn't sure what it meant.

"Extraordinary!" he said. "I'm fucking blown away."

Now, I had never heard Doc swear before. I wasn't sure how to take it.

"Let me explain," he said. "As a young man, I was fascinated with dreams. I was particularly intrigued by Freud and Jung's theories. In college, I read a few books about them. I even did an independent study on what drives dreams. That old fascination is what drove me to give you the third degree about your Berlin dreams. After hearing a few of them, I can tell you my appetite has grown. Your dreams go way beyond anything Freud or Jung ever wrote about in the books I read."

He took a deep breath and slowly let it out. Then he looked out the Electric Coffee Company's window. When he looked back at me, he asked, "Would you be willing to translate— in writing— each of the dreams you had about these Berlin folks? I mean all of them?"

I recognized that I'd stepped into something I had wanted to avoid— and I was sinking. I thought about what my buddy in Vietnam had said. He was probably looking down on me, laughing. Bruce had given me some solid advice, and I had ignored it. Now, I was paying the price.

I sat there, thinking about Doc, about my dreams, and about translating them into English.

I asked myself, *What would be the downside of spending a few days putting together those translations? I am retired. Since Mary passed, I've been here in a new city doing very little. I haven't formed any new friendships or relationships. And ever since I finished remodeling my home here in Great Falls, my life has been pretty empty. It is winter. Football season has ended. Baseball season hasn't started, and I have a ton of time on my hands.*

The other factor, I am embarrassed to admit, was that I was flattered by Doc's interest.

As I pondered how to respond, Doc continued to watch me intently.

What tipped the scales? I think it was my own curiosity. How would these dreams come off when read one after another?

"OK," I responded. "I'll type up translations on my laptop."

We agreed to get together in a week.

That was when Doc threw another gigantic fly into the ointment.

"After you complete those translations," he said, "could I borrow your journals for a few days? I mean all of the journals. I'll focus on your typed translations. But if I could also go through the rest of your journal entries, I would gain context for your dreams. I'll be better able to understand them."

This time, Doc had definitely asked too much.

I shot back, "No, Doc."

I paused and qualified my *no* (which was another error on my part). "I won't say *absolutely not*— at least not yet. I will give it some thought. But you are asking for a lot, Doc— too much. This is a big deal to me. You are a nice guy— I like you. But my journals are my most personal possessions. I'll give it some thought. I'll translate the dreams, which in itself is a big deal because I've never shared anything from my journals with anyone— ever. We can get together next week. I'll bring printouts of the translated dreams. When we get together, I'll let you know whether I'm willing to share anything else from my journals."

Doc thanked me. We finished our coffee drinks and headed off into our separate worlds.

2/3/2017— Translating Dreams

For the last couple of days, I've been working on translating my Berlin dreams for Doc. As I work, I keep coming back to the questions Doc asked me.

How is it that my memories of these dreams were so clear? How could the dreams that happened over multiple years link together almost like a television series? Was there any historical basis for the events I watched in those dreams? And how accurate were the details I saw of the city of Berlin?

I don't think I've ever read a book about Berlin or Germany's history. My grandparents' descriptions of the city were limited to personal experiences they had had— in their homes— and with their families. They never described Berlin's architecture or the people's styles of dress. And they certainly didn't describe the politics that took place during those years before Hitler came to power. In any case, they left Berlin long before those dreams.

If I weren't the one who had had the dreams, I would wonder if whoever told me about them might be making them up. I understand why Doc had his doubts, and I can't find an explanation for how those dreams happened as they did.

This is particularly on my mind today because last night, I woke up after having a different sort of dream.

In that dream, I was fixing up my house. But it wasn't my Great Falls home. After I woke up, I wondered if maybe the dream was about my home in Billings. However, that wasn't the case. The home in the dream was modern.

I woke up and sat on the side of my bed, wondering about the dream. I considered writing it up in a journal entry. But I couldn't remember enough of the dream to make it worth writing down. My memory of it wasn't nearly as clear as my recollection of my Berlin dreams. So, I just went back to sleep.

The next morning, I remembered the dream about fixing up a house. But all I could recall after I woke up was what I just described.

It occurred to me that I had been truthful when I told Doc that my Berlin dreams were always much clearer and easier to remember than my regular dreams. The skill of recalling dreams that Grandma taught me all those years ago is pretty much gone— except when I dream about Berlin.

I have no explanation for this.

2/8/2017— My Response to Doc

After I told Doc about my Berlin dreams, I started paging through my journals, identifying each of them. I've found fourteen separate Berlin dreams in the journals. I've gone ahead and translated all of these dreams into English. After I finished, I read through the series, one dream after another. I was blown away by how tightly they fit together into an almost seamless story.

Today, when Doc and I got together at Electric City Coffee, I handed him a folder containing the translations of my dreams.

He thanked me and said, "I've been looking forward to these since we last spoke. The three dreams you shared last week wet my appetite. Now, I'm excited to go home and read the complete set."

He hesitated, took a deep breath, and said, "As I told you last week, it would really help me understand your dreams if you allowed me to read through your journals. Your other journal entries might give me more insight into what other issues in your life might have inspired your dreams. Those entries would help me understand if your Berlin dreams were out of the blue or whether they were normal responses to other events in your life."

I'd thought about his request all week and was ready to respond.

"Over the past almost fifty years," I replied, "I have filled twelve journals with things I felt were important in my life. Before I let you read them, Doc, I need your word that you won't share anything from those journals with anyone. I'm not saying this because there are things in the journals of which I'd be ashamed. It's just that what is in them is so personal."

Doc gave me a serious look before saying, "I absolutely understand what you are saying, Hans. You have my word."

We shook hands on it. I told Doc he could stop by my place this evening and pick up the journals.

This evening, when Doc picked them up, he told me, "I read through the translations of your dreams. Geez, Louise! Hans. They fit together! This whole thing has turned into some sort of mystery that is so much more thought-provoking than I ever could have dreamt— no humor intended with my choice of that word."

I recognized his wording was an accident, but laughed anyway.

We agreed to get together for coffee in two weeks, at which point Doc will return my journals.

2/22/2017— Doc Offers One More Idea

Doc and I got together today.

We were at our regular table at the Electric City Coffee House, waiting for our coffee drinks to be prepared, when Doc said, "Your journals were totally engrossing. What an amazing window into your life! The entries also provide a frame of reference for your dreams. Your grandparents—particularly your grandmother— stand out. I see her inspiration for your dreams about Germany. However, that doesn't explain how the characters from your dreams got so developed or why they return to you in successive dreams— years apart— forming such a complete and continuous story!"

Doc looked down and shook his head before saying, "I kept asking myself as I went through the journals, *Where do these dreams come from?* I can't get my head around that question, Hans. I've reread sections from books by Jung and Freud and confirmed that neither of them ever referenced a patient with such a structured, continuous set of dreams. And the dream about Nietzsche? Hans. Where in the hell did you learn about Nietzsche?"

I laughed and replied, "I don't have a clue, Doc. I've heard people talk about philosophers all my life. In Nam, guys spoke about just about everything. I probably heard a few conversations about philosophy there. Names like Socrates, Aristotle, Kant, Thurber, Plato, and a few other names ring bells. I may have heard the name Nietzsche there. You know, some GI might have been talking about Nietzsche, and because I was so stoned, I don't remember it now. But honestly, I can't recall a time that I heard his name."

Doc chuckled as he said, "It's just amazing. By the way, Thurber wasn't a philosopher— at least I've never heard him called a *philosopher*. But the dream about Nietzsche makes my point. You dreamt a meaningful and informed dialogue about a complex philosophical issue. How can that be? It makes my point that your dreams are way the hell out there."

Doc paused, looked down while shaking his head from side to side again.

"Despite all you've said," he continued, "about your grandma having you recite your dreams, it amazes me that you were able to recall them so clearly. I know some people train themselves to recall dreams. But, as you said, you only remember your Berlin dreams completely. Why? If I didn't know you better— and if I hadn't seen you actually translate three of your dream entries—, I might accuse you of making this all up."

I heard my name called out by the barista, and I walked over and picked up my coffee.

After I returned to our table and took a sip of my latte, Doc threw another curveball at me. "That leads into my next brainstorm. Brace yourself. I've spent most of my waking hours since we last spoke reading and rereading the translations of your Berlin dreams and going through your journals. The more I read this stuff, Hans, the more I try to figure out how you did it— and the more amazed I become. Like I said, I just can't grasp it."

He stopped speaking. I figured he was trying to figure out what he was going to say next— or how to put it. I waited.

Doc began to speak in a measured voice. "What I want to suggest— and don't react to this too quickly— is that you take your Berlin dreams along with some other journal entries that highlight your family's background and assemble them into a single document— a case study. What you have experienced in your dreams, Hans, is so unusual, it would be a tragedy not to share it with others."

"A case study?" I asked. "Doc! First, you promise to never share any of my stuff with anyone. Then you want me to publish the whole damned series of dreams? Where are you coming from?"

I was upset— almost angry. This had quickly become something totally bizarre. Doc had begun to ask a lot more from me than was either fair or reasonable.

Doc replied, "Hold onto your hat, fella. I know that anything you write down— every aspect of your journals— they're yours. But I had this one more idea. I want to reiterate— I gave you my word I wouldn't violate your privacy in any way, and I won't. That being said, I am trying to encourage you to recognize what an unusual gift you have been given in these dreams— a gift that dream experts would be amazed by and could learn from. But that being said, they're your dreams. This is your life. I can come up with a lot of ideas. But you can ignore every goddamned one of them. I gave you my word that the journals— the dreams— are sacrosanct. I will respect that. But I didn't promise not to encourage you to share them yourself."

He stopped speaking and scratched his head for a moment.

Then he gave an odd look and said, "OK. My original idea was a case study. But I was just thinking that if you threw in some additional historical notes about Germany during that period— you know, about the Weimar Republic— you might be able to publish your document as a book. Your dreams tell a profound story of Germany in the 1920s and 1930s, a period with a bunch of similarities to what we are going through in the USA today."

By now, I was laughing. Any sort of serious response would probably have led to anger.

"Doc," I said, "I'm glad you're finding my journals interesting. But what you're suggesting here is just getting more nuts all of the time. I don't want to share my personal stuff. I'm no writer. I'm not a historian. And I like my privacy!"

Then I chuckled and added, "And I have no clue why you'd use a word like *profound* to describe anything I dreamt."

This time, Doc chuckled.

He shot back, "I hesitated suggesting the book idea because I anticipated that response. But you're wrong, Hans. You'd have a ball putting it all together. You've complained more than once that your life is empty since your wife passed away, that you wish you had a hobby. I am willing to bet that if you tried this, your life wouldn't seem so empty."

Doc looked at me for a second, then added, "And I'd he be glad— no, I'd be thrilled— to review your drafts— and to offer feedback. I'd actually edit your book— if you wanted. I've edited a series of articles about rural healthcare that were published by the University of Montana. And with my wife's assistance, I self-published a small book I wrote on ethical conflicts in modern medicine. Of course, no one ever bought the book. But writing that book was one of the most satisfying tasks I ever took on."

Doc stopped speaking and sat there, watching me. It was my turn to shake my head from side to side.

After a minute, he said, "Just consider it."

We drank our coffees in silence.

Doc slid over the shopping bag, which he was using to transport my journals as he returned them. As I reached down to pick the bag up, I saw two thick hardback books on top of the journals.

I took the two books out of the bag and held them up, asking, "What are these?"

"Whether you take me up on my suggestion or not," responded Doc, "you'll find these books interesting. They will give you some perspective on what you dreamt about—on life in Germany in the nineteen-twenties and early thirties. They might even give you some insight as to why I am so fascinated with your dreams."

One of the books was entitled *Before the Deluge; A Portrait of Berlin in the 1920s*. The other was *The Rise and Fall of the Third Reich*. I had heard of that book before.

I put the books back into the grocery bag.

Doc started speaking about a vacation he and his wife, Anne, were about to take. They were going on a two-week vacation to Hawaii. For that reason, he explained, we couldn't get together for a few weeks. As far as I am concerned, that is the best news he could have delivered. While Doc is sunning himself in the tropics, he can't be trying to manipulate me into writing some damn book about my personal dreams.

Doc looked at his watch and said, "I have to go now. I told Anne I would go with her to a community meeting. Thanks for listening to my ideas. I know I get ahead of myself sometimes. If you want to drop this whole thing, that's fair. I will respect your decision. But take a look at those two books. You might find them interesting."

A couple of minutes later, we headed out of the coffeehouse.

I'll look at the two books Doc lent me. They might be interesting. And I won't totally ignore his book publishing idea. But my strong feeling is that his idea just doesn't make any sense. During the time Doc and his wife are sunning themselves in the tropics, I'll be putting together a clear and convincing explanation as to why I won't be writing any books.

3/5/2017— Giving It Thought

It's been cold, windy, and snowy ever since Doc took off for Hawaii. I've spent the last few days sitting on my oak rocker, in front of the wood stove, sifting through a half-century of journal entries. As I read these entries, distant memories return; fleeting recollections of smoking dope and partying in Viet Nam; happy times with Mary and Jeannie; and the closeness and comfort given me by Dad and Grandma.

I decided I might as well read the books Doc shared with me. They may help me understand the circumstances that caused my grandparents to leave Germany. Both books were thick.

Even though I have just begun *Before the Deluge*, I can see that Doc was right. What the author wrote gives me insight into what my grandparents experienced. It also lends credence to the characters in my Berlin dreams. These books will help me understand the letters Grandma received from her sister, Ilse, who remained in Berlin after my grandparents left. Ilse's letters, in addition to laying guilt trips on Grandma for leaving, describe the challenges of living in Berlin during the Weimar Republic.

I keep thinking about Doc's suggestion that I write a book. As I consider the amount of time it would take, one thing stares me in the face— how empty my life has been since Mary passed. I do have the time. I haven't told anyone how depressed I've been, but it's hit me hard. I am here in a new town by myself, working to give each day some sort of meaning. There is no doubt that Jeannie loves me. But between her job and the kids, she's pretty busy. Jeannie recently suggested I should find a hobby.

And, I guess, that is what Doc did as well. He suggested writing a book. Doing that wouldn't cost a cent. And if I started to write a book, then decided it wasn't right for me, I could quit it any time I want.

Who knows? Maybe I could write an interesting book. As Doc said, my dreams about that young Berlin couple are sort of fascinating. And I have all of those recollections of conversations with my grandparents about Berlin after the Great War, as well as the letters Grandma received from her sister after Grandma and Grandpa came to Montana. I could even use information from the books Doc shared with me to make sure my historical notes are accurate. And Doc offered to provide free advice—, to edit the book.

But the major reason not to take on this project is that I don't know the first damn thing about writing a book. OK. I got good grades from Mr. DiPasquale in high school English. But DiPasquale was the sponsor of the school newspaper, and I worked harder on that newspaper than any other kid. He probably gave me the good grades just to keep me working hard on the paper.

And my PC word processing program will spellcheck and grammar check anything I write. Those were challenges I used to have with the paper. Still, I'm no historian. I got Bs and Cs in world history and haven't looked at a history book since high school.

If I want to start a project for which I am skilled, I could buy a run-down classic automobile. I've considered purchasing something like a '56 Chevy Bel Air. I could restore it. Now that's a project I've dreamt about taking on ever since I first considered retiring. And this is the perfect time to do it. Or I could build a garage. I have the space in my backyard. The winters are cold here, and I could really use a workshop. Building a garage would be a fun, low-risk project that I could do well.

On the other hand, if I decided to do the writing project, I could end the project whenever I felt like it. Even if I finished writing a book, which I expect would be mediocre, I could just burn the damn thing in my fireplace.

If I take it on, I certainly won't tell anyone about the project (except Doc, of course). Because any book I write will most likely be pretty bad.

3/6/2017— I Decide on a Plan

I need to remind myself how relieved I was after I sold the auto shop and retired. Working with my hands had become so painful! This morning, the arthritis in both hands was killing me. I took a couple of Ibuprofen; however, my hands still hurt. It's a good thing I haven't taken on a project to restore a car or build a garage. The physical pain resulting from either of those projects would overwhelm me.

After giving Doc's suggestion a lot of thought, I've decided I have nothing to lose by taking on the book project— nothing except for time, which I've got more of than I know what to do with.

I moved my laptop out of my bedroom and placed it on the kitchen table. Next to it, I've stacked my journals covering almost half a century of my life.

I'm ready to dig in.

I've begun the first step, which is to go through all of my journals and put yellow stickies on each page that has a journal entry that should be considered for inclusion in the book. I'll type up each of these yellow stickied entries into a Word document. Later on, I can figure out the order in which to put them.

Most of my journal entries will not be included. I began keeping a journal in July of 1969, and I'll include that first entry. But the next entry I've preliminarily tagged is dated a year later. It is at the end of that first journal.

I'll continue writing journal entries as I have in the past. New entries included in the book should be selected for inclusion in the book using the same criteria I am using for all of the old entries.

But what is that criteria? What is the theme of the book? Doc said he thinks the theme of any book I write will become *self-evident*. What the hell does that mean? I certainly don't have a clue. Maybe, if I ever finish the book, I'll figure it out.

Entries, Dreams, Letters & Historical Notes

8/27/1970— Mom's Illness

I received a letter from Dad today. He wrote that Mom's illness has taken a turn for the worse— a pretty ominous statement. I used a military radio patch to call Dad. He told me how ill Mom is. I told him I want to come home, that I could get an emergency leave.

"No, Hans," he told me, "I appreciate the offer, but there's nothing you can do to help. The folks at St. Anne's have been supportive, and Grandma is taking good care of me. Right now, it's a comfort knowing you will be coming home to stay at the end of your tour of duty next summer."

7/15/1971— Life Decisions

I enlisted in the army back in '67, right after I'd received my high school diploma. Since I was already a pretty skilled mechanic, they gave me a two-month crash course in chopper mechanics and assigned me to the Da Nang Air Base. I have been here servicing Bell Helicopters ever since. The choppers I work on transport troops into and out of combat. These missions are dangerous. The lives of troops and flight crews depend upon the quality of my work.

Now, after two tours of duty, I'm burned out, ready to return to Billings and settle down.

As soon as Dad was old enough to know the difference between a wrench and a winch, Grandpa put him to work in the service station. Except for the four years he served in

Europe fighting the Nazis, Dad has worked there ever since. When Grandpa died in '62, Dad took over the shop. A couple of years later, I started working there after school.

Dad told me he hopes that after I leave the military, I'll return to work at the shop. He said he'd make me a partner. At the time, I told him I'd think about it. I also considered enrolling at Montana State University and getting a teaching degree. In high school, I had a couple of really cool teachers who inspired me a lot. I gave some thought to becoming a teacher myself and passing on the excitement my teachers had given me.

But I'm already 22 years old. Starting college now doesn't make a whole lot of sense. I'm not willing to put off beginning my real life for another four years. I should be proud that I'm a skilled mechanic and not feel like I need to learn a whole new profession. I'm ready to get on with my life.

When I return home, I'll follow in the footsteps of Dad and Grandpa.

I went steady for three years with my high school girlfriend, Mary. We have continued to write to one another since I enlisted. During leave last winter, we went cross-country skiing and had a great time. We talked about maybe getting married someday. A couple of weeks ago, I wrote Mary and proposed.

Yesterday, I called her.

Yeah team! Mary and I will get hitched this fall.

11/10/1971— Mary and I Tie the Knot

Wow!

On Saturday morning, Mary and I said our vows. It was great that so many high school buddies could come to our wedding and to the reception at the Northern Hotel. It was so much fun!

A month ago, Dad blew our minds by giving us an incredibly generous wedding gift. He gave us a check for two thousand five hundred dollars! Dad's gift quickly turned into a down payment on the ten-year-old, three-bedroom rambler that Mary and I had been looking at. Our new place is on half an acre just outside of town. The lot is large enough to have a big garden and for me to build a two-car garage and workshop. And we are going to get a dog.

Mary and I are putting off our honeymoon for a few months. Instead, we will move into our own home next week.

Boy, am I ever excited.

12/1/1973— Some Special Letters

Grandpa died more than a decade ago. After that, Grandma moved in with Mom, Dad, and me. Grandma may be suffering from arthritis now, but her memory is still as sharp as a tack. I love spending time with her.

Since Dad's home is just a few blocks from the service station, I walk over at lunch each day and have a bowl of soup with Grandma. While we eat, Grandma tells me about her morning, and I tell her about mine. Grandma shares childhood memories of playing with her little sister, Ilse, and often reminisces about her beloved Berlin in the good old days, before the Great War changed everything.

Today, Grandma was telling me about the chaos that dominated Berlin after the war and how it caused her and Grandpa to emigrate to the US. I've heard a lot of that before. Grandpa used to angrily say that France, the communists, and the Jews used the Treaty of Versailles to destroy Germany. I remember him saying that if it weren't for that damn Treaty of Versailles, he and Grandma might still be living happily in Berlin.

Grandpa hated the Jews a lot. I challenged him once. I asked, "Why, Grandpa? What did the Jews ever do to hurt you?"

Boy, was that ever a mistake. Grandpa's face turned red, and he angrily told me the Jews were a bunch of devils, that they plotted to do all sorts of terrible things, and finally tricked Germany into surrendering to the Allies. Grandpa said that if it weren't for the Jews, Germany probably would have won the war. I never brought up the Jews to Grandpa again.

Yesterday, Grandma and I were drinking tea from the beautiful tea cups she had carefully transported from her home in Berlin. The gold-trimmed white china cups have red, pink, and yellow hand-painted roses.

As I sipped tea, I told her, "I love these cups, Grandma."

"Yah, Hans," she said. "The pattern is called Rosenthal Bavaria. Your great-grandpa and great-grandma received a set of these dishes as a wedding present. I remember how pleased I was when our Sunday dinners were served on that wonderful set. I am so appreciative that my father allowed me to bring these two cups and saucers with us when we came to this new world."

After we had sipped tea for a couple more minutes, Grandma began to reminisce about things her younger sister Ilse had written to her in letters years before. "Ilse was seventeen when Grandpa, your dad, and I left Berlin to come to America. Ilse's letters were my only connection with the old country— other than these cups and saucers."

This was the first time Grandma had mentioned receiving letters from her sister. I asked her if she still had any of the letters.

"Of course," she replied. "Of course, I have the letters. Ilse was my sister. You think I would throw away letters from my only sister?"

"Could I see the letters?" I asked.

Grandma gave a pensive look. Then, without another word, she slowly took her cane from where it was leaning against the kitchen table, stood up, and made her way back to her bedroom. Several minutes later, she shuffled back into the kitchen holding a stuffed, legal-sized envelope, which she handed to me.

I carefully slid out a series of neatly folded, handwritten letters from the envelope. I opened one letter and glanced at it. It was written on very thin paper in blue ink with a beautiful German script. I read through it quickly, then spent a few minutes glancing through the stack. Dates on the letters ranged between 1922 and 1950.

"Did you receive any letters from Ilse after 1950?" I asked.

Grandma didn't respond immediately. When she did, her voice expressed sadness.

"No, Hans," she said. "My sister Ilse never recovered from the illness she described in the last letter. She passed away a half year after she wrote it. Grandpa and I learned of Ilse's passing from the proprietor of her rooming house. Her letter informing us of Ilse's death included the name of the church that managed her interment. Grandpa contacted the church to learn the location of her grave. We were able to have a respectable headstone placed above my dear sister's remains."

We were both quiet for a while. I looked at my watch. It was time to return to work.

Before I left, I asked, "Could I borrow the letters, Grandma? I would appreciate the opportunity to read them."

Grandma made me promise to take good care of the letters and to return them soon.

This evening, after supper, I read the letters.

It was amazing to follow the changes in Ilse's life in Berlin between 1922 and 1950. The earlier letters described the difficult times she and her father experienced in the months after Grandma left. Later letters described economic, cultural, and political changes that occurred in Berlin before World War II. There was a gap in the letters between 1938 and 1945. She probably was unable to send letters to the United States while Germany was at war. After the war, the letters resumed. What a window into the past!

I will return the letters to Grandma tomorrow.

2/18/1975— Jeannie!

I'm a Daddy! Jeannie is so small— so delicate. When she cries, she demands my attention. Wow! Mary and I are the luckiest parents in the world, and we happen to have the world's most beautiful daughter.

Mary went into labor last night. It was two in the morning when she cried out from our bathroom, "Hans. My water just broke. Get dressed. Start the car." All of that planning for how we would calmly go to St. Vincent Hospital was quickly forgotten. I was suddenly filled with panic.

"Are you OK?" I asked.

"Yes. Warm up the car. I'll be out in a couple of minutes."

I threw on jeans and a sweatshirt, grabbed my wallet, keys, and the small suitcase Mary had packed weeks before, and headed out to start the car.

Fifteen minutes later, we pulled up in front of the St. Vincent Hospital emergency room. I got out of the car, grabbed a wheelchair, and rolled Mary into the emergency room. After wasting half an hour at the front desk giving our life histories, we were taken to a hospital room. A nurse instructed me to count the minutes between Mary's contractions. A short time later, the nurse returned and told us the doctor would be at the hospital in a quarter of an hour.

The nurse told me, "Your wife needs to pace herself."

I wasn't sure what the hell that meant. However, I was certainly wise enough not to repeat it to Mary.

A couple of hours later, at 5:30 in the morning, I was standing in front of Mary, holding our beautiful baby daughter. Mary was exhausted. But she looked up at us and smiled.

11/30/1975— Grandma's Passing

I've been really sad.

Grandma passed away last week. She was 83 years old.

The last few days have been tough. I've been thinking about the close connection I had with her and Grandpa. If you walked into their home when I was a kid, you might have thought you were in Germany. Grandma always was cooking something good in her kitchen. She prepared wonderful dinners for us of sauerbraten or Wiener Schnitzel, dumplings or spaetzle and gravy, and red cabbage or sour kraut.

Grandma never bothered to learn English. Once, she told me, "Why would I want to learn English? Who else do I want to speak with, except your grandfather, your father, and you?"

Grandma often spoke about her memories of Berlin. She described going for Sunday picnics in the Tiergarten; strolling down the Unter den Linden boulevard, where so many fashionable men and women paraded in front of high-class shops and hotels. She described what it was like to walk along the Spree on a sunny afternoon, watching families passing in small wooden boats. Grandma rarely emphasized the sadness of having been separated from her father and sister. But when she spoke about her family, her voice betrayed her. There was always a sadness.

Dad has said very little since she passed. Grandma was always so loving to him, and he depended on her so much after Mom died. Grandma kind of held everything together for him. Now, for the first time in his life, Dad is living by himself. This weekend, Dad will be here, sitting on the rocker, holding his baby granddaughter, Jeannie, while we watch the Packers play Chicago. And Mary will cook up a big Sunday meal for us. But it just won't be the same without Grandma.

We will all miss her.

Historical Note, 4/29/2018— The Weimar Republic

In reading *The Rise and Fall of the Third Reich* and *Before the Deluge,* the books Doc had recommended, I learned about the Germany that my grandparents chose to leave. Before reading them, I hadn't appreciated the circumstances my grandparents faced in 1922, and I did not understand the conditions that surrounded Hitler's rise to power. Based upon what I learned from these books, I put together the following high-level review of what preceded and followed my grandparents' departure from Berlin.

During the Great War, social and political changes were already affecting expectations of the German people. This was especially true in Berlin, where German activists, inspired by the Russian Revolution, wanted to overthrow the Kaiser. Meanwhile, Russian artists, intellectuals, businessmen, members of the Czar's former court, and non-Bolshevik socialists were flocking to Berlin to escape the radical changes happening in Russia. They brought with them cultural excitement and new political ideas.

The impact of the Great War on Germany was devastating— both spiritually and economically. Three percent of all Germans died in the war. Twenty percent of all Germans served at some point in the Kaiser's army. And when the war ended, ten percent of the German population was still in uniform at the front lines. When the war ended, the German people were shell-shocked, and Berlin became the epicenter of that distress.

In November of 1918, what had begun as a small strike by naval seamen in the Northern German port of Kiel spread across Germany. This strike grew into a revolution driven by Germany's defeat in the war, distrust of the Kaiser's government, economic hardship, and the desire for changes in the country's social and economic system. Most Germans favored gradual changes, but some pursued a socialist revolution similar to what had occurred in Russia.

On November 9, 1918, the monarch of Germany, Kaiser Wilhelm, abdicated, and his administrator, Germany's chancellor, resigned. The German monarchy had ended. Two days after the Kaiser abdicated, Germany and the Allies signed an armistice ending World War I.

However, the Treaty of Versailles, which formalized the end of the First World War, was not actually signed until July of 1919. This treaty was unilaterally imposed upon Germany (rather than negotiated). It dictated significant territorial losses for the German nation; limited the size and scope of future German armies; and established extraordinary financial compensation that Germany was required to pay to the Allies.

In January of 1919, the citizens of Germany voted to elect representatives to a new National Assembly, which was tasked with creating a new German constitution and government. This newly elected national assembly was dominated by moderates and liberals.

Due to political demonstrations, strikes, and assassinations occurring in the City of Berlin, the National Assembly met to convene in a small central German city named *Weimar. The Weimar Republic* was named after this city where Germany's new constitution had been written, even though, once complete, the country would be governed from Berlin.

The Weimar Republic's new constitution expressed many democratic ideals. It proclaimed the equality of all men and women; promised voting rights for all adult citizens; and protected freedom of the press and speech. This constitution guaranteed collective bargaining, unemployment compensation, and the rights of mothers and children. These rights were laid out in principle in the constitution. But few details of how they would work and at what level they would be implemented were spelled out. That ambiguity eventually led to huge political, economic, and social conflicts throughout the Weimar Republic.

This new democratic republic was to be run by an elected president who would appoint a chancellor and cabinet. The president, chancellor, and cabinet would be accountable to a democratically elected parliament.

The constitution included a major escape clause. If the president of the republic declared an emergency, the constitution granted him or her the power to authorize the chancellor to govern the country by decree. That meant that once an emergency had been declared by the president, the chancellor could establish or change laws that governed the country without any parliamentary review. Emergency authority was enacted by the republic's president in 1930, three years before Hitler came to power. This eventually became one of the primary tools that allowed Hitler, once he had become chancellor, to establish totalitarian rule.

The amount of Treaty of Versailles reparations that the Allies dictated to Germany was thirty-three billion dollars. That is the rough equivalent of two-thirds of a trillion dollars today— an enormous amount for a country that had just seen its wealth and economy devastated by the Great War. This debt required annual payments which resulted in extraordinary inflation in Germany and overwhelmed the country's economy during the early 1920s. Inflation was so severe that in November of 1923, one American dollar was worth over four trillion German marks! These reparation payments drove an ongoing weakness in the German economy which eventually became a critical factor in the far right's toppling of the Weimar Republic.

5/30/2017— Background Note on Ilse's Letters

I got together with Doc this morning to discuss a section of my book draft that I had shared with him last week.

After we sat down at our table, rather than asking how I was doing or making any comment about my writing skills, Doc asked, "Do you have access to Ilse's letters?"

"Sure," I responded. "After Grandma passed away, I asked Dad if I could have them. He'd never even seen the letters and had no interest in them. Dad told me, 'Go ahead. Take them.' I did, and I've had them ever since."

Doc replied, "You might want to include a few of them in your book."

My gut reaction was that these letters were private correspondence— between Grandma and her sister. However, after considering his suggestion, I've realized I could review the letters, make sure there isn't anything in them that is too personal, and if not, they might fit nicely into the story I am trying to weave.

I hadn't even looked at Ilse's letters in years. When I got home, I went down to the basement and retrieved them. After reading through them, I realize that Doc's suggestion is good. Some of those letters should definitely be included in the book.

This evening, I will start translating Ilse's letters.

Ilse's Letter, 5/30/1922—Her First Letter

Dear Gisa,

This morning, I received your letter. It gave me joy to hear that your voyage to America was safe and that you have arrived in Montana. When I read how Dieter became so ill during the ocean voyage, I was fearful. Learning he recovered before arriving in Billings was a relief. The boat trip across that vast ocean and the train ride across America's endless plains sound amazing. America is so large!

It is wonderful that Dieter found employment so quickly. Will he try to acquire a farm soon?

I have so many questions. Is the rugged western frontier safe? Are there savages? Are Americans as rude as I have been told? I heard that they are especially hateful to Germans. Is that true?

The two paper dollars you enclosed with your letter were a wonderful gift. You said you regretted not having more to send to us. But you should realize that this amount made a huge difference for Papa and me. It was sufficient to pay our grocer the amount we owed and to buy cabbage, potatoes, and sausage sufficient for a large pot of *kohlsuppe.* Papa and I will savor that soup throughout the coming week. I promise to think of you, Dieter, and your lovely son as I taste each spoonful.

Each day, Papa receives his pay in paper Reichsmarks. I wait to meet him as soon as he leaves work. We immediately shop for whatever affordable provisions we can find in the grocery bins. Without Papa's modest earnings, we would surely starve.

On the day you left Berlin, I watched your train slowly pull away from the *Hauptbahnhof*. I was so sad. I knew I would miss you so much. But my real dread was that I would have to bear Papa's angry fits alone. Indeed, Father's moods are as difficult to manage as ever. One day, he will tell me how angry he is that you and Dieter left us. He often refers to you as his *selfish daughter*. But a day later, he will tell me how much he misses you. You will always be his special angel.

How smart you were to leave this crazy city and our even crazier father.

However, my difficulties here in Berlin should not be your problems. I don't blame you for leaving. You and Dieter have your lives ahead of you. You will find wonderful happiness in America. My challenges will be my fate.

One month from tomorrow, I will complete my studies at the lyceum. Father agrees that I must end schooling and seek employment. I am fearful I will not be successful. There are so many soldiers who fought valiantly in the Great War who still have not found work. I am fortunate that Father is secure in his position driving the trolley. God save us if he were unable to work.

I miss you so much, Gisa. Please write as soon as you can.

Your loving sister, Ilse

A Dream, 9/14/1976— A Student and a Demonstration

I woke up at four this morning. I had just had a remarkable dream.

The dream took place in a city. At first, I had no idea which city this was. I just felt lost— almost dizzy. I was walking along a narrow thoroughfare with shops and cafes on one side of the street and a large office on the other. All of these businesses had signs with German names. An old-fashioned automobile and an occasional horse and buggy drove past me. The vintage of the cars told me that the dream was probably taking place in the nineteen-twenties.

I didn't recognize any of the people who walked past me. They were all dressed in an outdated manner. Many of the men wore old-fashioned bowler hats or newsboy flat caps. Some were in suits, others in workman's outfits. Most of the men had mustaches or beards. Women wore long skirts or shapeless dresses that went down well below their knees. Many of them had on old-fashioned hats.

At the end of the street, I could see a crowd of men chanting something while marching along a wide, tree-lined boulevard that intersected the narrow street I was on. I walked toward them. Some women near me on the sidewalk hurried away from the marchers.

When I arrived at the boulevard, I saw expensive-looking restaurants and shops fronted by large glass windows full of merchandise. There were even a couple of grand-looking hotels to my left. Every business had a company name printed in large letters on its front window or on the sign hanging over its front door. All of these names were in German.

In front of me, hundreds of men marched down the broad boulevard carrying signs protesting their government's reduction of benefits for people in need. The marchers were chanting in German, "Stop Breaking the Constitution's Promises." Some marchers, dressed in worn jackets and old-fashioned newsboy caps, looked like rank-and-file workers. Others, dressed in wool coats and dark bowlers or fedoras, appeared to be of a higher economic class. When I looked off to my left, I realized I was in Berlin, Germany. Several blocks away was the city's most famous monument, the Brandenburg Gate. Then I realized that the thoroughfare in front of me had to be Unter den Linden, Berlin's central boulevard.

I heard a commotion and looked behind me. Another group of men was advancing toward the boulevard. Its members were tough-looking fellows dressed in worn clothing— some of them were in old military coats. Many of these men carried large sticks and clubs. They ran past me shouting slogans as they passed me and emerged onto the boulevard. When they got there, they attacked the marchers I had seen at the beginning of my dream. Those men fought back. It was a vicious battle. Men were knocked to the street. Some from each group were injured, their faces dripping blood, their shirts turning red. And all around this confrontation on the boulevard were police dressed in old-fashioned uniforms. They pointed their rifles down at the ground as they watched the battle— and made no attempt to stop it.

A clean-shaven young man stood next to me, watching the action on the boulevard. He had a knapsack on his back and wore a leather jacket with a flat cap.

"Karl," one of the marchers from the first group yelled at him. "Karl Becker. Why did you choose to abandon us the moment the nationalist thugs arrived?"

The young man turned to the marcher, raised his arms with open palms facing the marchers, and hollered back, "Sorry, Yorg. I cannot afford to be arrested again. If I miss one more class at the university, I have been told I will be expelled. And, if my factory boss learns I participated in another demonstration, he will remove me from my job. Sorry, Yorg, I cannot afford to get thrown out of the university or to lose my job. I have no choice. I must leave."

The young man named Karl Becker turned his back on the chaos and walked away.

I woke up and lay in bed, marveling at how everything in the dream had seemed so clear. I looked over. Mary was still asleep. I quietly got out of bed, grabbed my journal, tiptoed out of our bedroom, and went downstairs. I sat down at our dining room table, where I am now finishing a description of the dream in my journal.

2/10/1978— Dad is Gone

I'm grieving as I write this entry. Dad died this morning. I am at a loss. Both of my parents are gone now. My grandparents— they are gone. Life seems so empty. Everything seems suddenly to be so utterly strange.

The ringing of our phone woke us up at three this morning. The hospital nurse told me Dad was having trouble breathing. She said I should come right away. Mary and I were at Dad's bedside within half an hour. He was struggling to breathe. It was painful to watch. Minutes later, it was over. My father was gone.

Dad moved in with Mary, Jeannie, and me two years ago. We enjoyed having him here. At dinner, Dad would quiz Jeannie about her day and ask me how the business was doing. On weekends, Dad and I would watch ball games together, drink a few beers, and demolish a huge bowl of buttered popcorn.

Dad and Grandpa were the ones who taught me how to repair engines. Even after Dad retired, he'd come into the shop at least once a week, look over my shoulder, suggest which wrench I should use, and sometimes tell me to advance an engine's timing a little bit or adjust the carburetor's idle mixture. I would stop whatever I was doing and listen. Afterwards, I'd thank him. I loved having him visit the shop. I'm going to miss that.

Jeannie will be three in a few days. She is too young to understand that her grandpa won't be with us anymore. Mary's folks passed away years ago. She had a special bond with Dad. I see she is hurting as well. But she sets her pain aside and has been supportive of me.

Mary understands how empty I feel.

Life can be hard.

2/19/1987— Jeannie Rebels

Jeannie is twelve. She is an excellent student, has plenty of friends, and plays clarinet in the school band. But Jeannie tends to know it all and regularly tests our patience.

After dinner this evening, Mary asked her to clear the table and put the dirty dishes in the dishwasher. Jeannie told Mary that she just didn't have time— she had to go out to meet a friend. Mary didn't like that a whole lot and told her as much. Jeannie responded that things have changed since Mary was young, that she has to have some freedom, and that a twelve-year-old needs more spending money than we give her.

Things escalated. Mary asked Jeannie why she needed more money. Jeannie's face clouded up and she said she doesn't need anyone to tell her how to spend her money— or any other advice for that matter. Then Jeannie broke down in tears and headed up to her room— ignoring the dirty dishes.

Mary told me I need to speak with Jeannie. Needless to say, that conversation didn't go really well. There were tears. And after that, there were more tears.

Jeannie is right. Things appear to have changed since Mary and I were her age. I am not sure I like the changes.

Ilse's Letter, 6/3/1923— Life in Berlin

Dearest Gisa,

It was wonderful hearing from you. I am happy that you and Dieter have found such a beautiful apartment. It is also wonderful that Dieter prospers in his employment.

Life here continues to be full of challenges. I have been trying everything imaginable to make the days more bearable for Papa and me. Your generous gifts have made a huge difference. The five dollars you send us each month is so important for our survival. It seems that the dollar bills grow in value every day compared to the German mark.

You would be proud of me, Ilse. I am no longer your plump baby sister. The benefit of not being able to buy more food is that I eat less. My body has become thin! I look much healthier. Some have said I look sexy! Now, if I only could afford to purchase a fashionable outfit.

Unfortunately, hard times continue for the German people. Each day brings new challenges. You and Dieter were so smart to leave Berlin. As I ride the tram to work each day, I see so many hungry men. They stand at street corners looking for handouts. Many of these men still suffer from injuries incurred in the war. Some have lost an arm or a leg. Each wounded warrior must be hoping someone will stop and give him a few pfennigs to buy a piece of bread.

Why must the French and the Belgians punish the German people? Why can't they reduce the amount of poison in the Treaty of Versailles? What hate motivates them to cause our pain? Even worse, I have heard at work about Germans— people who live among us— hateful communists and scheming Jews— who find delight in the way we suffer— in seeing the oppression that grips the Fatherland.

Each month after I receive the five one-dollar bills you sent, I go to the money changer to exchange those dollars for Reichsmarks. Then, with my handful of currency, I rush to the market because the marks I received from the moneychanger always quickly diminish in value. Sometimes, I cannot even find meat, cheese, or eggs. Papa and I have gone without so many things we once took for granted. We stopped drinking real tea months ago.

I was fortunate to find employment at the James-Klein Revue Dinner Club on Friedrichstrasse. I am embarrassed that the club provides a type of entertainment to men that I do not condone. Female employees perform inappropriate dances for drunken men. However, I can assure you, dear sister, I am totally respectable in my behavior.

Each evening, I watch fat men guzzle liter after liter of beer as they stare at the half-naked dancers. I serve these pigs huge plates of meat, potatoes, vegetables, and gravy. When I walk home late at night, I always carry a napkin full of leftover scraps taken from what they left on their plates. Those morsels become breakfast for Papa and me on the following morning.

It has been a year now since Papa has been unable to work. The hardening of his arteries seems to have worsened. He becomes angry more often, more confused each day. He is sometimes unable to recognize me. When I leave our apartment for work at midday, I am always full of fear that Papa will injure himself while I am serving patrons at the dinner club. In exchange for a few marks, Frau Schmidt, the widow from the apartment above us, looks in on Papa several times each evening.

But on Sundays, Papa and I still walk in the Tiergarten after church. Those walks, my dear sister, are the highlight of my week.

I love you and miss you so much.

Your only sister, Ilse

Historical Note, 4/25/2019— The James-Klein Revue Dinner Club

I searched in the library for information about a *James-Klein Revue Dinner Club.*

I found information and learned about the club from a book called *Voluptuous Panic; The Erotic World of Weimar Berlin,* written by Mel Gordon. The book describes the *James-Klein Revue Dinner Club*'s entertainment as "Crass. Expansively lewd. A touch of inflation-era madness mixed with Parisian Music Hall nudity. One critic referred to the James-Klein-Revue as 'a pornographic magazine come alive....Mostly lavish nude tableaux— or meat shows— arranged around a comic theme."

The description in *Voluptuous Panic* concludes, "Any activity that is sexually over-the-top in Berlin is frequently labeled a *miniature Klein-Revue.*"

Ilse's Letter, 10/1/1925— Sad News

Dear Gisa,

I write this letter to share sorrowful news. Papi is no longer with the living. Our father surrendered to the hardening of his arteries, the condition that caused him so much suffering. Two nights ago, Papi awoke in the middle of the night. I went to his bedside. He thought it was Mutti, sitting at the side of his bed. Papi spoke to our dear, departed mother as if she were alive. He asked her to take the children— he mentioned your name and mine— to the Tiergarten this coming Sunday after mass.

It was terrifying listening to him speak, pausing after each utterance, seeming to listen— almost as if Mutti was responding to him. As I watched, tears fell from my face.

Suddenly, Papi sat up. He bent his head forward, at an angle, and covered his face with both hands. Then Papi wept. A moment later, our father's body relaxed. He folded back onto his pillow, and a peacefulness came across his face— a look with no tension— a calm I had not seen in him in many years.

By morning, our father was gone— released from his pain. I am alone.

I sold the wedding ring that Papi wore on the fourth finger of his right hand for so many years. The proceeds paid for his burial arrangements.

I feel so alone, Gisa. There are no relatives here with whom to share my sadness, no one to grieve with me. My friend from work, Jürgen, has been a wonderful comfort. He helped make funeral arrangements and will stand next to me at Papi's graveside service on Friday morning as I give my final goodbye to our father.

My manager at the James-Klein Revue Dinner Club has been sympathetic. He told me I should tend to Papi's burial and not bother to return to work until Saturday. I am so fortunate to have that job.

I feel so alone and miss you so much,
Your sister, Ilse

Ilse's Letter, 12/4/1927— Jürgen

Dear Gisa,
Such an exciting time! So much to share! My previous letters briefly introduced you to Jürgen, my friend from work. Jürgen and I often see one another. He has become quite dear to me. Since Papi's death two years ago, Jürgen has been my only comfort. News that you may have already guessed is that your baby sister is happily in love. And yes, last week, Jürgen asked me if I would become his wife.

Of course, I joyously responded, "Yes!"

We have not yet set a wedding date. In the meantime, to stretch our limited resources, Jürgen has moved into my apartment. It is so wonderful not to be alone anymore.

I have told you very little about Jürgen. He is six years older than me. He served with distinction in the Kaiser's army during the Great War. That experience embittered him toward those who stabbed both the German army and its people in the back by gifting the Allies all that the Kaiser's army had achieved through such sacrifice. Jürgen will never forgive nor forget that treachery. Too many of his comrades gave their lives fighting for our great nation.

A year ago, Jürgen had to give up his job as a waiter at the Haller Review Dinner Club. He was asked to leave because a part-owner of the nightclub (a Jew) read an article in the *Berliner Tageblatt* about a political demonstration in which Jürgen participated. The protest was against communists and other enemies of the fatherland who are plotting against the German people. The article referenced Jürgen's heroic actions to defend his comrades against a gang of communists that tried to interfere with a peaceful demonstration.

A few weeks after leaving the Dinner Club, Jürgen was offered a position as a construction worker. However, he was also given a different opportunity with the National Socialist German Workers' Party, the organization for which he was already volunteering. Jürgen chose that position even though it pays less. Jürgen explained that the National Socialist Party represents the future of Germany.

Jürgen organizes worker rallies, distributes notices for meetings, and provides other support to the party's Berlin leadership. He is proud to assist the National Socialists as they reclaim Germany for the German people. Jürgen's patriotism makes me so proud.

Berlin's economy continues to improve. The Reichsmark has retained its value now for three years, a relief after those horrible years of severe inflation. I can now go to the market and purchase sausages, bread, and other basics at affordable prices. That being said, the small amount you send me each month is what allows us to buy these foodstuffs and thus, not be hungry. Your help gives us confidence for the future.

Please congratulate Dieter for me on establishing his own automobile repair business. Jürgen and I wish him great success.

The new house Dieter purchased for you seems magnificent. I look forward to hearing more about it. We are happy for you, Dieter, and little Mathew.

Thank you for being such a wonderful sister, Ilse

11/9/1988— Kristallnacht School Assembly

Jeannie is in the eighth grade at Lewis and Clark Middle School. Students from all Billings middle schools occasionally gather for large assemblies at the Shrine Auditorium.

The other day, Jeannie came home from school and told me there would be such an assembly on November 9th to commemorate the anniversary of Kristallnacht, the Night of the Broken Glass, when the Nazis terrorized Jewish families. Kristallnacht occurred across Nazi Germany fifty years ago. Jeannie told her teacher that her father was German and that she wanted to invite him to attend the assembly with her. Her teacher welcomed my attendance.

I actually didn't want to go. But Mary told me that Jeannie would be hurt if I turned her down. So, this morning at ten, I met Jeannie and her class at the Shrine Auditorium. The assembly's speaker was a Jewish man who had been a teenager living in Frankfurt on Kristallnacht.

I ended up finding the presentation meaningful— and shocking. The guy's speech made me feel fortunate that my grandparents and dad got out of Germany when they did.

At dinner this evening, Jeannie told Mary and me she was upset about what she had learned. She asked me, "How can some human beings do things like that to other human beings?"

She wanted me to tell her more about what happened in Nazi Germany. I told her what I know— which isn't much. I added that I want to learn more about the holocaust.

I need to go to the library and find a book that will tell me more about Kristallnacht, as well as give me more information about Adolph Hitler and the Third Reich.

A Dream, 9/16/1987— Someone Else's Daughter

I woke up a few minutes ago from an amazing dream. I sat on the side of the bed for a few minutes, totally blown away by my dream. Then, it occurred to me that the dream was similar to one I had about a decade ago. It is just after three in the morning.

In it, I was standing in a crowd of pedestrians on a busy boulevard. The location seemed familiar. I looked to my left and saw the Brandenburg Gate. It was about five or six blocks from me. I realized this was Berlin.

Pedestrians around me were looking back and forth, up and down the boulevard. Two groups of protesters were coming from opposite directions. Members of the first group carried flags and banners with hammers and sickles. One sign read, *Increase Payments to the Unemployed.* Another sign said, *Nazis Divide Germany.*

The other band of demonstrators waved flags with swastikas and carried signs accusing other German groups of being traitors. One sign read, *Jews and Communists Backstab Germany.*"

Marchers from both groups carried clubs and sticks. They were holding them as if they were weapons. When the two sets of demonstrators got within fifteen feet of one another, the marchers from each group began to holler insults at the other group, rushed forward, and a battle began. Their fists, sticks, and clubs drew blood.

On the sidewalk next to me, there was a girl watching the battle who looked to be in her late teens. Next to her was a tall and thin older man dressed in a three-piece suit. His thick, bushy moustache stands out very clearly in my memory.

The two were arguing. As I listened, I realized that the man was the girl's father.

The girl had tears running down her cheeks as she screamed at him, "Papi, you and Mutti no longer can control me. I will date any man I wish to see. You can no longer treat me as a child. I am a grown woman. I demand respect! I will never enroll at the university. And Papi, today I choose to stand up against the Nazis. You cannot stop me from doing this!"

The father bit the back of his hand, looked back over his shoulder at the bloody conflict, and said in a hushed voice, "Greta. These political events are dangerous. I hate Hitler and his followers as much as you do— probably a lot more. But we must be cautious. You are so young and naive. Even though you feel you are a full-grown adult, you have very little understanding of the danger that is growing around us."

I learned from their conversation that Greta had recently graduated from her lyceum and moved away from home. Her father made clear that he did not approve of the girlfriend with whom Greta shared a room. I watched the father and daughter as they walked away from me, continuing to argue with one another.

That was when I woke up. I grabbed my journal, headed to the dining room, and began to document the dream. The level of clarity with which I was able to recall every detail in the dream was weird.

I am going back to bed now.

A Dream, 6/25/1988— A Strip Club

It happened again. I had a dream that took place in Berlin.

There were no marchers, no demonstrations. But what was strange was that I recognized two people from my past dreams. After I woke up, I sat on there, on the side of my bed for several minutes, recalling the dream, considering how weird it is that it connects with the others.

The young guy in this dream— Karl Becker— was in a dream I had more than a decade ago. He was at a demonstration in Berlin. The girl was from a more recent dream. Her name was Greta. The first time I dreamt about her, she was arguing with her father. In this dream, she wasn't quite as young.

While I was sitting on the side of the bed, visualizing what I had just dreamt and recalling the earlier dreams, Mary woke up. She asked if anything was wrong. I told her *no*. She rolled over and went back to sleep.

My alarm clock said it was 5:30 in the morning. I had to get up in half an hour anyway. So, I grabbed my journal and headed down to the dining room table to write up the dream.

In the dream, the guy, Karl, was walking down a German street with a bunch of other young men. They were in a neighborhood full of bars and strip clubs. Karl and his buddies obviously had been drinking. They were slapping one another on the back, making snide comments about wanting to have sex with some of the women they had just seen.

The group was standing in front of a cabaret with a large sign that said, *The Stork Club*. They walked in through the club's front door. A maître d' led them to a table in the back of the crowded cabaret. They ordered beers and began to ogle women dancing on a small stage. Those women were dressed in skimpy black negligees and nylon stockings and were doing raunchy dances to the accompaniment of an out-of-tune piano. It seemed like every man in the audience was shouting lude comments at the half-naked women, and Karl's friends had enthusiastically joined in.

After the women finished their crude dances, they stepped down from the stage and began to circulate throughout the audience of the packed cabaret. They were selling postcard-sized photos of almost naked women. A young dark-haired woman approached Karl's table. One of Karl's buddies asked her if, instead of a photo, she would give them some special entertainment.

She said *no* and offered to sell him a picture postcard of an almost nude woman.

Karl's friend responded, "No, luscious," he said, "Not a photo. I'd like to see you without that cheap outfit you are wearing. Or better yet, why don't you take a seat on my lap for a minute— give me some of your most special entertainment."

A stein half-full of beer sat on the table in front of Karl's friend. The dancer picked up the stein and turned it upside down over the lap of Karl's friend, emptying all of its contents.

"There, you hot little bull," she said, "there's your entertainment. That should cool you off."

Karl's friend jumped up and started cursing the dancer.

The maître d' ran over to the table, apologized to Karl's friend, and told the dancer, "Get out of here, Greta. You have offended your last customer in my cabaret. You may be a cute piece of ass, but you are also a sick cow. Leave now and never show your ugly body around this club again."

The young woman, tears in her eyes, replied, "You are an animal, Peter, a horrid, ugly animal. You treat us girls as if we have no value. I am lucky to escape this barn, which you call a cabaret."

The maître d' yelled, "Get out of here before I have Leo throw you out on the street!"

He looked over his shoulder at a plump dancer with short blond hair and hollered at her, "Elsa! Get over to this table. Give these handsome men some special attention."

The dancer, whose negligee had slid, revealing the nipple on her right breast, trotted over to the table and began to flirt with Karl's comrade.

Meanwhile, Greta was walking out of the club. She must have grabbed some clothing from a back room. But as she walked out of the cabaret wearing a dark blue coat, Karl spotted her. He jumped up from his table and rushed out of the restaurant after her. When Karl got outside the cabaret, he looked up and down the street. Greta was nowhere to be seen.

And I woke up. That was the whole dream. It seemed so real!

It's 6:15. I need to get ready for work.

Historical Note, 4/25/2019— Berlin's Permissive Behavior

I read in *Before the Deluge* that before World War I ended, Berlin was already regarded across Europe as a city that had a very permissive attitude toward sexuality. That situation became even more pronounced after the armistice, as women who had come from across Germany to work in Berlin's factories during the war were replaced in their jobs by returning soldiers. At the same time, women whose husbands had died in the war needed a source of income. The inflation and uncertain economics that followed the war added to the urgency for women to make money any way they could.

Many Berlin women found a source of revenue from prostitution and employment at Berlin's nightclubs and revues. This situation attracted male tourists from across Europe (along with their stronger currencies) to visit Berlin to sew their oats. All of this contributed to the growth of Berlin's intense sexual industry.

Prompted by my dream about the strip club, I returned to the book, *Voluptuous Panic; The Erotic World of Weimar Berlin*, in which I had found information about the dinner club where Ilse worked.

I was blown away to discover that there really had been a club called *The Stork's Nest*. It was in business in Berlin until 1930. Its entertainment was described in the book as, "In sequence, each cabaret performer leaves her chair and moves downstage to replace the last entertainer just as she is completing her solo. Audience members traditionally send up steins of beer to the chanteuses when they completed a number.... The female singers specialize in prostitute-songs, patriotic war ditties and other standard cabaret fare."

I was taken aback that the cabaret had really existed. I wondered, *How can this be? Greta was a product of my dreams.*

The only possible explanation I have come up with is that the *Voluptuous Panic* book referenced *The Stork's Nest Cabaret* as being the model for the club depicted in Marlene Dietrich's movie, *The Blue Angel*. Maybe I had heard someone in Nam talking about *The Blue Angel*— maybe even seen the film while I was in the service?

I asked Doc what he thought.

Doc just shook his head from side to side, rolled his eyes, and said, "Your guess is as good as mine. This whole series of dreams you had is so far out there, Hans, that I wouldn't even try to venture a guess as to where the hell your inspirations came from."

A Dream, 2/4/1989— Nietzsche and the Professor

I just had another Berlin dream. After I awoke, I realized I had had two related dreams in the past. Years ago, in my first Berlin dream, a student named Karl Becker had been participating in a street protest in Berlin. He walked away from the protest. In a second dream about Karl, he and his friends were at a strip club in Berlin.

Right now, I am at my dining room table, diligently documenting the dream. It is 2:30 in the morning.

In the dream, Karl Becker approached a tall man with a thick mustache. This man was wearing a grey three-piece suit. As I wrote this, I realized that I actually recognize the tall guy from a third Berlin dream in which he was with his daughter, Greta.

In this dream, a tall, blonde man who also appeared to be a student was standing in the background, watching and listening to the conversation Karl had with the tall man.

"In your lecture this morning, Professor Bauer," said Karl, "you stated that Nietzsche believed God was dead, that his beliefs were a response to that conviction. I have tried to plough through Nietzsche's texts. But I am not at all sure that I understand much from them. I think that Nietzsche's perspectives were different from what you described in your lecture. I think Nietzsche was horribly depressed, and his depression drove him to give up his belief in the Savior. Nietzsche ended up blaming his pain and sadness on society rather than taking ownership of it as his own personal condition."

The man whom Karl referred to as Professor Bauer closed his eyes and was silent for a moment before responding to Karl.

"Nietzsche does not easily lend himself to interpretation," replied Professor Bauer. "The man may have been profoundly intelligent, but he is very difficult to understand. There is an interpretation of his works that commends him for elevating the need for a moral structure that surpasses traditional Western values. That interpretation also gives him credit for being willing to create and develop such a value system. However, another perspective condemns Nietzsche for being a drug-addicted victim who suffered from serious mental and physical illnesses. That reading is probably closer to your own interpretation. I am not sure I know which explanation is correct."

Professor Bauer gave a nervous glance at the tall blonde student who continued to pay total attention to their conversation.

The professor looked away from that other student, gave a soft shrug, and continued to speak. "As a child, Nietzsche was faced with the death of his father as well as the loss of his younger brother. The pain of those losses permeated his life. And yes, he was perpetually depressed. This depression, accompanied by the pain and limitations of serious physical maladies, caused Nietzsche to question the strong Christian faith of his youth. He was, of course, inspired by the questions Schopenhauer asked."

Bauer paused before adding, "Keep in mind that Nietzsche actually had enrolled in a seminary with the intention of becoming a minister. But disillusioned, Nietzsche instead searched for a way to justify the pain of his life experience."

Bauer took a deep breath and exhaled before saying, "However, Nietzsche found an intellectual solution. He postulated that a human being has the capacity to rise above the pain of existence— to embrace a higher meaning in life— to reach a superior state of being which he refers to as *the overman*. But we need to keep in mind that Nietzsche also, at times, suffered from loss of sanity."

Bauer glanced nervously at the tall blonde student who continued eavesdropping on their conversation.

"As Nietzsche rationalized his pain," the professor continued, "as well as dismissed his personal failures, some believe he ignored— rather than understood— the dilemmas of human existence. Some argue he was willing to substitute his own role as an outcast philosopher with the role he, himself, previously had credited to Jesus."

At this point, the tall blonde student, who had been auditing their conversation, interrupted. "I am sorry, Professor Bauer, but I believe you have seriously misunderstood Nietzsche. What this brilliant truth-seeker did was to explain that human beings can overcome the obstacles of human frailty. This is important to recognize, particularly in light of the Führer's leading the German people toward that goal. We must embrace the fact that the Aryan people are capable of a purity of existence that transcends the weakness of other races around us. I believe the German people, professor, personify *the overman*.

That ideal is also well expressed in Wagner's Der Ring des Nibelungen."

The tall blonde student paused, looked at Karl for a moment, then back at Bauer before finishing his statement. "Don't you agree, Professor Bauer, that this is a much more profound— and appropriate— interpretation of Nietzsche? Adopting such a vision will allow the German people, and I quote Nietzsche here, 'to go beyond the world of good and evil?'"

Bauer looked at the tall blonde student who had interrupted his conversation.

"Thank you, Eric," he said, "for your clearly stated interpretation of the great Prussian philosopher Nietzsche. As I observed to Karl, Nietzsche lends himself well to multiple interpretations. Your thoughtful restatement of the Aryan interpretation of Nietzsche's philosophy is well explained and deeply appreciated."

Turning back to Karl, the professor said, "Now, Karl, we must leave. Our dinner will be getting cold, and my wife will be anxiously awaiting our arrival. Let me grab my coat and briefcase, and we shall depart."

Karl looked a little confused, but responded. "Why certainly, Professor. I have been looking forward to meeting your wife for some time."

Professor Bauer went into an office and returned a moment later wearing a dark tweed overcoat and carrying a bulging leather briefcase. He turned to the tall student and said, "Then until we see one another again, Eric, good day."

Without another word, Karl and the professor walked to the wide marble staircase, descended it, and left the building.

When I woke up, I grabbed my journal and pen and headed down to the dining room. It had been an amazing dream.

But now, it is time for me to go back to bed.

Ilse's Letter, 2/1/1929— Prosperity

Dearest Gisa,

The Ford Motor Model T Coupe, which Dieter purchased for your family, sounds wonderful. Thank you for telling me about it. I am so happy for you both.

Jürgen and I are also doing better as the German economy continues to strengthen. I look forward to the day when Jürgen and I can afford to make a wonderful acquisition similar to yours— perhaps even a beautiful Mercedes? When I walk along the Unter den Linden and see fashionable women and men enjoying their marvelous vehicles, I dream of that day.

The healthier German economy has resulted in larger tips for wait staff at the Haller Review Dinner Club. For the first time, Jürgen and I will be able to take a small vacation to a spa in Bavaria. I look forward to that journey.

Gisa, I am married to such a strong and wise man. He is doing well in his work for the party. While initially, Jürgen wore a brown uniform and was assigned small tasks, his leaders' confidence in him has grown, and Jürgen's responsibilities have expanded. He is now trusted with countless important tasks by the Berlin office of the National Socialists. Jürgen looks so dashing as he departs for his duties each morning dressed in his elegant black uniform.

Jürgen has even been included in some high-level party meetings. He recently drove Joseph Goebbels, the leader of the National Socialists' Berlin region, to engagements in Bamberg, Frankfurt, Hamburg, and Munich. Jürgen told me the strong and able leaders he has met on these trips have inspired him.

At the Hamburg rally, Jürgen shook the hand of our party's leader, Adolph Hitler! Later that evening, the Führer eloquently predicted to thousands of loyal followers that Deutschland will once again gain the respect of the world. However, the Führer was quite clear that to accomplish this, those who have impeded our nation's progress must be removed from positions of influence. Jürgen explained to me that our leader was referring to the communists, the Jews, and others who have continued to not just stand in the way of progress, but have schemed to undermine the exciting future we all deserve.

The past few years have included some very tough times. But once again, it is exciting to be German and to have a leader who promises to make things better.

I look forward to hearing from you soon.

With much love,

Your sister, Ilse

A Dream, 2/12/1989— Dinner with the Bauers

It is not yet midnight, and I just woke up.

Work was hard today. A customer threatened to sue me. He blamed all of the problems of his Chevy Vega on the muffler I installed a month ago. I finally told him to go ahead and do whatever he needed to do— I'd rather speak with his attorney than him.

I went to bed at 8:30 and awoke a few minutes ago after another Berlin dream. These dreams are fascinating. But I cannot afford to lose sleep every time one occurs. That being said, I grabbed my journal and headed downstairs.

Mary was sitting in the living room finishing a glass of Chardonnay. She had been watching reruns of *All in the Family*. She asked what was up. I told her I had had a weird dream and wanted to write it down. Mary asked if I wanted to speak with her about the dream.

I told her, "No, I'll just write it up and go back to bed."

Mary finished her glass of wine and headed to bed.

Once again, my dream is tied together with previous dreams. A week ago, I had a dream in which a student, Karl Becker, was invited to the home of his professor, Klaus Bauer. As that dream ended, they headed off to Bauer's home to have dinner. (I am not sure how I remember all of these names, but I do).

Anyway, when they arrived at Bauer's apartment, the professor's wife called out, "I am glad you made it, Klaus. I was worried you were going to work late at the office again. Greta and I have almost finished our soup and are about to start on the meat dumplings and fried potatoes."

Bauer hung Karl's coat up on a coat rack and called back. "I have invited a guest for dinner, Esther. Please set another place at the table while my guest and I wash our hands. We will join you and Greta shortly."

A moment later, Karl sat down at the table in front of a delicate china bowl full to the brim with a soup of broth, potatoes, carrots, green onions, and chicken.

Professor Bauer introduced Karl to his wife, Esther, and to their daughter Greta. Karl gave a double-take as he shook hands with Greta. It looked like he recognized her as the dancer he had encountered at the Stork's Nest Cabaret in my prior dream.

However, Karl acted as if he had not met Greta before. And Greta, her face flushed, gave no indication of having met Karl in the past. Moments later, as her father and mother bowed their heads while saying a prayer of thanks for their dinner, Greta mouthed the words *danke schön* to Karl before quickly bowing her head and joining her parents in saying grace.

While Karl and his host family ate, I surveyed the Bauers' impressive dining room. Two large oil landscapes hung on its walls. A plush oriental carpet covered most of the hardwood floors, and the dining table and chairs were beautifully crafted. However, the detail that jumped out to me was the place settings on the table. I recognized the pattern of the china. It was *Rosenthal, Bavaria.* That was the pattern of the tea cups Grandma had carried from her home in Berlin, the cups and saucers from which Grandma and I used to drink tea.

Esther Bauer interrupted my musings about the china pattern by asking, "Why were you late, Klaus?"

Her husband chuckled before responding. "Karl and I were discussing Nietzsche. We had the misfortune of having the close attention of our dear old friend Eric."

Mrs. Bauer scowled as she said, "That little Nazi bugger."

"He is not so little, Esther," said Klaus Bauer. "And I must be cautious. I cannot ignore the danger we all live in during these precarious times. While I am hopeful that that little crazy-man Adolph will never achieve the power he so obviously dreams of, one never knows. People like Eric might someday become powerful."

"Don't worry, Klaus," his wife responded. "Everyone will soon realize the little mustached midget is nuts. It is only a matter of time before he is discarded by the fools who now allow him to grow in public visibility."

"Don't be so sure, Esther. Foolish biases are often difficult to remove from frightened folks' heads."

There was a somber silence at the table before each person returned their attention to their dinner.

Klaus Bauer turned to his guest and said, "Karl. You study business and philosophy. Greta studies poetry. Greta hopes to someday be a great poet. You two live with such different ambitions, but you are both good people. You should get to know one another."

"Please, Papi," said a blushing Greta. "I come to have dinner with you tonight, to greet you, and to tell you how I am doing. I am not here to discuss my ambitions or to be fixed up with a date. I would be interested in Karl telling us what he does for pleasure."

It was Karl's turn to appear uncomfortable.

"I study at the University and work in a factory," he replied. "Someday, I hope to run my own factory and create my own designs of beautiful pottery. But at this point, I just try to survive. And today, I struggle to understand if Nietzsche is a Nazi, a depressed adolescent, or a visionary."

Greta asked, "Have you made pottery yourself?"

I didn't hear Karl's response because I woke up. After I awoke, I was a little confused as to what I had just witnessed. I lay there in bed for a few minutes before realizing that Mary had not yet come to bed. That was when I got out of bed and decided to head downstairs to see what was up with Mary and to document my dream.

A Dream, 9/30/1990— The Coffee Date

Today is Sunday. After an intense week at work, I was relaxing on the living room couch. It didn't take long for me to drift off to sleep. When I woke up about an hour later, I was aware that I had just had another Berlin dream, one which included the same characters as were in my other Berlin dreams.

I went into the kitchen, poured myself a cup of coffee, and stuck it in the microwave. While the coffee was heating up, I went up to our room and grabbed my journal. Mary was resting on our bed, reading a book.

"Oh, sleeping beauty is awake," she said.

"Yup," I responded. "Any plan for supper?"

Mary smiled and replied, "Jeannie is off with her friends this evening. Want to have some prime rib tonight? We could go to Montana's Rib and Chop House. You always like it there."

That sounded good. I told Mary as much and asked if we could wait an hour before we left. She agreed. I headed downstairs to write up my dream.

It started with Karl leaving a classroom along with a bunch of other students. In the hallway, he spotted Greta, who appeared to be about to leave the building. He called out, "Heh, Greta Bauer. Could you wait for just a moment and let me catch up?"

Greta turned around. When she saw who had called out to her, she laughed and said, "I am not sure if I should. However, I will take the risk and wait for you."

A moment later, Karl was standing next to her and asked, "Can I buy you a hot drink and a piece of apple cake?"

A few minutes later, the two young people were sitting in a coffee shop, waiting for a waiter to deliver drinks and desserts.

"Thank you, Karl, for not embarrassing me in front of Papi and Mutti. The whole Stork's Nest episode is one I certainly wish to forget. It only lasted a few days— a dumb experiment of which I am deeply ashamed. I am just fortunate my parents never learned of my stupidity."

"I appreciate that, Greta," said Karl. "We all explore sides of life we eventually wish we had never seen. I appreciate that you are not angry with me for my companion's behavior that night. That was the only time I ever went out with Reinhard and his friends. They are not people whom I respect in any regard. It was stupidity that got me into that situation— and also, perhaps, a bit of luck."

Their coffee and apple cakes were delivered by a plump waiter. The two new friends turned their focus to their apple cake and hot drinks.

After several minutes, Karl said, "Your father is a great teacher and your mother is a gracious hostess. That was the best meal I have had in some time."

"Yes," said Greta. "My parents are wonderful. Do your parents live in Berlin?"

"No and no," replied Karl. "My father died in 1916, in the Great War. I was only a small boy and have no memory of him. My mother— she was a wonderful parent. But she died from consumption in 1928, right after I completed gymnasium. Mutti and I lived in Dresden. I came to Berlin after her death to find work and hopefully gain admittance to the University."

"I am sorry for asking such an ignorant question," said Greta. "It is too easy to assume that others have had the same stable set of life circumstances that God has given to me."

"I should try to make you feel very guilty," Karl joked, "but we all struggle with misperceptions and unanticipated discoveries. For example, I went into a strip club and found a beautiful poet. Who would have guessed that would be the outcome?"

And that was when I woke up. It had been a pleasant dream. Karl and Greta seemed like such nice people.

Mary came downstairs. She told me she was hungry and ready to go. I need to throw on a jacket, and we can be on our way out to dinner. I am starved and cannot wait to bite into a thick, juicy slice of prime rib.

8/18/1993— Jeannie Turns Eighteen

Jeannie will head off to college next month, to the University of Montana in Missoula. Time for her to spread her wings. I'm happy for her.

Our lives won't change a whole lot. Mary and I use most of our energy in our jobs. Our time at home is more about recovery than celebration. Given that, it seems like a shame that between eating out, purchasing new cars, and replacing appliances, we haven't gotten ahead financially.

Ilse's Letter, 2/28/1930— The Economy

Dearest Gisa,

My apologies for not writing you in months. I am healthy, but things have been difficult for Deutschland. The economic collapse that hit much of the world has now come to Germany and has impacted me personally.

The Haller Review Dinner Club went out of business with no warning to anyone. I arrived at work on a Tuesday in early January. All of the doors to the club were locked. A handwritten note posted on the door stated that all operations for the club have ceased. I have since learned that no employee was warned and that our final paychecks will never be distributed.

Even though the Weimar Republic's constitution requires unemployment compensation, those of us without work understand that the small amount we receive each week makes this legal requirement seem like a bad joke.

Jürgen and I are unable to afford sausage. Our diet is made up of soup, potatoes, cabbage, and bread. I can only thank God that Jürgen continues to receive a modest paycheck from the Party. The Berlin Region of the National Socialists continues to rely heavily upon his efforts.

Goebbels recently established offices in Magdeburg and Cottbus. Jürgen has been asked to spend at least two days a week in each of those offices. He recruits party members and organizes local demonstrations, which call for the Weimar Republic to be more responsive to citizens' needs during these hard times.

Before losing my job, I had been employed without a break since studying at the lyceum. I have never had so much time on my hands, for which I have no use. Each day passes slowly.

I read in the Berliner Tageblatt about the difficult business conditions in America. Will Dieter's automobile service station survive during these challenging times? I pray that he will continue to be successful and that your family will prosper.

You have been a wonderful and generous sister. It is shameful to ask you this now, but any financial additional assistance you can provide to us during these horrid times will make such a difference.

I miss you so much, dear sister. Please write to me soon.

Your loving sister, Ilse.

Historical Note, 5/30/2019— Hitler's Rise

Understanding the path of Hitler's climb to power was proving challenging for me— particularly during the climactic years of 1932 and 1933. However, using information gleaned primarily from *The Rise and Fall of the Third Reich*, I came to understand how the Weimar Republic failed and Hitler's dictatorship began.

Paul von Hindenburg was originally elected to a seven-year term as president of the Republic in 1925. Before that election, von Hindenburg's reputation was driven by his role as field marshal overseeing German forces during World War I. He was seen by the people of Germany as a trusted elder statesman.

The economic crash that began in 1929 in the United States affected much of the world. Germany was hit particularly hard. By the early 1930s, problems in the Weimar Republic's economy were severe. Unemployment was over 30% and the political battles between the Nazis, communists, and supporters of the then-current government were violent and ongoing.

As von Hindenburg's second term was coming to its end in 1932, he was eighty-four years old. In spite of his aging condition, he chose to run for reelection. Adolph Hitler also chose to run for the presidency. Von Hindenburg was backed by the army as well as Germany's centrists. The other major candidate (besides von Hindenburg and Hitler) ran under the Communist Party banner.

In the March 31, 1932, presidential election, a clear majority was required to win the presidency. Von Hindenburg received 49.6% of the votes. Hitler received 30.1%. The communist candidate received 13.2%. Several minor candidates received the remaining votes. In a run-off election held on April 10, 1932, von Hindenburg received 53.0% of the vote, Hitler got 36.8%, and the communist candidate received 10.2%. That 36.8% vote percentage was the largest portion of any Germany-wide vote that Hitler ever received.

A key responsibility of the Weimar Republic president was to appoint Germany's chancellor. This position led the German government on a day-to-day basis. As von Hindenburg aged during his first term, he delegated more and more control over the government to his chancellor.

Less than two months after being reelected, von Hindenburg requested the existing chancellor to resign. Among the candidates to become chancellor at that point were Hitler and Franz von Papen, a Prussian nobleman. Von Hindenburg didn't trust Hitler and appointed von Papen as chancellor. But on December 2, 1932, von Papen resigned from the chancellorship, anticipating he would be reappointed and allowed to select a new cabinet.

But von Hindenburg appointed a military leader as chancellor. This general survived as chancellor for less than two months. On January 30, 1933, after Hitler agreed to limits on who would serve in his cabinet, an unenthusiastic von Hindenburg appointed Adolph Hitler to the chancellor position. Hitler and his trusted political advisor, Joseph Goebbels, had done a brilliant job of navigating their way through a chaotic period of political intrigue and deal-making.

What stood out was how effective Goebbels was in advising Hitler. It was Goebbels who convinced Hitler to run for the presidency in March of 1932, when Hitler felt it might be premature to make that move.

It was Goebbels who excelled in managing National Socialist/Nazi Party communications and artfully utilized Hitler's public speaking skill— the Führer's unusual ability to gain trust from his rank-and-file followers. Once Hitler had taken full control, Goebbels's skills and innovations as Germany's Minister of Propaganda allowed the Nazis to effectively manage public opinion.

Historical Note, 5/30/2019— The Reichstag

The Reichstag was the Weimar Republic's national assembly. One of the Reichstag's primary duties was to provide strong oversight over the Weimar Republic's executive branch of government.

Reichstag members were elected from many different political parties. Those parties included, among others, the Communist, Catholic Center, Social Democrat, National People's, and National Socialist (Nazi) Parties.

In 1928, the Nazi Party held only 12 of 608 seats in the Reichstag. That number grew to 107 in 1930 and to 230 after a July election in 1932. However, the Nazi elected representatives decreased to 196 in the November 1932 election. That was the last parliamentary election prior to Adolph Hitler being named the Reich Chancellor.

Thus, when Hitler became the chancellor of Germany in 1933, less than one-third of the Reichstag members were from his National Socialist Party.

Historical Note, 6/12/2019— The Reichstag Fire

The Rise and Fall of the Third Reich described the period between Hitler's appointment on January 30, 1933, and the parliamentary election which occurred a month and a half later as follows:

> "By the beginning of February, the Hitler government had banned all Communist meetings and shut down the Communist press. Social Democrat rallies were either forbidden or broken up by the SA rowdies and the leading Socialist newspapers were continually suspended. Even the Catholic Center Party did not escape the Nazi terror...the leader of the Catholic Trade unions was beaten by Brownshirts when he attempted to address a meeting...."

On the night of February 27, 1933, the German Reichstag building, the meeting place of Germany's Reichstag, went up in flames. This was shortly after Hitler became chancellor and two weeks before new parliamentary elections were to be held. A Dutch communist was arrested at the Reichstag building and charged with arson. A broad communist conspiracy was alleged by Hitler. Years later, Hermann Göring, one of the highest-ranking Nazis, bragged that he and his storm troopers were the ones who had set the Reichstag on fire.

As it does in the United States Constitution, the Weimar Republic constitution specified the authority and limitations of the executive branch. In the United States, if the president's legal or constitutional authority is exceeded, Congress or the courts have the authority to challenge and end the misuse of power. If Congress and the courts both refuse to limit the executive, the United States could end up with a dictatorship.

The Weimar Republic constitution also spelled out the powers of the executive branch as well as its limits. However, the constitution also stated that if public security and order were endangered, the president of the Reich was authorized to take measures deemed necessary without the consent of the Reichstag.

To put it simply, under this constitutional provision, the Weimar Republic president could suspend constitutional civil rights. This special authority was designed to give the president the flexibility to respond to an emergency. But it served as the Achilles heel of the entire constitution. Hitler was smart and aggressive enough to take advantage of this weakness.

On February 28, 1933, the day after the Reichstag was burned, Chancellor Hitler asked President von Hindenburg to sign a decree suspending civil rights in Germany. Hitler stated that his intent was to protect the German People from those who would destroy their government. This document is often referred to as *the Reichstag Fire Decree.*

Once von Hindenburg signed it, Hitler's regime was authorized to arrest and jail political opponents without specific charges. This virtually ended freedom of the press and free speech. With that authorization, Germany became, for all intents and purposes, a police state.

One week after the Reichstag fire, Germany held its last democratic election for seats in the Reichstag. Even though the communist party had been publicly blamed for the Reichstag fire and campaigns of Nazi political opponents were severely limited using the Reichstag Fire Decree, the Nazis only received forty-four percent of the votes cast.

After that election, the Nazis still needed additional Reichstag votes to gain the authorization Hitler sought. German political and economic leaders had the opportunity to refuse to give Hitler that authority. But other parties and legislators did not take Hitler on. Instead, they backed off, either afraid of Nazi violence or accepting Hitler's vague promises about how he would manage Germany. Hitler's opponents thus gave up their power, one by one, until the Führer was in a position to destroy all of them.

During the years before achieving his dominant position of power, Hitler had been strategic in his use of diplomacy and alliances. His political tactics and intrigues were skillfully employed. But when there was no better tactical tool to utilize, Adolph Hitler never hesitated to use violence and the brute force of the SS and SA.

Ilse's Letter, 2/2/1933— Wonderful News

Dearest Gisa,

Such wonderful news!

Jürgen keeps me updated on political events that may affect our future and on the intrigues of ambitious politicians who seek to block the Führer's brilliant plans for Germany's future. These pieces of information, over the past year, have alternately filled my heart with hope and despair.

On January 30th, however, our dreams were fulfilled. Afterwards, Jürgen described to me the extraordinary chess game that had taken place at the highest levels of power within the Fatherland. The Führer acted brilliantly in devising and executing his strategies. Now at last, I can tell you that Bruning, Schleicher, and von Papen have all failed. President von Hindenburg had no choice but to recognize the will of the people. The Führer has been appointed chancellor of Deutschland, and the corruption that has plagued our wonderful Fatherland is about to end.

Jürgen carries himself with a confidence that is a joy to behold. I have never seen him so jubilant. He looks so handsome in his black Schutzstaffel uniform.

Jürgen has been offered a position in the new government. He is finally being rewarded for his sacrifices and hard work. We will move out of this apartment, in which I have spent my entire life, into a grand home. We will have an automobile— a necessity because Jürgen's work will require him to often travel across our beautiful country.

I received the letter you sent in October. Do not feel bad, dear Gisa, that you are unable to send more dollars to assist Jürgen and me. I know it has been difficult for you. I am hopeful that Dieter will be able to retain his business and that the two of you will hold onto your lovely home.

Perhaps, after Jürgen is installed in his new position, we will be able to send some marks to assist you during your difficult hours in much the same manner as you generously assisted us.

I must end this letter. This evening, Jürgen and I have been invited to attend a National Socialist Party victory celebration at the Hotel Kaiserhof. It is located near the Reich Chancellery. I have never been inside such a grand hotel. I have acquired a beautiful sequined gown to wear to this special celebration.

Please write soon, darling. Tell me how you are doing. I will also write to update you on all of the exciting things happening in our beautiful Berlin.

Your loving sister, Ilse.

5/1/1996— **Jeannie is Engaged**

Last night, Jeannie called Mary and me to tell us Bob asked her to marry him. Jeannie accepted. Our daughter is so happy! She and Bob will be married in July.

Mary and I were a little taken aback. Jeannie had brought Bob home for Thanksgiving last year, and he seemed pretty nice. But we had no idea they were that serious. Jeannie is finishing her junior year at the University of Montana. Bob is a senior. He plans on attending dental school at the University after graduation.

Jeannie is excited and in love. That pleases us. I wouldn't have minded if she had taken some time finding herself after graduating before she decided to get married. But that is Jeannie's decision. Mary and I are so happy for her.

A Dream, 4/26/1997— Brown Shirts and Burning Books

This morning when I woke up, I felt distressed. At first, I wasn't sure why. But after sitting on the side of my bed for a few minutes, I realized I was upset because of a dream I'd just had— about Berlin. It's been years since I had one of those dreams. I grabbed my journal and headed downstairs, and began to write.

In the dream, the two young Berliners I'd dreamt about in the past, Greta and Karl, were holding hands. They were standing near the back of a crowd on the outskirts of a large square. Behind them was a large cathedral. In front of them were what had to be thousands of people fixated upon a huge bonfire. The festive mood of the crowd seemed almost like a political rally, football game, or rock concert.

As I watched, I started to understand what was happening. In the center of the square were men in light brown shirts being assisted by boys in dark shorts and white shirts. They were throwing armfuls of books onto the large bonfire, which, I suddenly realized, was entirely made up of books.

And the crowd was roaring in approval.

After seeing Brownshirts beat up a man in a suit who had been standing near them, Karl and Greta slowly moved back out of the crowd. Greta had a bewildered look on her face. Karl glanced at her and whispered, "We must leave, Greta. This is not good. It is dangerous."

"No, Karl. This is something we must observe. The world is going crazy, and we must bear witness to this evil."

At that point, a voice over loudspeakers congratulated the men who were tossing books onto the bonfire. The voice said something like, "The time of dangerous Jewish minds is over. Future Germans will not lose themselves in the dangerous lies of books. They will be men of character. For tonight, Berlin puts to flames the evil of the past!"

Greta was standing on her tiptoes, watching a small man in an overcoat who was giving the speech.

"I see him," she said. "That is Goebbels. I have heard him often enough on the radio. But I have never seen him in person. Joseph Goebbels is such a small, ugly man."

As Goebbels completed his speech, excited members of the crowd lifted their right arms into the air in an emphatic gesture and called out repeatedly at the top of their lungs, *Sieg Heil!*

Karl pulled Greta away, saying, "We must leave, Greta. You have seen the spectacle. Now, we must go."

"I am so afraid, Karl," she replied. "So afraid. I did not tell you earlier, but today, I saw men in brown shirts beating and kicking an old man on the street in front of the University. I think I recognized him. I believe he is Jewish— maybe also a communist. I don't know. But I did recognize him. He was a colleague of Papi's at the university. I am so fearful. Let's go to your home. Tonight, I do not want to sleep alone."

Karl pulled Greta back further from the crowd, and the young couple left the square, walking past the cathedral and disappearing into the shadows of a small side street.

And my dream was over. I've been sitting here in the dining room for several minutes. I finished describing the dream, but I am in shock. I described what I saw in the dream. But words cannot fully convey the ugliness of what I observed.

Historical Note, 9/17/2023— The Berlin Book Burning

Last week, I was watching NBC Nightly News. They were reporting on an Iowa school district that outlawed a list of books, which they labeled *un-American*. The NBC reporter said that the school district's list included *The Grapes of Wrath,* the *Harry Potter* series, *Huckleberry Finn*, and *To Kill a Mockingbird*. The reporter referenced the Nazi book burnings of May 1933.

When I saw that news story, I was reminded of a dream I had a couple of decades ago.

I pulled out *Rise and Fall of the Third Reich*. There it was. On May 10, 1933, twenty-five thousand 'un-German' books were burned in an "Action against the Un-German Spirit."

Forty thousand Berliners gathered in Berlin's Opera Square to hear Germany's Minister of Public Enlightenment and Propaganda. Goebbels said in his speech that "exaggerated Jewish intellectualism" was over. He emphasized the need to rid Germany of "intellectual filth."

I was amazed. Forty thousand people celebrating the burning of literature and history books? I thought to myself, *Were the Nazis trying to repeat the Middle Ages? Are we following their lead?*

Ilse's Letter, 4/10/1933— Great Changes in Deutschland

Dearest Gisa,

Life in Berlin continues to be thrilling. Every day, Jürgen tells me of a new plot or intrigue by enemies of progress. Again and again, they attempt to undermine the wonderful changes the Führer is bringing to the Fatherland. But each time they try to stop the progress, our leader outsmarts them.

You have probably read in your United States newspaper that the communists set fire to the Reichstag on February 27. A communist culprit was discovered near the building after the fire. He admitted to being a part of a plot to set the fire. I have no idea what the communists might have hoped to accomplish with that action. Perhaps it was a crazy attempt to topple our government?

I have seen leaflets that accuse the Führer of lying to the people and of the commission of terrible acts. Some newspapers have even been so bold as to accuse the National Socialists of threatening to end freedom in this country. Jürgen has assured me these words of betrayal are the acts of liars who hate Germany, who do not wish to see the Fatherland restored to the prominent world position it deserves. Jürgen told me these traitors will be silenced, their lies defanged by the great successes that Germany is about to achieve.

Our leaders are so strong, Gisa. President von Hindenburg has authorized the Führer to pursue those who plotted against our country. Hundreds of communists, Jews, National Socialist traitors, and radical sympathizers have been arrested. Many of these scoundrels have admitted their betrayal of the Fatherland.

The SS continues to identify secret plots and is arresting the perpetrators. Jürgen returns from work late each night. In the morning, he shares new information and tells me how the SS is rooting out those who have tried to undermine the nation's progress.

By a strange set of events, the parliamentary election occurred just days after the Reichstag fire. That vote by the German people resulted in a government dominated by the National Socialists. I have difficulty following how quickly everything is changing. But I am assured by my wonderful husband that each step along the path has been another huge success for the Nazis.

As I mentioned in my last letter, Jürgen and I will be moving into another apartment. Jürgen was able to secure a lovely five-room flat in Prenzlauer Berg. The old brick apartment building into which we are moving is near a park and home to many distinguished residents. The former residents of our apartment have left the city, and we are thrilled to be the new occupants of this lovely flat. The furnishings in the apartment are antiques, and there are beautiful paintings hung throughout. And the greatest luxury? The apartment has two bathrooms!

Jürgen told me about a shop that sells used furnishings quite inexpensively. Its merchandise was confiscated from dissidents who chose to leave the country. While we have little need for furniture, Jürgen and I went to peruse the shop's inventory. And what a surprise! I found a partial set of Rosenthal, Bavaria china— the pattern of china our parents received as a wedding gift. I know Papi gave you two cups and saucers to bring with you to America. Jürgen and I have replaced those cups and saucers in our set and supplemented it with beautiful serving pieces, a lovely teapot, and a matching coffee pot. In addition, Jürgen found an impressive set of silverware which we purchased for a very reasonable price.

We have also acquired an automobile! Jürgen must drive to meetings in cities across Deutschland. He needed a dependable vehicle for these journeys as well as for our personal errands about town. Jürgen's superiors offered him a choice between two automobiles. One was a luxurious four-year-old Mercedes 630 Tourer. The other was a one-year-old BMW 3/20. Even though the Mercedes was quite dashing, Jürgen felt the newer vehicle, the blue and white BMW, would be a more practical choice because the Mercedes had a canvas top. I totally agree.

Jürgen and I send you so much love. We are prospering and full of hope that all is well for your family.

Please give my love to Dieter.

Your loving sister, Ilse

A Dream, 9/14/1997— The Family Dinner

Today is Sunday. I worked in the auto shop until late last night completing work on a couple of complex repairs on a 1968 BMW. This morning, Mary didn't wake me up when she got up and headed out to mass. I woke up a few minutes ago— after another dream about Berlin.

In the dream, Greta and Karl were having dinner at a small restaurant with her parents, Esther and Klaus. I gleaned from Greta's casual conversation with her parents that Karl and Greta were now living together.

A waiter wearing a white jacket and black bowtie came to their table and put down a platter of bratwursts as well as two large serving bowls. One bowl was heaped with roasted potato salad, and the other was full of red cabbage. Esther filled each person's plate and passed it to them. The waiter returned a moment later, carrying glasses of white wine for Greta and Esther. A moment later, he returned to the table again, this time with two large steins overflowing with beer. He put one stein in front of Klaus and the other in front of Karl.

After the waiter left, Esther looked down, shook her head from side to side, and spoke to her daughter.

"Since Hitler became chancellor," she said, "things have gone from bad to worse."

"I know, Mutti," Greta responded. "It's just horrible. It seems as if his appointment as chancellor has changed everything in just a matter of months. Thank you for calling me yesterday to set up this dinner and for letting me know that Papi has decided to leave the university."

She turned to her father and said, "But why, Papi? What happened? Why have you chosen to leave your position at the University?"

Klaus Bauer took a long swallow of beer, looked at his daughter, glanced at Karl, then said, "Mutti was being gentle in how she described what occurred. Last Friday, Greta, I was fired from my position."

Esther interrupted her husband to quietly, but angrily say, "We are certain the person who is responsible for all of this is Eric."

Klaus Bauer sighed.

"Maybe," he said almost inaudibly. "Maybe Eric contributed to my calamity with his complaints to party officials, accusing me of embracing socialism. Maybe he damaged my reputation with his constant whining to the dean about my interpretation of Nietzsche. Maybe. But finally, Esther, I own the responsibility for what has occurred. Last week, in our regular monthly meeting, we were informed that Professors Levine and Goldblatt have been relieved of their courseloads. That means they were asked to leave their positions. I was foolish enough to state that the removal of all of the Jewish professors from our programs has lowered the quality of the education we can offer. The dean gave me a cold look and said, 'Professor Bauer. When you live in a glass house, you must be cautious about when and how you choose to throw stones.'"

There was silence at the restaurant table.

"Friday afternoon," Klaus continued, "I was grading papers in my office when there was a knock on the door. It was the dean's secretary. She informed me that Dean Schmidt had requested that I visit him in his office. Moments later, when I entered his chamber, the Dean looked up from the paperwork on his desk and said to me in an expressionless voice, 'Don't bother taking a chair, professor. It is my duty to simply inform you that you are relieved of your duties— effective immediately. Please vacate your office by the end of the day.'"

The professor took a deep breath and slowly let it out. Tears streamed down Esther and Greta's cheeks.

"How can they do that to you, Papi?" asked Greta. "You are the most highly respected professor of philosophy at the university."

"Greta," her father responded. "These are the times we live in."

My dream ended.

I am now sitting here, at my dining room table, still in shock. My dream characters have begun to feel like my family. The terror they experience is extremely upsetting.

7/1/1998— Jeannie and Bob

Jeannie's husband, Bob, has finished his dental degree. I always thought that after he finished school, the two of them would end up here in Billings. Mary and I were looking forward to being near our granddaughter and seeing her more often.

Today, Jeannie called us. Bob has been offered a position with a Great Falls dental office. Jeannie and Bob are moving to Great Falls. Jeannie explained that Bob grew up there and his uncle owns the dental practice that hired him.

So, the die is cast. We are disappointed.

This evening at dinner, Mary suggested that after we retire, maybe we should move up to Great Falls.

Historical Note, 9/30/2019— Night of the Long Knives

I was confused about the differences between the roles of all the named Nazi paramilitary organizations— the Brown Shirts, the SS, the SA, the Storm Troopers, and the Gestapo. It took me a while to figure out which group was which. Below is a quick summary of what I learned about each group's name and its corresponding organization.

The SA is an abbreviation for the *Sturmabteilung,* in English, the *Storm Troopers.* As the Nazi Party grew and came to power, the SA was its violent paramilitary force. They were often called the *Brownshirts* because of the color of their uniforms. The SA was utilized to terrorize Germany during the 1920s and early 1930s. Unemployed men, often veterans of the Great War, were recruited into the SA. Their membership brought them into a sort of brotherhood and gave them a license to express their economic frustrations in violent acts against Jews, Communists, and other adversaries of Nazi leadership. By the time Hitler became chancellor in January of 1933, there were more than two and a half million SA members. Their chief, Ernst Roehm, had been the close friend, political soul-mate, and loyal ally of Adolph Hitler during the formation of the Nazi Party.

Within the SA/Sturmabteilung, there was an elite security section named the SS or *Schutzstaffel*. *Schutzstaffel* literally means Protection Squadron. SS officers wore black uniforms. While the SS's original responsibilities were to protect Adolph Hitler, under the leadership of Heinrich Himmler, over time its numbers and power grew significantly. The SS, in their black uniforms, were the Nazi officers who ran and staffed the Gestapo.

In 1934, the political winds shifted. Chancellor Hitler was working to become an ally of the German Army which felt threatened by the SA's size, power, and aggressiveness. In addition, Hitler feared Roehm was plotting with others to overthrow his leadership of Germany and the Nazi Party. On the night of June 30th, 1934, Hitler directed the murder of one hundred and fifty senior SA/Sturmabteilung officers, including Roehm. Other political opponents of Hitler were murdered on that night and in the days that followed. This night of killings and the violence that followed is referred to as the *Night of the Long Knives*.

After the Night of the Long Knives, the Schutzstaffel or SS became the primary violent arm of the Nazi Party and of the German nation, and the SA/Sturmabteilung or Brownshirts was disbanded. Many SA members were incorporated into the SS under the control of Heinrich Himmler who reported to the chancellor, Adolph Hitler.

A Dream, 4/1/2001— Esther's Distress

I have the flu and feel awful. Mary went to work, but I stayed home. When I awoke, it was noon. I had another dream about Karl and Greta. Even though it's been several years since I had a Berlin dream, Karl and Greta's story continued as a seamless continuation of the other Berlin dreams.

In the dream, Karl was kneeling in a small kitchen, placing chunks of coal into a small, cast-iron cook stove. The door behind him opened. Greta entered the room. Still facing away from her, Karl asked how her day at work had gone. Greta gave no reply. Karl turned around and looked at her. Greta's eyes were red, and it was clear she had been crying.

"What happened?" asked Karl.

Greta, who appeared to be holding back tears, responded, "It was slow this morning. Construction on our street to make the area beautiful for the Olympic Games keeps customers away from the café. I took a break and sat down at a table with a cup of tea.

"The door to the street opened, and Mutti came into the cafe. I saw in her face that she was upset about something, and asked her what was wrong. Mutti told me yesterday morning, a man came to their door and informed Papi that he must report to the Gestapo station for questioning. Papi had no idea what officials might want to ask him about. Mutti told him he must not go. But Papi said he had no choice— he had done nothing wrong, so he should not fear going in. He put on his suit and left for the Gestapo station, a half hour's walk from my parents' apartment."

Tears were now flowing down Greta's cheeks.

She wiped them away and continued. "Papi did not return home yesterday evening. Mutti did not sleep at all last night. She told me she was considering going into the Gestapo station to explain that Papi is a loyal German. I told her not to do that. A while later, some customers came into our café, and I had to return to work. When I looked for her, I saw that Mutti was gone. I don't know what she plans to do. I don't know what I should do."

My dream ended. I got out of bed, grabbed my journal, went down to the kitchen, and heated a cup of coffee.

Then I began to write.

I have been sitting here at the dining room table for half an hour, thinking about my dream. Based upon the reference to the Olympics, the timing had to be late in 1935 or early in 1936. Of course, having read several books about the Third Reich, I know the sorts of things that were happening in Nazi Germany at that time. But even though it was just a dream, I am quite upset. I feel like I know Karl and Greta— that they are my very close friends who are going through this crazy horror.

A Dream, 4/1/2001— Greta's Pain

After documenting the dream in my journal, I went into the living room and turned on CNN. I watched an information piece about recognizing when you have COVID. Afterward, I realized I was a little stuffy. That was worrisome. I went into the bathroom and grabbed a COVID test— one of the free ones the government has distributed.

I was concerned. What if I get sick? What will happen to the auto shop without me there to run it? I had been careful to wear a mask whenever anyone other than family members was around— but who knows?

I opened up the COVID test package and carefully followed the instructions on the box. Twenty minutes later, I gave a huge sigh of relief when I saw the negative test result.

I returned to my bedroom, laid down, and immediately fell asleep. That was when I had my second Berlin dream of the day.

In this dream, it was dark outside. I was watching Greta and Karl. Greta was entering an apartment building. Karl was right behind her. They walked up a wooden flight of stairs to the second floor. Greta unlocked and opened a door.

I recognized that they had arrived at Greta's parents' apartment. Greta called out for her mother, then for her father. She received no answer. Greta and Karl walked through each room of the apartment. Everything was neat and tidy. But no one was there.

Greta said, "Wait. I will check to see if Mutti's handbag is here. Mutti always takes it. If something bad happened, she might have forgotten it—", she swallowed and added "or not been allowed to retrieve it."

Greta went to a large bureau in her parents' bedroom and opened the top right drawer. She did not find a handbag.

"What do we do now?" asked Karl.

Greta sat down on the side of her parents' bed, pursed her lips for a moment, and said, "Mutti often speaks with the widow in the apartment above us. Wait in the parlor. I will go up and ask her if she knows where Mutti is."

Greta walked up a flight of stairs and knocked on an apartment door.

A hushed voice inquired, "Who is there?"

Greta responded, "It is me, Frau Müller, Greta, the Bauers' daughter."

An elderly woman opened the door a little more than a crack. She did not invite Greta into her apartment.

"Frau Müller," said Greta. "Do you know where Mutti is? I spoke with her earlier today. She was concerned because Papi did not come home last night after he was asked by officials to go into a Reich Security Office for an interview. But now, Mutti is not in our apartment either."

Frau Müller opened the door a little further and peeked out into the hall. She carefully looked to the left— then to the right— as if to see if anyone else was present, listening to their conversation.

Frau Müller's voice turned to a whisper. "I spoke with Esther early this morning. She told me that yesterday, your father had received an invitation to speak with some official people. Your mother told me your father went to see the officials and had not returned. She asked what I thought she should do. She asked if I knew what might have happened to the Professor? Your mother wondered if she should go to the station where your father had gone. Maybe she could inquire about him? Perhaps even explain that your father is a loyal German who fought bravely for the fatherland in the Great War?"

Frau Müller sighed before adding, "I did not know what to say, Greta. What could I recommend to her? I told her as much. After that, your mother returned to her apartment."

"Is there anything else you can share with me, Frau Müller?" asked Greta.

The neighbor peeked out again into the hallway, carefully looking, as she had before, to the left, then to the right.

In an even more hushed voice, Frau Müller said, "An hour after Esther spoke to me, I glanced out my bedroom window. Your mother was walking briskly down the street, her shoulders leaning forward, her scarfed head gazing down at the pavement as she walked. I fear, Greta, that your mother may have gone to speak with the officials. I have neither seen nor heard anything of her or your father since."

Greta returned to her parents' apartment and updated Karl. After the apartment, she closed the door and fell to the floor, weeping. Her entire body was shaking. As she cried, Karl kneeled on the floor next to her, his arms around her.

Greta was silent for a while. Then she stood up, and they were about to leave the apartment. She raised a finger and went into her father's study. A moment later, Greta returned to Karl. She was carrying two photo albums.

I watched the young couple leave the apartment, their faces expressing dismay.

That was when I woke from the dream. I was covered with sweat. My heart was beating rapidly. I put on my robe, grabbed my journal, and headed downstairs to document the dream.

A Dream 4/2/2001— The Bauers' Apartment

Yesterday, a little while after I had written down my second dream of the day, Mary called from work, asking how I was doing. I told her it felt like I'd gotten over the flu and was really hungry. I didn't mention the two Berlin dreams to her, even though I couldn't stop thinking about them. These Berlin dreams have been so strange. I have been constantly worrying about the Bauers— concerned about the challenges facing imagined characters from dreams! How's that for weird?

Anyway, Mary stopped at Ciao Mambo on her way home and picked up an order of linguini and meatballs for me and one of fettuccini with shrimp for herself. After dinner, I was exhausted and turned in. I slept like a baby— until about 3 AM when I woke up— after another dream.

I must have been unconsciously worrying about the Bauers because this was the third Berlin dream in a row. Mary was fast asleep, so I quietly got out of bed, grabbed my journal, and headed downstairs, where I dutifully began to write.

This dream had to have occurred the following morning. Greta and Karl were arriving at her parents' apartment. When they opened the door, they saw that her parents' apartment had been trashed overnight. Drawers had been opened and contents thrown all over the floor. In the kitchen and dining room, dishes from the Bauers' set of china had been smashed into pieces. Dr. Bauer's books were pulled from their shelves and tossed around the room, chairs had been broken, and mirrors smashed.

Greta was stoic. She said nothing. Instead, she righted a chair that had been thrown down but was still serviceable and sat down upon it. Her face was pale. After a couple of minutes of silence, she stood up and went into her parents' bedroom.

A moment later, she returned to Karl.

"All of Mutti's jewelry is gone," she said. "The frames from our wall-hung photographs have been broken, the photos torn. My parents' oil paintings and oriental carpets have been taken, and the silver is gone. I don't care about any of those things. I just worry what this means...."

She took a deep breath before saying, "I will go to speak with Frau Müller. She may have seen or heard something."

Karl remained seated in the dining room while Greta left the apartment to speak with her parents' upstairs neighbor.

When Greta returned, she had a serious look on her face.

"Frau Müller was not eager to speak to me about anything," she said. "She seemed afraid and didn't want to talk at all. I placed my foot in the door and wouldn't allow her to shut it. Finally, Frau Müller told me the Brownshirts had come here last night. She stayed in her apartment as she listened to the sound of furniture being thrown around and dishes being broken. She told me that after about half an hour of the ruckus, one of the Brownshirts knocked on her door. She said he was a tall, young blonde man. The brownshirt told her that Papi was a communist who had been plotting against the fatherland— that Mutti was a Jew who had conspired with Papi and other radicals. The tall blonde Brownshirt warned her not to speak with me should I come looking for my parents."

While the look of worry on Greta's face was intense, she seemed calm. In a serious, but unemotional voice, she whispered. "Frau Müller does not know I live with a man. I told her I had given up my room in the Kreuzberg District and that I was leaving later today to live with relatives near Munich. As I left, I told her, 'I must hurry to catch my train now.' Frau Müller was only too glad to see me leave."

Greta slowly gazed around the dining room before looking back at her partner and saying. "Karl, you need to leave the apartment building before anyone sees you. I will follow in a few minutes. Let's meet at the stop where we catch the tram. Go now— quickly."

And the dream ended.

7/1/2009— Mary is Retired

I never told Mary, but Sears always took her for granted. The company's managers are a bunch of jerks.

Last Friday, Mary was laid off. She had spent her entire career working for that company, selling whatever they asked her to sell. Over the years, that included dishes, appliances, pots and pans, appliances, tires, children's clothing, and even Craftsman shop tools. Sears has been failing for some time now. Its management clearly didn't have a clue how to compete with the big box stores on appliances, with the small shops on customer service, or with the internet on the price of everything else. Mary has been telling me for the last few years that unless Sears advertised a big sale, whichever station she was working had no customers.

While we are losing her income, we have savings put away for retirement and no debt. Mary told me she is actually relieved. She said working at Sears for the last few years was like sitting in the hospital next to a sick relative— waiting for death to arrive. She is looking forward to spending her days in our garden and in our family room, sewing dresses for our granddaughters.

This is the beginning of big changes for both of us. It won't be that long before I sell the service station and retire. Mary told me that once that happens, she would like us to move up to Great Falls and live near Jeannie, Bob, and the kids.

A Dream, 7/15/2009— Greta Quits her Job

I haven't dreamt about Greta and Karl since the day after her parents disappeared. But last night, I had another Berlin dream.

In it, Greta was sitting next to Karl at a round oak dining room table. They must have been in their apartment. Greta was speaking about her job as a waitress.

"I always enjoyed my regular customers," she said. "They would sit in my section and always greeted me by name. I would wish them a good day— using their name as well. For some of my patrons, especially in the morning, I knew exactly what they would order. I would bring them their usual cup of tea or whatever they ordinarily drank before asking, *Would you like the regular toast or muffin with your tea?*"

Greta paused and looked off with a soft smile on her face. I wondered, maybe she was visualizing those customers?

"I was always careful to avoid conversations with Nazi officials," she continued. "Of course, I was very polite to them. But I never gave the fascist salute. No. Not that. And after they took a seat, I would try to stay away from their table. Once, I heard an arrogant Gestapo officer laugh and say, 'Jews may think they are the chosen people. But my question is, chosen for what? They do not seem very happy when we choose them to be interrogated.' His comrades all laughed."

Greta was silent for a moment before adding, "Who knows? Maybe that pig was involved in the arrest of my parents?"

"A week ago," Greta continued, "Eric— the student who interrupted your conversation about Nietzsche with Papi— came into the café. When I saw him, I told Ketrina, the other waitress, that I must take a break. Before I went to the back room, I glanced at him. He was sitting there, in his neatly pressed black uniform, proudly chatting with the other SS officers. Eric gave the air of someone important, and it seemed like the other SS officers treated him as if that was indeed the case. I stayed in the back room, out of sight, until Eric and his buddies left the café."

Karl asked, "Do you have any idea why Eric was always so hateful to your father?"

Greta bit her bottom lip and gazed off for a second before replying, "I actually met Eric many years ago. His father taught math at my lyceum. Eric visited his father's classroom from time to time. He was a couple of years older than me, tall and handsome, even then. Eric would arrogantly parade around in his neatly pressed Nazi Youth shirt. He often flirted with me. I was younger than he was and was both embarrassed by the attention and put off by his arrogance. So, I just ignored his flirting. I think he took that as a judgment that I felt my father, a university professor, was so much more distinguished than his father, who taught math at a mere lyceum. In any case, Papi told me once that the disrespect Eric showed for him was apparent the moment Eric first walked into his classroom."

Greta had a lump in her throat as she said, "I think I was to blame, Karl."

The couple sat quietly, sipping their coffees.

Greta put down her cup, took a deep breath, and continued, "Still, I was stunned yesterday when Ketrina warned me that a Gestapo officer had asked her questions about me. I have no idea whether that was because Eric had seen me and wanted to hurt me, or if it was because the Gestapo had some knowledge that I was working with the Catholic League's Resistance Group. Reich officials may have discovered I was distributing leaflets disclosing the real facts about all of the innocent people who have been disappearing. In any case, once Ketrina told me about the Gestapo Officer's questions, I realized I had to resign immediately."

She paused and added, "I am so relieved I never shared your name, Karl, or our address, with my employer at the café."

I woke up. My dream had ended. I headed down to the kitchen with my journal. Mary came downstairs a moment ago and started to make coffee.

"What are you doing?" Mary asked.

"Just writing another journal entry," I told her.

Mary smiled and said, "That's good, honey. Can I pour you a cup of coffee?"

Ilse's Letter, 7/15/1935— Political Turmoil

Dearest Gisa,

I hope all is well for you, Dieter, and Mathew.

My life continues to be full of change. Of course, I have enjoyed our new apartment. Having so much space in such lovely surroundings can only raise one's spirits. Unfortunately, many of our neighbors have been less than welcoming to Jürgen and me. This is to be expected in a building where so many people have known one another for so many years. Hopefully, as time passes, we will make friends with our neighbors.

How is Mathew doing? Is he enjoying school? Does he still help his father in the automobile service business? I'll bet he has grown so tall that I would not recognize him if I saw him. Please send me another photograph of Mathew.

The consolidation of power and responsibility under our Führer seems to be completed. Those who objected to progress have been removed from the government. The violent street demonstrations that we endured for over a decade have ended. We tolerated the communists, Jews, and others who wished to overthrow our government for so many years. It is a relief that those conflicts are now simply distant memories. But it took the strength of the Führer to end those actions.

It distresses me that I have gained weight. At first, I thought I might be with child. But that is not the case.

Jürgen and I continue to hope that I will be able to bear a child, a son we can name after his father. But so far, we have not been given that blessing. I do not know if this is because of medical issues or just a consequence of Jürgen's responsibilities requiring him to work away from home for so many weeks at a time. Jürgen's responsibilities are, of course, confidential. But he continues to shoulder special duties in the program for which he works near Munich. I only know that Jürgen provides reeducation to German citizens who have not been supportive of the Reich.

Recently, however, Jürgen was promoted to an even more important unit. He explained that his prior captain had been disciplined and that the officer to whom he now reports is much more capable. Jürgen is hoping to be reassigned in the coming months to duties nearer our home.

I apologize for not writing so often. Jürgen recently suggested that since the visibility and stature of his role have grown, it would be better for me not to write so often to those whose allegiance is to others outside of the Reich. Instead, my husband has encouraged me to make friends in the building, in our neighborhood, and to participate in events sponsored by the National Socialist Women's League, which offers many interesting programs.

I look forward to hearing from you, dear sister. I wish you and your family only the best.

Your loving sister, Ilse

A Dream, 7/4/2010— Picnic at the Tiergarten

Today is the fourth of July. Bob, Jeannie, and the grandkids are staying with us for a few days. Mary is putting together a picnic for this afternoon. We will take the meal to Lake Elmo State Park. When we get there, the grandkids can go swimming while Mary, Bob, Jeannie, and I each open a can of beer and take it easy.

I slept in this morning but woke up after another Berlin dream. It's been a while since I dreamt about Greta and Karl. I had pretty much stopped thinking about them. Maybe our family's Fourth of July picnic inspired this dream?

Mary has gone out with Jeannie to do some shopping. Bob is taking a nap and the kids are playing video games.

I will stay in our bedroom while I write down the dream in my journal.

Greta and Karl were relaxing on a blanket in a park next to a small lake. In front of them was a picnic basket. Greta took slices of cheese and sausage from the basket and divided them onto two cloth napkins. Next to the cheese and sausage, she placed a brötchen roll and a small tomato. Karl opened a bottle of apple wine and filled a metal cup half full. He handed it to Greta, poured wine into a second cup, and raised it toward her, saying, "To a wonderful picnic on a beautiful sunny day."

They each took a drink of the apple wine as they began their picnic lunch.

"I have such fond memories of coming to the Tiergarten with Mutti and Papi," said Greta. "There is a bigger lake ten minutes from here. They rent wooden rowboats. Papi, Mutti, and I used to go there after we finished our lunches. I was so proud when we were out on the lake because Papi would let me row the boat. Would you like to go there after we eat? It is a lovely day to go out on a boat."

"That would be nice," responded Karl.

Then Greta began to sing a song in a happy, lighthearted voice. I am stunned that I can remember the words.

> *In a lovely little brook*
> *There swam with joyous speed*
> *A whimsical little trout*
> *Who passed us like an arrow.*
> *I stood upon the bank*
> *And watched in utter joy*
> *As that happy little fish*
> *Swam in the lovely little brook.*

In spite of the fact that I was dreaming, I recognized the song. Grandma used to sing it to me when I was small. I have heard the melody other times since then. It is *The Trout Quintet* by Franz Schubert.

In my dream, Karl and Greta packed their basket, stood up, and walked away from their picnic spot, hand in hand.

The dream ended and I woke up. Mary had just gotten home. She asked me to pack the car.

I'll put my journal away and we will head out to our picnic at Lake Elmo State Park.

Ilse's Letter, 9/1/1937— A Postcard

Dearest,

I am sending a brief message on this picture postcard from Magdeburg. Do you recognize the ancient castle in the card's photograph? Mutti, Papi, you, and I visited this city in 1919. We stayed at the Hotel Magdeburger Hof. Isn't that a wonderful memory?

My husband is always working so hard. It is a special joy for us to relax and enjoy the spas and fine dining available in this wonderful city. My husband has been reassigned to a location much closer to home. He continues to work hard and speaks so highly of the progress the Reich has made toward full employment and a healthy economy.

The terrible things that some say in secret about what is happening in Germany— they are all lies. Our leaders face great challenges from within and from across the world. They lead us with courage and conviction.

Sorry for not writing sooner. It has been a busy time for me. I hope to find time to write a much longer letter soon.

I hope you are doing well. I miss you,
Your sister

My Note about this card: This brief picture postcard didn't include any names— not who it was sent from nor whom it was sent to. It was simply addressed to "Auto Service Station" using Grandpa's service station address, which Grandma had probably sent to Ilse at some point in the past. The card gives no information that would identify Ilse or Jürgen. My explanation is that Ilse wanted to let Grandma know she was doing fine, but was afraid to identify herself in any way. The politics of the time may have made her worry that any communication from a family member of a Nazi to Americans would be viewed as suspicious.

A Dream, 5/1/2011— The Photo Album

Mary is spending the weekend visiting Jeannie and her family in Great Falls. It's Sunday afternoon. I took a nap and woke up a few minutes ago after a pleasant dream about Greta and Karl.

Greta and Karl were sitting at the same dining room table that was in the dream I had a couple of years ago. Each of them had a cup of tea. An open photo album rested on the table in between them. I recognized it as one of the albums Greta had taken out of her parents' apartment the day her mother disappeared. Greta was commenting on the photographs in the album.

"This snapshot," Greta said with a soft smile, "shows Mutti and Papi cuddling on a sleigh. I remember Papi telling me the photo was taken on their honeymoon. They were in Gstaad, Switzerland. Papi told me he had to talk Mutti into going down the slope on the sled. The picture was snapped just before they pushed off. Don't they look like lovebirds?"

Greta turned the page of the album. There was a photograph of Esther Bauer sitting next to a small child. Klaus was standing behind them.

"I was two years old when this photograph was taken," said Greta. "I almost remember that one-piece pajama suit. Look how young my parents look in the photo— and how focused they are on me. I am afraid to say that I was probably more than a little spoiled. But I loved the attention— still do."

She looked up, and Karl blew her a kiss.

A few more pages were turned. I didn't catch the images on those pages. However, Greta stopped on another page. Karl bent over and studied a photograph of Klaus and Greta wearing thick sweaters and knit caps. They were standing on wooden skis in the snow.

"This is Papi and me in Gstaad," said Greta. "We only went skiing that one time. Mutti stayed home. She said she didn't like the snow. But Papi and I had a wonderful time. He taught me how to ski." She paused and added with a smile, "Even though I fell several times, I felt like an Olympic champion."

She turned the page. There were two round-faced girls with large, sweet eyes and innocent expressions. They were sitting next to one another on a white bench. One of the girls looked to be about three years old, the other about five. They were each dressed in white lace dresses and wore dark boots. Each of the girls had a white ribbon in her dark, carefully combed hair.

Greta continued, "These are my cousins Edith and Lizzi— Mutti's sister Liselotte's daughters. Aren't their eyes big and beautiful? We visited them in Frankfurt in 1919. Liselotte's husband, Herman, is a Rabbi at Frankfurt's Westend Synagogue. Mutti's family was proud that Liselotte married a rabbi. A year later, they were shocked when my mother married Papi, a devoted Catholic."

Greta paused while gazing at the photograph. She touched the two girls with the pointer and middle fingers of her right hand, took a deep breath, let it out slowly, and said, "I haven't seen these sweet little girls in more than fifteen years. I wonder how they are doing during this time of hate for the Jews."

She turned the page. There was a grinning young Greta dressed in a white clown suit with big black buttons and large ruffles around her neck, wrists, and ankles.

Greta smiled as she described this photo. "Here I am dressed as Pagliacci. I felt so sophisticated wearing this outfit which imitates the lead character of the Italian opera. I wore that clown suit for Fasching two years in a row. I loved it."

Greta closed the album, and the couple sat silently.

After a while, she said, "It was so fortunate I remembered to take these albums on that horrible evening after my parents disappeared. I don't miss the other things in my parents' apartment. I can forget about the china and chairs that were destroyed, the paintings and jewelry that were stolen, and the other things that we may have just left behind because we feared.... Well, we had no choice but to go. However, it fills my heart each time I page through these albums. It's just that I miss Mutti and Papi so much, Karl. They were the bright lights in my life— along with you."

She stopped speaking before adding, "I wonder— where Mutti and Papi are now? Might they be in a re-education camp? Wouldn't it be wonderful, Karl, if one day, we heard a knock on our door— and it was Mutti— and Papi— that they had returned to Berlin? Wouldn't that be wonderful?"

She shook her head and looked down at the table.

My dream ended.

10/14/2014— **Mary's Passing**

I just don't know what to do. I have never felt so alone— so empty.

Mary is dead.

She complained about a headache last Tuesday. I called to check on her from work, but she didn't answer the phone. I went home for lunch to check on her. When she wasn't in the living room, kitchen, or backyard, I checked our bedroom. I found her there, lying on the bed.

The doctor says he believes Mary had an aneurysm. He said her death probably happened pretty quickly. I feel so guilty about going to work that day— about leaving her at home. I should have taken her to the doctor then and there.

Everything has been crazy. Jeannie has come down here and been a great help. Between a sense of guilt and all of the legal tasks I must take care of, I haven't had a chance to figure out how I feel.

I think the word *bad* begins to sum it up. *Bad* on steroids.

Jeannie has been supportive. She is experiencing her own heartache, but has focused on me.

I am not sure what the future will bring. Jeannie told me I should sell the service station and move to Great Falls. She said the kids would enjoy having me there.

I don't know what to do. I am just confused.

5/1/2015— I Sell the Shop

Yesterday, the sale of the auto shop closed. Mac has worked for me for over a decade. He deserves a shot. I think he will be successful.

I can retire now, whatever that means.

I promised Mac I would work half-time in the shop for a couple of months to provide a bridge to all of the various vendor and management connections.

I've thought about booking a cruise to Hawaii to celebrate my retirement. But who feels like celebrating? Instead, I need to start making some serious decisions about my future.

Life has been empty since Mary passed. Jeannie continues to encourage me to move up to Great Falls. To be honest, there isn't a whole hell of a lot left for me here in Billings.

I probably will take her up on it.

8/10/2015— Personal Decisions

The house has seemed so empty ever since Mary died. Jeannie has visited several times. She and Bob kept encouraging me to move up to Great Falls to be nearer to them and the grandkids.

After taking a couple of trips to scout out Great Falls, I have decided I will make the move. In addition to being nearer to Jeannie and the kids, Great Falls seems like a nice place to live. To top it off, home prices seemed lower up there.

I fixed my place up to get it on the market. I began by doing all of the things Mary had told me she wanted me to do, but I never got around to doing. My realtor added a few improvements for me to make. After that, the spiffed-up house went on the market. I drove up to Great Falls during the open house weekend last month and narrowed down the neighborhoods in which I would shop after my home here in Billings was sold.

I decided I want to purchase an older, smaller place within walking distance of downtown Great Falls.

When I returned to Billings after the open house weekend, I learned I'd received two offers. A deal got wrapped up quickly. The sale will close on the first of October.

This all has been happening pretty fast. Now I need to find a place in Great Falls— and go through forty years of all the things that Mary and I accumulated. I'll have to decide which things to keep and which to give away.

And then I will pack up my life, put it onto a rented truck, and start over again.

10/16/2015— Great Falls

Once I had a firm offer on my home in Billings, I focused on finding a place in Great Falls. In mid-September, I purchased a nice little bungalow. It's a fixer-upper just a few blocks north of downtown— a fifteen-minute walk from the River's Edge Trail that goes for miles along the banks of the Missouri. The house is about 900 square feet, not including the unfinished basement and attic. That's plenty of space for me. The lot has a big backyard— plenty of room for a dog or a garden if I get ambitious. But it doesn't have a garage. Maybe I'll build one someday. There certainly is room for one.

The woman who lived there for the past sixty years probably didn't make a single renovation to the place during all of those years. The appliances remind me of my grandparents' home.

The house needs a lot of care. But its skeleton is rock solid. There are a lot of projects that need to be completed before I can move in. I've rented a studio apartment for a few months while hired contractors reroof the place, install insulation into the attic, and replace the house's furnace and original knob and tube wiring. After that, I will move in and do the rest. The home's floors are beautiful old cherry that'll be a joy to refinish. There's easy access from the unfinished basement to replace the plumbing. And I'll install a new water heater, appliances, and bathroom fixtures. Then, bingo— that hundred-year-old house will be my like-new home.

3/30/2016— Last Details of the House Project

I bought myself a six-pack of Heinekens and a mushroom and sausage pizza yesterday evening to celebrate the completion of my home renovation. Before moving in, I tore the place up pretty good with a few dust-raising repairs. Now that I've been living in it for several months, the projects have gotten smaller and smaller. This week, a new washer, dryer, electric range, dishwasher, refrigerator, and microwave oven were delivered. They're all in place now and functioning perfectly. I am as happy as a clam.

The house is every bit as nice as I had hoped it would be. Over the coming summer, I'll put in a vegetable garden and get the lawn in shape. I'll probably also plant an apple tree or two and maybe even put in a few blueberry bushes. But I'll take my time doing those tasks. At this point, projects should be more about enjoying the place than about having to get them done.

I have always been willing to take on big projects. Part of why I'm fearless about taking them on is that I always get things done. At the right point on each big project, I can identify the remaining steps, knock them off, and call the project complete.

So, my new home is complete— and boy, am I ever thrilled!

7/1/2016— St. Anne's Cathedral

My grandparents and parents were devout Catholics. As a child, I attended weekly services with them at St. Patrick Church in Billings. St. Patrick is a beautiful cathedral with a wonderful history.

Mary was deeply religious. Our family rarely missed communion. I attended funerals for my grandparents, my dad, and my wife at St. Patrick. I missed my mom's funeral because I was in Nam.

I appreciate what the Catholic Religion meant for my family. But after Mary passed away, I stopped attending church. It wasn't that I had a change of heart about God. I had always gone to mass because it was expected of me. I am not sure that attending weekly services makes any difference to me at all. I believe in the teachings of Jesus Christ. But I think it is the actions one takes in their life, rather than how one spends Sunday mornings, that make the difference.

When I moved to Great Falls, Jeannie asked me to attend mass at St. Anne's Cathedral with her and her family. I told her I wasn't interested. I think she was a little hurt. I tried to explain my feelings. I told her it was nothing against her, her family, St. Anne's, God, or the Catholic religion. St. Anne's is an absolutely beautiful church. I respect the people who go there, or to any house of worship to find truth through prayer. It just isn't going to be part of my life anymore.

Maybe it's because there is too much hypocrisy all over. Maybe it is because I see too much pain in the world. I don't know. But on Sunday mornings, I tend to go for a walk by myself.

9/15/2016— Grandfathers and the Roundtable

After going to last month's Coffee Roundtable, I told Ronnie I would like to participate in his coffee group on an ongoing basis. This morning, the Roundtable had its monthly meeting. Ronnie and I walked over to the Electric City Coffee House together. We were the last two to get there. Ronnie treated me to a latte and a cinnamon roll.

As we sat down, the others were making predictions for the upcoming NCAA football season. I said nothing. I've never followed college football that much. Most of the group figured Alabama would walk away with the national championship. Steve summarized their views when he said, "Alabama should just say, *Screw the NCAA*. We're joining the NFL."

At that point, Ronnie took over. He told the group, "As I let you guys know on the phone, Hans has decided he will be a regular member of our Roundtable. We all know one another— probably a lot better than we care to— but we're all newbies to Hans. I thought it might make sense for each of us to tell him a little about ourselves. Let's go around the table. Each of you can say a little about yourself— you know, give some personal history— or one or two factoids that might be interesting. That way, Hans will realize what a mistake he made joining our group. After we're done, we'll ask Hans to do the same."

Everybody nodded and indicated they were on board with Ronnie's plan.

"OK," said Ronnie. "I'll start. Hans knows a little about me already because we live next door to one another. Hans, what you didn't know about me is that I played the trombone in the high school band. I was first-chair trombone for two years before graduating. In the military, I ended up in Vietnam along with some of the other guys around the table. But I brought my trombone with me and would play morning reveille occasionally. My army buddies didn't appreciate my musical skills. One morning, I returned from breakfast. My trombone was wrapped around one leg of my bed. My factoid is that Sandy and I began to go steady in the 9th grade. We wrote to one another weekly while I was in the service and got married a month after I got out of the service."

Jim was sitting on Ronnie's left. Ronnie nodded to him, indicating he ought to go next.

"Hey there, Hans. I'm a member of the Little Shell Tribe of Chippewa Indians. You won't find me speaking a lot about ancestry. But I am very proud of my ancestors and our rich history. One little factoid about me is that in 1966, I made all-conference as an offensive guard even though I weighed only 145 pounds. So, Doc here, and I guess Ronnie as well, owe me big. I saved them from getting mashed a lot by our opponents' defensive lines. Another factoid is that I make the best buckwheat pancakes in all of Montana. At least that's what my grandkids tell me."

It was Doc's turn. "During my senior year," he said, "I was the Bison's varsity quarterback. I broke my right leg in the fourth game of the year— just a hairline crack on the tibia. It didn't occur to me or anyone else to X-ray the leg until the beginning of basketball season. At that point, the doctor told me it was just too late for him to do anything about it. It had pretty much healed. I made all-conference point guard during that basketball season. My factoid is that my grandfather came out to Great Falls to work on The Great Falls Gazette. In the 1930s and '40s, Grandpa had a regular column in the Gazette. In 1950, he got an interview with Harry Truman. To get that, Gramps received a thorough secret service body search before being allowed to board Truman's railroad coach."

Steve smiled and said, "Morning, Hans. My personal history lesson for the day is also about my grandparents. They came here from Scotland right after they got married. Their dream was to find great wealth. Instead, Grandpa ended up going to work for the railroad. He eventually became a railroad engineer and traveled all over the Northwest. My factoid is that my grandpa was in a train wreck in 1938. His train was crossing a long bridge over a river. The bridge trestle's foundation had just been washed away by a flash flood. The trestle collapsed and the train fell into the river. My grandpa died. Grandma ended up having to go to work cleaning homes of wealthy families here in Great Falls to raise my dad and his two sisters."

Jack took it from there. "That's amazing, Steve. My mom told me about that trainwreck. Her aunt was on the train, but was only injured. Wow!"

Jack took a drink of coffee, then spoke. "You all know I sold the hardware store a few years ago. My grandparents began it as a general store in 1922. In the 1930s, things got really tough around here. My grandparents struggled to keep the store open. But they always were willing to give their regular customers a break when they couldn't afford to pay for necessities. Grandpa converted the store to a hardware store in 1940 and made a go of it. Selling the store was tough for me to do. But I really had no choice. You get old and you just have to hang up your spurs."

Jerry went next. "My great-grandpa came out to this neck of the prairie from Saint Louis in the early 1880s. He was a skilled horseman who became a ranch hand on a few of the big spreads around here. When he retired, he moved to Great Falls and became a good pal of Charlie Russell."

Jerry paused, shrugged his shoulders, and continued. "My grandparents had a small ranch east of here. When the depression hit, the bank took the place. Grandpa came into town and got a job with the police department. When Dad came back from the war, he followed Grandpa's lead and got hired as a cop. I guess that sort of explains why I joined the State Patrol. My factoid is that my wife's parents were members of Jim's tribe— the Little Shell Tribe. I remember visiting her grandpa and grandma in a cabin they had north of here. They were really good people. Her grandpa gave me a bobcat skin. He'd shot that bobcat himself, skinned it, and tanned the hide. I think that was the nicest gift anyone ever gave to me."

It was my turn to tell the others about myself. While listening to them, I had wondered what I was going to say. I decided that if everybody else was going to speak about their grandparents, I ought to do the same.

I told them about how my grandparents came here from Germany, hoping to have a farm or a ranch, and that instead, Grandpa started a service station. I told them how my grandma took care of me when I was young and that she never learned to speak English. I explained that as a result, I could speak German like a native. I said I was humbled to be a part of their coffee group, that they each seemed really interesting, and I appreciated their sharing their personal stories with me. I finished up by saying I looked forward to getting to know each of them better.

After the around-the-table sharing was done, the conversation turned back to NCAA football. And after that, the month's Coffee Roundtable was over.

As we walked home, I thanked Ronnie for inviting me into the group and told him how fascinating I found each member's story about their life.

Ronnie gave a kind smile as he responded, "To be honest, it was fascinating for me as well. I learned something new about each of these guys— things I'd never heard, even though I've known them for over fifty years. I'm glad you joined the Roundtable, Hans. There will be many more interesting conversations to come."

Ronnie turned onto the walkway to his home, and I turned onto the walkway to mine.

10/20/2016— Who will be my Candidate?

A few days ago, Ronnie called all the Roundtable members to let us know that at our next meeting, we would be asked to share who we are supporting for president and why. They have done this every four years before the presidential election.

I had already been wrestling with who I would vote for. My challenge? I dislike both candidates. I need to be ready to tell the others at the Roundtable what I think.

Yesterday, I watched the third presidential election debate between Hillary Clinton and Donald Trump.

I saw the two prior debates as well. The first debate was dominated by Clinton. She threw out policy positions as if she were a government analyst on steroids. Trump continually interrupted her, behaving like an angry teenager. Clinton accused Trump of being a racist and, I guess, if the shoe fits.... In any case, I just didn't think Trump was ready to be president.

In the second debate, it seemed that both candidates were trying to prove that their opponent was a horrible person. I didn't like Trump's statement that he would have a special prosecutor go after Clinton. That's banana republic stuff. Hillary got a couple of points for her attacks about him not paying any federal taxes and for his record on women. But Trump landed some pretty good blows as well. I think Clinton is pretty much a puppet for a lot of wealthy types, and I've gotten tired of hearing about all of the rich Hollywood folk who are endorsing her.

In the third debate, Trump finally seemed presidential. Clinton accused him of being a pawn for Russia. He responded aggressively— but what did she expect?

Now I need to decide how I'm going to vote. Which of these two creeps do I like least? If there was a halfway decent third-party candidate who had a chance of winning, I might support him. But no such candidate exists.

Our borders need to be toughened up. People are crossing into this country willy-nilly and being allowed to stay. I'm not sure that building a wall makes any sense. But at least Trump promised to try to do something to address the problem. And Trump comes out and says middle-class folk are struggling. He is right.

Things aren't going that well in this country for most people. Problems are being ignored, and there is a lack of leadership. Trump calls out problems and promises to solve them. OK— he doesn't tell us how. But listening to him say he wants to make America great is a hell of a lot better than listening to someone else tell us everything is great and we should just relax.

I think I'm voting for Trump.

10/21/2016— Coffee Roundtable Politics

Our Coffee Roundtable had its monthly get-together today. It was the final meeting before the election. As we waited for Ronnie to show up, we spoke about the upcoming Cubs and Indians World Series.

Even though the coffee group has no officers, it was clear after the first meetings I attended that Ronnie is the group's leader. I gather he's been in that role since the Bison Roundtable started in 1975.

Ronnie got there about fifteen minutes late. Once he arrived, the baseball discussion stopped. Everybody looked at him to see how the meeting would proceed.

"Sorry, I'm late," he said. "I had to give Sandy a ride to the hairdresser. Her Thunderbird's in the shop. As I was driving over here, I was trying to figure out how the election will go and what you all will say today. What do I think? I think it looks like we are finally going to get a president who is not woke."

Doc replied, "That's your opinion, Ronnie. I think Trump is a total moron."

"Hillary Clinton is the real moron," responded Ronnie. "She doesn't have a clue that this country has real problems. She has no idea what we need or any sense of the difficult times average Americans are facing. Hillary hangs out with her rich Hollywood pals, drinks sparkling white wine, and calls the rest of us a bunch of deplorables."

I had already figured out that Doc was the only strong Democrat in the group. But I hadn't anticipated that the gloves would come off so soon.

Ronnie turned to process as he said, "Let's go around the table. Each of you tell who you support, why, and who you think is going to win. Does that work?"

Jack said, "Let's go for it."

Nobody objected.

Jerry was sitting on Ronnie's right, so Ronnie said, "Jerry, why don't you kick it off?"

"You know how I feel, Ronnie," said Jerry. "Donald Trump is going to win because he is a political outsider. He has been saying what no one else has been saying. And, I have to be frank. Hilary Clinton is an arrogant bitch. If it weren't for her husband having been president, she never would have been nominated. I recognize that Trump is a little over the top. But sometimes you need someone who is a little outspoken to break old habits. Trump is committed to fighting crime, to stopping gangs from coming in from Mexico— and I think he will build the wall. But one thing we all know, Trump will not be directed by a bunch of gay radicals who think white working-class Americans are stupid. Trump will, as he says, make America great again."

"Who do you think will win?" asked Ronnie.

"Oh," responded Jerry. "It's a slam-dunk. Trump is going to destroy her."

"Steve," continued Ronnie, "you're on."

"You guys know I'm a Democrat," said Steve. "But the economy has been awfully hard on a lot of people, including my kids. Obama hasn't figured that out. What do I have to lose with Trump? My rent's gone up. My groceries are more expensive. And I don't see an end to it. Trump is new to government and has a background in business. Maybe he'll try something that hasn't been tried. We can't continue to let the middle class in this country be destroyed."

Steve paused and added. "And who do I think will win? Beats me. I think it looks like a horse race."

Jim, who was sitting next to Steve, looked around the table at the others before taking a big breath and saying, "I don't like how Trump gets away with shooting his mouth off so much. As a person who's not white, it troubles me that Trump always blames people of other colors, other religions, and other backgrounds for our problems. Many of his criticisms of the way things are— well, he's right about them. Things do cost too much, and it's getting worse. Immigrants are taking our jobs and keeping the wages low. And the bad thing is that nothing is changing."

He took a deep breath. It seemed like Jim might still be trying to decide who he would vote for.

"I don't have a clue," said Jim, "who's going to win this election. I don't like Hillary. But I have a big problem voting for a racist."

He paused again, then said, "I guess I'll be voting for the Democrat."

Doc was sitting on the other end of the table from Ronnie. Everyone turned to him. I think they were ready for a confrontation between him and Ronnie. Jim told me there had been some lulus in the past.

Doc looked down at his latte for a moment, then shook his head from side to side before saying, "In the 1930s, there was a big drought in Montana. My dad told me how a lot of farmers around Great Falls were struggling to hold onto their spreads. A guy from Texas showed up who was going from town to town, having these big come-to-Jesus meetings in a tent just outside of each town he visited. This guy promised rain that would end the drought if people prayed with him— and if they gave him money. Ranchers who ordinarily wouldn't have bought into that sort of crap attended his revivals. They threw hard-earned cash onto his collection plate. They hoped that the guy would pull it off— that the rain would come. Well, the rain didn't come, and most of those people ended up feeling foolish. A lot of them eventually lost their spreads. When changes finally came, they weren't delivered by a huckster. They were accomplished by Roosevelt and the Democrats."

Doc gave a brief look at Jim, then Steve, and finally me before continuing.

"Now," he said, "I know Hillary's no FDR. I agree she's as arrogant as can be and doesn't have a clue how hard it is for someone living from one check to the next. But at least she understands what the government is supposed to do. Hillary would be working with people who've been involved with programs that have made a difference in the past. She's not promising to give us the metaphoric rain. Your man Trump is. And his record should tell you he has always lied to working folk— and he cheats them. I haven't seen or heard one thing that makes me think he's changed. I'm voting for the Democrat. I think she will win."

Ronnie rolled his eyes but said nothing— yet.

Jack was next. "You guys know where I stand. This country was founded upon Christian values. But we've been drifting for years. The courts have authorized all sorts of crap that devalues life, including allowing abortion and denying that marriages should be between a man and a woman. Donald Trump is man enough to take on this crap. He'd have to be. I think the Donald will be elected and things will change."

Ronnie looked to me. It was my turn. I generally haven't discussed my political beliefs with anyone other than Mary. I might have been a little long-winded in what I said, but I wanted to explain where I stood.

"Back in the day," I told the others, "Grandpa and Dad both supported Roosevelt. It's hard to argue with what Roosevelt accomplished— I mean, social security, the WPA, electrification, and all of the other programs he introduced in the thirties. And Roosevelt had it right on Hitler. He led us to victory. My Dad went to Europe after Pearl Harbor. He fought the fascists. After World War II, when Grandpa was worried about the communists, Dad talked him into trusting Ike. My family went ahead and became Republicans. And one more thing, we all know our federal government is inefficient. I believe our leaders tend to line their pockets while us regular folks have to pay for it. At some point, the federal government needs to stop taking our money and actually solve some real problems. So anyway, I pretty much agree with what most of you said. I intend to vote Republican."

Then I added, "But I agree with Jim. I don't know who will win."

It was Ronnie's turn to speak. He was brief.

"I agree with everyone here," he said, before laughing and adding, "except Doc. But it's a free country. And Doc, I think you need to watch a little bit less MSNBC and a little bit more FOX. You might actually learn something."

Doc just chuckled.

Ronnie continued. "I think we have problems in the federal government that are constantly being glossed over. Trump, I will admit, is a bit of an asshole. He has a big mouth and seems to be disrespectful to so many things that have been off-limits to speak about forever. But I think that attitude will empower him. I anticipate Trump is going to win big and that we are going to see some serious— and good— changes in this country. I'm voting for the Trumpster."

Ronnie was quiet for a minute. Then he looked at his watch and said, "Next time we get together, this will be resolved, the World Series will be over, and we can start doing some serious arguing about the NFL."

That gained a few laughs and a couple *you betchas*.

The Roundtable for the day was complete, and everyone went on their way.

11/16/2016— The Roundtable and Trump's Victory

The election is over, and I'm relieved. Trump won. Hillary Clinton would have been awful. That being said, Trump is a wild card. I'm hoping he does not overdrive his headlights.

I had hoped the Coffee Roundtable would move right back into discussing sports again. However, when we met for coffee this morning, Ronnie rubbed the results into Doc.

"You've just gotta admit, Doc, you were wrong," he said. "Hillary lost and Trump's going to make America great, just like he promised. We'll get the wall. You'll see manufacturing jobs return. Your shiny Toyota, Doc— you'd better prepare yourself. Because your next car is going to be a GM or a Ford. I suggest you check out my Cadillac. You might be able to afford one of these babies because Trump is going to cut your taxes instead of raising them like Hillary would have done."

Doc took a deep breath, slowly let it out, but didn't respond.

Jim ended the stalemate by saying, "I don't care about Trump or Hilary. The truth is, Aaron Rodgers is the best quarterback in the National Football League."

Jerry gave him a sharp look and shot back, "How can you say that, Jim? Tom Brady is so much better than Rodgers that it hurts my brain to even think about it. Brady's the best quarterback— probably— ever."

The political discussions we've had in the Roundtable have been uncomfortable. I am relieved the election is over. Everyone at the table seemed to breathe a sigh of relief that the subject had been changed.

As we left the coffee shop, Jim whispered to me, "That competition between Doc and Ronnie isn't new. They both wanted to be the quarterback on our high school team. Doc won that battle, and Ronnie had to play halfback. Ronnie never forgave Doc for beating him out."

6/15/2017— A Name for My Project

I have been making a lot of progress identifying and assembling the pieces that will make up my book. One of the things I've been giving a lot of thought to is naming the book. The other day, while Doc and I were at the Electric City Coffee House, drinking coffee and casually chatting about the book, I referred to it as *The German Journals*.

Doc stopped speaking, his back stiffened, and he gave me a strange look.

"That's it, Hans," he said. "*The German Journals* would be a pretty snazzy name for your book. When did you come up with it?"

I was a little taken aback. I thought about it for a moment. Calling my book *The German Journals* made a lot of sense.

I laughed and replied, "Just now— and totally by accident."

Doc took a sip of coffee. Then he sat up even straighter and stared intensely out the window. When he looked back at me, he had a smile on his face.

"You know," he said with a sly look, "A book with the name *The German Journals* could refer to any period in Germany's history. That's a lot of time. It just occurred to me that there might be a more— how can I put it— a more specific title you could come up with. *The German Journals* is just too broad. Can you think of a title for the book that tells your reader a lot more?"

I paused, trying to figure out what Doc was getting at. At first, I wondered if maybe he was suggesting calling it *The Berlin Journals*. But Berlin is also a pretty old city.

That name wouldn't narrow down the historical time period, just the location.

Then it hit me.

I asked, "Are you getting at my naming it *The Weimar Journals?*"

Doc gave a big smile and replied, "What do you think?"

I laughed and replied, "Sounds like a plan."

9/30/2017— Becoming a Student Again

Between my walks along the river, getting together with Jeannie, Bob, and the kids, working in the yard, and learning to cook, I've kept much busier than I was after I first moved to Great Falls.

Working on *The Weimar Journals* has been like beginning a college education and majoring in history. Reading the two books Doc lent me quickly confirmed how ignorant I had been about the Germany my grandparents and father emigrated from in 1922.

Before the Deluge, by Otto Friedrich, introduced me to the severe economic and political turmoil in the Weimar Republic at the end of the First World War until Hitler emerged as chancellor. It detailed the cultural richness of Berlin throughout that period.

Before the Deluge impressed on me that, in addition to its connections with my family's history, the City of Berlin is fascinating. I need to go there someday.

The Rise and Fall of the Third Reich, by William Shirer, explained how Hitler and his henchmen took advantage of Germany's turmoil and how they turned a democratic republic into a totalitarian state, and how they mobilized it to devastate the world. These two books gave me context for my Berlin dreams. They helped me build a better understanding of the letters Grandma received from her sister Ilse.

I found a few other books at the library that added to my insights into the Weimar Republic during the period between World War I and when Hitler came to power. Interestingly enough, the group of books I read about Germany has also given me insight into events occurring in the United States today.

3/25/2018— The Project's Structure

Doc and I got together this morning at Electric City Coffee to discuss how my book should be organized— I mean, the order in which the different entries, dreams, letters, and notes should be placed.

We were trying to come up with the best approach when Doc told me he had discussed how the book should be organized with his wife, Anne. Doc said she was more experienced in editing than he was and explained that when he published an article and tried to publish a book, she had been his main helper. Doc asked if I was uptight about the fact that he had let her review my draft.

I thought about it for a couple of minutes. A few years ago, I would have been really upset. But now that we are thinking about actually publishing a book, it seems a little crazy if I also don't want anyone to see it— especially if that someone might be able to make the book better.

I told Doc, "Go for it. The more the merrier."

He chuckled and said, "Sort of hard to put the horse back in the barn anyway. Isn't it?"

I laughed and agreed.

After Doc had gone over his wife's input and given his own thoughts, we decided that the journal entries I had identified should, for the most part, be placed in the order I'd written them— with a few exceptions. My dreams, Ilse's letters, a couple of news clippings, and my historical notes will each have a brief title that includes the date they were originally written. I will try to place each of them next to a journal entry that sort of corresponds to it.

I actually have been trying to organize the book that way all along. But stating it in words helps me have a clearly defined approach.

10/15/2018— The Supreme Court

The Bison Coffee Roundtable had its regular get-together this morning. We have two new members. They came to our last meeting and afterwards, each said they planned on continuing. Both were members of the 1967 Bison High School Football Team.

Lee Thomsen is a big guy. He played center on offense and tackle on defense. Lee is a retired mechanic who spent his entire career working for a local Ford dealer. Lee didn't say a lot today or in the last meeting.

Tom Benson is a semi-retired rancher. His son is his partner in running his ranch. Tom is religious, pretty conservative, thinks the government should spend less of our money, and should stay out of our business.

There was a lot of small talk up front. We talked a lot about the World Series. It seems like everyone in the group is hoping Boston wins. After that conversation, Steve shared that the Billings High School football team has really improved. There were a few snide comments about getting better being a permanent condition that had never been achieved. After that, Ronnie updated us on the cruise trip he and Sandy had taken near Greece.

It got interesting after that. Doc made the mistake of saying that it was unfortunate that the country now has a beer-drinking sex offender on the Supreme Court. Ronnie quickly reacted to that.

"It is better," he said, "to have a beer drinker who likes women on the court than a white wine drinking liberal who's probably a homosexual."

It went downhill from there.

Jack jumped in, saying, "When Trump was elected, he promised to get some conservatives on the court to undo the damage the liberals have done over the years. He did it. What bugs the Democrats about Trump more than anything else is that he's keeping his promises. For too long, Democrats had packed the court with liberals. Those liberals changed the way this country operates. Kavanaugh may be a good old boy. But what's so bad about drinking a few beers? I know I did when I was young, and I'm pretty sure the rest of you did as well. At least Kavanaugh will work to get rid of all of the woke conspiracies."

Up to this point, I hadn't heard Tom Benson participate in any political discussions. But here, Tom added, "Amen to that."

Jerry, who always seems to take Ronnie's bait and run with it, added, "I have to admit that the last thing we need on the court is some goddamned homosexual."

I didn't say anything. But I have noticed that Jerry dumps on gays and lesbians a lot. I had an employee at the auto shop who was gay. He was my hardest worker and always treated our customers well. While I'm not big on gay rights, it tires me out listening to people preach against them. What's the big problem?

Doc, who was obviously more than a little pissed at this point, looked at Jerry and put it out there. "Why are you always so damn insecure about other people's sex lives, Jerry?"

Before Jerry could respond— and I know he was about to— Jim changed the subject to Oklahoma's Quarterback Kyler Murray. Jim predicted Murray would win the Heisman Trophy. After that, our Coffee Roundtable was off to the races on who was the best college football quarterback and most deserved the Heisman for being this year's best college football player.

Lee Thomsen spoke up for the first time. "I don't know why the Heisman always goes to a quarterback. Defensive and offensive linemen win your games. Quarterbacks only lose them. For every four quarterbacks who get taken in the first round of the NFL draft, three flame out. On the other hand, when a guy from the trenches gets taken in the first round, there's a ninety-nine percent probability he will become a successful fixture for the future."

Everyone at the table pretty much agreed with Lee's assessment. Our debate about the Supreme Court and morality was forgotten.

9/7/2019— Philosophizing with Doc

I've been working on the renovations to Jeannie's kitchen since January. Like most remodeling projects, it has turned out to be much more complicated than I planned. But the result is great, and Jeannie is happy as can be.

While I was working on her kitchen, I didn't look at any of my old journals or even think about the Weimar Republic. However, now that the kitchen is complete, I'm turning my attention back to the book.

Doc and his wife, Anne, just returned from a month-long trip to Europe. Doc was telling me about how much they enjoyed Spain, Italy, and France. After that, he went on to tell me about their visit to Berlin. He talked about how, after being dominated by fascists and destroyed by the war, Germany focused on embracing the things to be learned from the mistakes of the past. He spoke about Berlin's memorial to Jews, the museums he visited, and how much the city had been rebuilt since the war. Doc was particularly taken by the differences in post-war reconstruction between East Berlin and West Berlin.

"It was a wonderful trip," he said. "I learned a lot that I didn't know before about the city. I was there once before. But I think my interest has been piqued by all of the research you've done about the Weimar Republic— and by our discussions. Anne told me she can't understand why you haven't gone there. I agree. You should make that trip. It would be fascinating to see the land of your grandparents. It would also probably influence your book."

I told him that I'd thought about making the trip and would give it some more thought— maybe go ahead and do it. I asked him to thank Anne for her suggestion.

I turned the conversation back to my book. "While you were on your vacation, I didn't work on the Weimar Republic. Instead, I finished Jeannie's kitchen."

I showed Doc a few photos on my phone, and he gave me some nice compliments on my craftsmanship.

"But now the kitchen is done," I said, "I am ready to dig into my book project. A couple of weeks ago, I started reading a pretty dense book called *The Weimar Republic*. It goes into a ton of detail discussing Weimar Germany's political intrigues, economic challenges, and the social conflicts that were going on in Germany at that time on in Germany. As I read the book, I couldn't stop thinking how similar the Weimar Republic's problems were to the political chaos we are experiencing here in the US— I'm referencing things like the Russia Probe, state abortion bills, immigration battles, and the Democrats' efforts to impeach Trump."

I paused, waiting for Doc to respond.

He looked at me and said, "OK, tell me more about what you are thinking."

I thought about it for a moment.

"With the exception of Adolph Hitler," I said, "who understood that the Weimar Republic's chaos was his path to power, it seems as if all of the German leaders were busy battling one another and didn't figure out what was being destroyed. They didn't even understand it was happening. The politicians, labor leaders, businessmen, soldiers, and statesmen were so into their strategies for obtaining power, that it— I mean, getting power— became more important than anything else in Germany. I think that is how Germany lost its democracy."

I waited again for Doc to respond.

After taking a sip from his latte, he said, "Yup, Hans. I couldn't have said it better. I will add something— drawing upon my experience as a healthcare provider. When a person doesn't take care of themselves— when they misuse their body and ignore the consequences of their behavior— the probability increases that they will become seriously ill. If a person does drugs, smokes, or they drink a lot, if they eat too much fatty food or don't exercise, most people realize that that person is abusing their body. But this principle not only applies to physical health. It is true for anyone abusing their own spiritual health. Don't you agree?"

I did and said so.

"Ok," Doc continued. "What you were telling me is that when politicians take advantage of their political system, when they are careless about preserving citizens' rights, and when they disrespect the integrity of governmental processes, they are not just abusing their political system; they are abusing their country. And yes, I agree that is what happened in Germany. Everyone was interested in the country's future— but only on their own terms. They were willing to gamble that their country would survive. But it didn't."

Doc paused. There was fire in his eyes as he said, "And you are also right that that is happening here in the good old USA. Irresponsible people are gambling with what we have— they are abusing the freedoms we take for granted— putting it all at risk— to pursue their personal vision of how things should move forward."

1/5/2020— I Decide to Visit Berlin

Doc and I get together at least once a month to go over drafts of my book.

This morning, he said, "Last fall, I suggested you take a trip to Berlin. Have you thought more about going?"

I told him, "Yes. I've never been to Europe. I want to see the city in which my grandparents lived, and I'm curious about some of the places in Berlin that Ilse wrote about in her letters. If I took the trip, I could check out some other things— you know, from my Berlin dreams. They seemed so real. So, yes. I've thought about making the trip, and I agree, going to Berlin seems like a good idea. It would be an adventure."

Inspired by Doc's comments, I ordered Rick Steve's Berlin Guidebook when I got home. Later, I went to Expedia.com and started looking for dates for flights and hotels later this year— maybe in early July.

I just made reservations for the trip from the tenth to the twentieth of July. I can hardly believe it. I'm going to Europe! I'm totally stoked about the plan!

Next, I need to apply for a passport.

3/26/2020— COVID Hits the Roundtable

The Bison Coffee Roundtable met this morning. Steve hadn't missed a meeting since I joined. But today, he wasn't there.

Ronnie explained his absence. "Millie, Steve's wife, called me yesterday evening. She told me Steve's got some sort of flu, probably the Chinese Flu. Millie said Steve wanted to come in anyway. But she laid down the law. She ordered him to stay in bed."

There were a couple of chuckles.

The conversation turned to the Chinese Flu.

Everyone looked to Doc to see what he had to say. Doc was wearing some sort of black surgical mask, which covered his nose and mouth.

"I've been reading about it," he said. "This is an awful lot like the flu that hit the world after World War I. That was a really big deal. It killed 25 million people. The World Health Organization has already declared COVID an international emergency. Trump pronounced it a national emergency on Friday, the 13th. That date is pretty ominous right there. This is one of the few times I've agreed with Trump on anything. It could end up getting pretty scary. The big pharmaceutical companies are working on a vaccine. But for now, we don't know what COVID is and have no way to stop it."

Everybody looked around the table at one another. We were all worried.

Doc continued. "I heard that the Governor is going to force most businesses to shut down in the next couple of days. We'll probably have to stop getting together for a while."

Ronnie interrupted. "Everybody needs to relax a little. Trump also said that the whole COVID outbreak is the Democrats' new hoax."

He paused and looked around the table before saying, "OK. A lot of people will get the Chinese Flu. But they'll recover. There is a new flu every year that people die from. Trump said he figures more people will end up committing suicide because they are freaking out about the bad things they hear about the Chinese flu from fake news channels than will actually be killed by the disease. In fact, Trump said that by Easter Sunday, the churches will be full again. I'll bet you he is right. Like I said, we need to relax a little."

Jerry added, "Amen. We need to relax."

Doc replied, "Well, I am worried. I love you guys, but I don't think we should be meeting today. I'm going to take off. I advise the rest of you to do the same."

I spoke up. "I need to be careful. I don't want to infect my daughter's family. Doc is right. We should hold off for a while."

Doc stood up. I joined him, and so did Jim.

Jim said, "My wife didn't even want me to come here today. Let's take a break, Ronnie. This'll end soon. We can get back together when we know everything is safe."

Ronnie replied, "Look, I don't know what's going to happen either. I am glad to hold off, quit for today, and skip next month's meeting. By then, we should be ok. Does that work for everyone? I'll call everyone and let you know when we will meet again. OK?"

Everyone nodded. The rest of the group got up, and we all headed toward the door.

As we left, Doc said, "Heh, Ronnie. Give Millie a call. Tell her we're all thinking about Steve and tell her to wish him the best."

4/9/2020— Roundtable Update

I spoke with Ronnie over the fence this morning. We were both working in our front yards. Ronnie told me he spoke to Millie last night. Steve is doing a lot better. He plans on being at our next Bison Coffee Roundtable get-together. Ronnie said he was relieved. A week ago, Millie had told him Steve was having difficulty breathing and that she was scared. That's good news, but what Steve went through says to me that this whole COVID thing should be taken seriously.

5/10/2020— Trump's COVID Press Conferences

I've watched a few press conferences on CNN in which President Trump rattled on about COVID. I guess the guy just likes yammering in front of a television camera. Even an auto mechanic like me can tell he doesn't have a clue about COVID.

One time, Dr. Anthony Fauci, his CDC infectious disease expert, giggled and rolled his eyes after Trump lashed out at the State Department, calling them the *Deep State Department*. In another weird statement, Trump suggested treating the body with ultraviolet light or injecting disinfectant into a sick person's body to kill the virus.

This coronavirus is serious. I wish Trump would back off and let the experts handle it.

6/1/2020— Trip to Berlin Cancelled

This morning, I cancelled my Berlin flight and hotel reservations. Given COVID, I had no alternative. I am really disappointed. I spent a lot of time reading Rick Steve's guidebook, Googling Berlin to learn more about the city, and imagining what my trip was going to be like. The more I thought about visiting Berlin, the more excited I became.

Hopefully, I'll be able to make the trip next year. Right now, however, with so many people getting sick (and a bunch of them dying), I need to be cautious.

What a bummer.

6/5/2020— Bison Roundtable Zoom

As a result of COVID, I haven't spoken with hardly anyone over the last couple of months. I've seen Jeannie's family, spoken with Ronnie over the fence, and saw Doc once when he stopped by to discuss my book. I've also spoken briefly to grocery clerks when I pay for my groceries. Other than that? Zilch.

The Coffee Roundtable hasn't gotten together since early April. Ronnie called last week to let me know he'd set up a video conference for this week using a program called *Zoom*. Meeting with a group of people on a computer will be new territory for me. I've never been on a video call. I downloaded the program onto my laptop yesterday, then tested it to make sure it was ready to go.

When I logged onto Zoom this morning, I saw Ronnie, Doc, Jim, Jack, Lee, and Tom on my laptop screen. A couple of minutes later, Jerry appeared. He complained about the complex technology. The rest of us just laughed at him, as Lee put it, for being technologically illiterate.

After all of these weeks of solitude, the call was satisfying. Each person told the others about how they were dealing with the pandemic. We agreed that COVID is harder to deal with for our kids than for us. Our kids are either working from home or have been laid off. It hasn't been so tough for us retirees except for Jack and Lee, who complained they had to babysit their grandkids, and that their grandkids are spoiled.

Steve told us about his illness and recovery. He said anyone who compares COVID to the regular flu doesn't know what they're talking about. He had a temperature of

103 degrees, a cough that wouldn't quit, a sore throat, and lost his sense of taste. Steve hasn't been able to smell anything for over a month, and he also still gets tired a lot.

Jim told us about a couple who'd gotten infected. The husband got COVID first, and his wife took care of him. After he had recovered, she got it and died.

Jack spoke about the services his church held on Zoom. He said one of the parishioners started making wisecracks about the pastor's sermon, not knowing that his microphone was turned on. The guy went on for more than five minutes and used a bunch of four-letter words to describe the pastor. We all laughed pretty hard. But I felt sorry for the guy.

Jerry said he'd heard that wearing a mask didn't help. He told us he wasn't going to ever wear one.

Doc told Jerry, "Lotsa luck, pal."

Jerry replied, "You're just panicking along with all the other liberals, Doc. You guys need to relax."

Tom threw in that he read that the virus got started in some Chinese laboratory. A website he visits regularly stated that the virus is some new kind of Chinese war on Western civilization.

Lee told us that what he missed more than anything else was watching major-league sports on TV. We all agreed

I said I hoped the pandemic would end soon. Doc told us that some sort of immunization should be available later in the year and would probably do the trick. Jerry commented that there was no way in hell he would let any government bureaucrat poke him in the shoulder.

The conversation turned to how the economy is slowing down because of COVID. Then it moved into a discussion of Trump vs. Biden. That discussion included all of the same old stuff.

10/16/2020— A Roundtable Discussion

It's been nice having our Bison Coffee Roundtable get-togethers back at the Electric City Coffee House. Today was our second in-person gathering after several Zoom calls. Last month, we had an intense discussion about wearing COVID masks. We finally agreed that each person will decide whether they want to wear a mask, and no one should complain about what another person does.

Everyone was present except for Jack. Jack is the third member of our group to get the virus. Ronnie reported that Jack is feeling better and plans on being with us next month.

Jerry missed last month's meeting because he had COVID. On our Zoom call the month before he got sick, Jerry told us he thought the virus was a hoax and that he would never wear a mask.

Jerry was with us today and said, "OK. I was wrong. I admit it. This COVID virus is tough. I almost had to go to the hospital. I can assure you. It's no hoax."

I noted that Jerry was wearing a mask.

When Ronnie called each of us before the meeting, he gave us a heads-up that he was going to ask for our opinions on the presidential election. So, everyone had a chance to plan what they wanted to say.

One member of our group, who will remain unnamed, saw me taking notes. He said he was worried that I would quote him in my book. (The word has somehow gotten out to the others that Doc and I are working on a book.) I told this guy (everyone else was paying a lot of attention) that I would just summarize the reasons members liked one candidate more than the other. I promised not to give any information about who said what.

I could see from the body language within the group that that issue had been discussed amongst them. There appeared to be general relief with my response.

In that spirit, below is my summary:

The reasons Coffee Roundtable members will vote for Biden are:

- Trump is a threat to democracy;
- Biden is honest and Trump is a liar;
- Trump's first presidency was too unpresidential;
- Trump uses racist language and admires authoritarian strongmen; and
- Trump didn't manage COVID well.

Reasons given to vote for Trump included:

- Trump understands the threat from wokeism by the intellectual elite;
- The networks and newspapers are biased and criticisms of Trump are mostly fake news;
- Trump has challenged worn-out political traditions that needed challenging;
- The country was doing well until we got hit with the Chinese Flu;
- Biden is called Sleepy Joe for a reason— he is a tired old idiot;
- Biden is a radical leftist who would lead us toward communism;

- Biden will unfairly favor brown and black people and discriminate against white Christians.
- Trump will stop immigrants from a) coming into this country, b) bringing in drugs, c) committing crimes, and d) taking American jobs.

The one thing I can say that ties everyone together is that the main reason each of us will vote for our candidate is because we dislike the other candidate more.

Ronnie called for a straw vote.

When I didn't raise my hand for either candidate, Ronnie asked, "Aren't you going to vote, Hans?"

I said something like, "I've been giving it a lot of thought, but I haven't decided who I'll vote for. I have the same reservations about the Ds I've always had. But Trump's first term in office was a complete clown show."

That was the truth. I am between a rock and a hard place, not sure how I'll vote.

So how did the vote go? I promised only to write in my journal— and then include in my book if I ever complete it— that a majority of Bison Coffee Roundtable members favor electing Donald Trump.

I was prepared for more conflict in the meeting, especially between Doc and Ronnie. But it never materialized. As we walked out of the coffee house, Doc told me that he and Ronnie had made their peace. They also had agreed that any strong differences between them would not be voiced in front of the group.

10/28/2020— My Vote

Since our last Coffee Roundtable discussion, I've had two follow-up conversations about my vote.

The first was with Doc when we met as we often do to discuss *The Weimar Journals*. We generally begin with Doc giving me feedback on the latest draft I'd shared with him. Today, we discussed my dream entries and right-wing critics of the Weimar Republic. It was an interesting conversation.

As that discussion ended, Doc gave me an odd look and asked, "Have you decided how you're going to vote yet?"

I told him, "No."

"Can I give you my thoughts?" he asked.

"Sure," I responded. "Go for it."

"First of all," Doc said, "I know your family has always voted Republican— at least since Roosevelt. But you shouldn't be letting what your grandfather and father decided control how you vote. The world is changing."

He gave me a thoughtful look, probably trying to judge how defensive my reaction to his statement might have been.

"You've been working on your book for some time now, Hans," Doc continued. "Doesn't what happened in the Weimar Republic frighten you? Don't you see similarities between how Hitler controlled the Nazis, how he manipulated the German people, and how Trump dictates to the Republican Party and tries to intimidate any American who disagrees with him? Isn't it obvious that Trump wants to be an emperor? In *The Rise and Fall of the Third Reich*, did you notice the book's epigraph? *Those who do not remember the past are condemned to relive it.*"

He paused and let that sink in.

"I saw that," I replied. "The thing that's difficult to deal with is that so many accusations have been made about Trump. The press describes him as corrupt, an incompetent fool, and an idiot. But I know the economy was doing quite well until COVID hit."

Doc chuckled and said, "Fox News is the only television station telling the truth, right? The Democrats rely on *fake news* to try to destroy Trump. Do I understand where you are going with this?"

I had to admit, "Not completely, but there is at least some truth in what you say."

"OK," Doc said. "Why don't we talk about fake news? We can start by looking at the Weimar Republic. It was pretty liberal. When Adolph Hitler criticized the Republic's leaders, promising to restore Germany to its place in history, his followers were comforted. Hitler never acknowledged the problems that the Republic was saddled with at the end of the First World War or addressed the Weimar Republic's successes. He blamed the Republic's leaders for the economic challenges Germany faced— as if the Weimar Republic had created the worldwide depression. Hitler continually criticized and blamed Germany's leaders while promising his followers he would solve all of Germany's problems without explaining how."

"Once Hitler was in power," Doc continued, "anyone who criticized his regime was imprisoned for telling lies about the fatherland. Any newspaper that criticized Hitler was accused of being anti-German, of lying, and was shut down— one way or another. The Nazi version of *fake news* was calling criticisms *lies*. Anyone who repeated those criticisms was eliminated— again, one way or another."

Doc paused, took a deep breath, and continued. "I don't need to go through the whole story. You've read *The*

Rise and Fall of the Third Reich. The thing you should recognize is that what happened in Germany is not unique in history. When a totalitarian wannabe establishes a repressive regime, their first step is to silence their critics; to call them liars using one name or another to put them down. Look back at history and see how often, after being criticized, autocrats eliminated their critics. Do you think Stalin encouraged honest discussion and legitimate criticism within his country? Do you think he allowed freedom of the press? No. That's where his gulags came in. Do you think that Mao permitted intellectuals to teach or newspapers to exist that did not support his regime? Of course not. He reeducated them. Il Duce in Italy? He used violence. How about repressive kings? Do you think that King George encouraged the American colonies to have a free and open press? Of course not."

Doc gave me an intense look. He may have been waiting for my response to his rhetorical questions. But I wasn't going there. I just waited.

"Do you think Putin allows freedom of the press?" he asked. No. His critics are all liars. They often fall out of hospital windows. Repressive regimes always begin by eliminating the voices of those who question their repression. In a nutshell, they accuse their critics whose viewpoints threaten them of being liars. Then they jail them, reeducate them, or assassinate them. They demolish physical printing presses, shut down the internet, or just sue the hell out of them with an army of attorneys. Repressive regimes never like criticisms— especially valid criticisms. They eliminate— one way or another— statements and their authors who challenge their autocracy."

I was surprised. Doc had gotten himself pretty worked up. His face had become red. He was showing me a passion I'd never seen from him. I stayed quiet.

"I want to assure you," he went on, "if a news report about Trump is dismissed without a response to the underlying facts, if it is just called *fake news*, that report is probably threatening and probably uncomfortably true."

Doc gave a much softer look before finishing up. "When it's all said and done, Hans, you personally don't decide who becomes president. You only contribute one vote. But when you go to the polls, you should feel like your vote is the decision for the whole country. That is the principle that makes democracy work."

*****

Another political discussion occurred on Sunday morning. I was raking some leaves when Ronnie called over the picket fence that divides our yards, "Wanna watch the Green Bay game? Sandy's out, and I ordered a pepperoni and mushroom pizza."

I won't spend a lot of time reviewing Ronnie's pitch. After he had poured each of us a beer, he hit all of the things about Biden that were mentioned at the coffee group— being weak, wanting to be a leftist dictator, and being soft on aliens. But he didn't offer any arguments for voting for Trump other than that Trump is an outsider, he's built a wall, and he isn't Biden.

I asked Ronnie what Trump was going to do to stop COVID and how he would fix the post-COVID economy. He told me Trump deserves credit for the COVID vaccinations being created in the first place. He initiated Operation Warp Speed and wasn't getting proper credit for it. He added that COVID was almost history, and that Trump had saved the economy once and would do it again.

I asked Ronnie about things Trump had said, such as denying making comments about grabbing women by the pussy even though there are videos of him saying it.

Ronnie said, "Fake news, Hans. You should know better than to trust the liberal press. They take everything out of context, manipulate it, or make it up. CNN? MSNBC? The New York Times? They are owned and managed by a bunch of liberals who don't give a damn about you, me, the truth, or this country. They are manipulating you as they build up their own wealth and power. Those reports are just fake news."

I counted. In his defense of Trump, I think Ronnie used the term *fake news* six times.

*****

I've got a few days to decide. I think I may end up voting for Biden. Doc's points about the Weimar Republic are compelling. That being said, we all feel that the devil we know is always worse than the devil we haven't met yet.

And I really don't know that much about Biden.

11/9/2020— Biden is Elected

On election night, Trump declared himself "the winner" before votes had been counted for many states. When the television networks reported that Biden was ahead, the Tribune quoted Trump as saying, "This is a fraud on the American public. This is an embarrassment to our country. We were getting ready to win this election; frankly, we did win this election. We did win this election."

Over the past few days, I've been listening to Donald Trump continue to complain that the election was stolen from him.

Joe Biden won. I'm not really celebrating. I just hope I won't end up regretting that I voted for him.

11/18/2020— Bison Coffee Roundtable, Post-Election

The Coffee Roundtable got together today.

Ronnie started things off by pointing out that Doc wasn't there, which was fairly obvious. We all had assumed Doc would be taking his victory lap. Ronnie explained that Doc called him last night and said that his wife, Anne, had the Coronavirus. Anne is getting better, but Doc didn't want to leave her alone and had to miss our get-together.

Ronnie asked if anyone wanted to say anything about the election.

Jerry and Tom took turns telling us how the election had been stolen from Trump.

There were no comments on what they said. I think group members were generally disappointed with the results, but also burned out on politics. They don't want to talk about Trump or Biden anymore.

Jim changed the meeting's tone by bringing up the 2020 NCAA college football season. He complained that, without any fans due to COVID, there was a lack of intensity in the games. Once our group started complaining about COVID's impact on football, our collective energy picked up.

I was relieved the presidential election wasn't mentioned again and that no one asked who I voted for.

12/12/2020— Roundtable Economic Discussion

The Bison Coffee Roundtable got together today. Ronnie sent us an email a couple of days ago saying he wouldn't be able to make it. He and Sandy are visiting friends in Portland. Ronnie encouraged us to go ahead and meet without him, suggesting that since the Ds had won the presidential election, Doc ought to run the meeting.

Doc started the meeting by saying, "Let's take a different approach today. We've all known one another for a long time. We didn't always agree on everything when we were kids, and we certainly don't agree on everything today. But we're good friends, and one of the reasons for that is that we listen to one another. Today, I'd like to do some listening."

Doc had everyone sitting up straight and paying close attention. No one was sure where he was going with that statement.

"Last week," he continued, "Anne and I were having a drink and I was telling her about the politics of the Bison Roundtable. Anne said, 'Your friends are smart. On top of that, they're honest people. Do you know why they support Trump even when they know he cheated just about everyone he's ever come into contact with?"

Doc stopped speaking and took a sip of coffee. The group was now even more intrigued with where Doc was going with this.

"I thought about her question," he said. "Anne is awfully perceptive. After a while, I realized she had a point. I've heard you guys say that Trump is great and that the Democrats are awful. But I know it's not that simple. I know all of you are honest and principled. You wouldn't support someone like Trump unless you had a good reason. So, that is what I would like to discuss today: *Why Trump?* Let's stay away from slogans and policy cliches. I'm willing to bet you voted the way you did for good reasons. I'd like to hear them. So, I'm asking you now, *Why Trump?*"

Nothing was said for a couple of minutes. Then Lee, one of the newer members of our group and someone who I'd learned generally doesn't say a whole lot about politics, started it out.

"I appreciate you asking, Doc. I am going to be pretty up front. First of all, I voted for Obama twice. In 2016, when it came time to decide if I would vote for Hillary or Donald, I asked myself, *Should I go with the Dems again?* I gave it a lot of thought. What I want from the government is safety and economic security. I know I'll never be rich, but I don't want to worry about whether I can hold onto my home. So, how I would vote in 2016 came down to personal economic issues."

Lee stopped for a moment. I could see he was jotting some numbers down on a pad of paper in front of him.

When he stopped writing, he said, "When I do the math, it's painfully obvious that Leslie and I are getting totally crushed by the economy. I'm going to go through the numbers for you. First of all, we depend upon social security for income— that's a total of about thirty-nine thousand dollars annually between the two of us. Seems like a lot, doesn't it? And since I own my home— we've been in it since 1978— there is no rent. In being able to say that, I recognize we are doing better than a lot of people."

He looked around the table before saying, "But I need to pay another two and a half thousand each year for property taxes. I also have a car payment of a little over three hundred a month— that's four grand a year."

He looked down at the numbers on his scratch pad before saying, "Insurance for my home, car, and our Medicare policies— that's about another three grand. Fuel for my furnace, electricity, water, garbage pickup, and sewer— they take about six grand a year. After all of those expenses, twenty-one grand is left. Still sounds pretty good, huh?"

I was tracking with Lee because I go through a similar budget exercise every year.

"So, what's left?" he asked. "The answer is plenty— cable TV, cell phones, and gas for my car. They cost about three grand a year. My tithe to the church takes another thousand. Then the big one— Leslie and I spend about nine hundred bucks a month on groceries. So, after all of those costs, we have about seven thousand dollars a year available— dollars that are not committed. That's about six hundred bucks a month— that goes to home repairs, insurance deductibles, gifts to my kids, clothing, and anything else we want to buy."

He paused, looking around the table before saying, "I used to get a little extra cash by filling in when someone was on vacation at my old auto shop. But my back problems finished that off. Leslie works occasionally at the nursing home— but that's minimum wage, and it's not regular. Managing our budget is a little like walking out onto a lake in early November. The ice is awfully damn thin.

Lee had everyone's full attention.

"In 2016," Lee continued, "My vote for president was driven by my finances. My choices were to vote for a rich woman who said everything was peachy-keen and who promised to keep it that way or a rich man who admitted that things were tough for average Americans and said he was going to do something about it."

Most of the other members of the Bison Coffee Roundtable nodded their agreement.

Lee finished up. "That's what I faced four years ago. This year, even though the Dems had a different candidate, their message didn't change. No disrespect to you, Doc, but you're in a different economic bracket than me. I'm willing to bet that the things you worry about at night are different from the things I worry about. Now that the election is over and Biden won, I hear him say all the right things. But I've been listening to the Dems say all of the right things all of my life. I don't believe them anymore. Doc, I can't afford to take another risk. The ice is too damned thin. I am afraid of going through it into the frozen water. If things don't get better, Leslie and I aren't going to make it."

When Lee stopped speaking, Steve said, "Amen, brother."

There was quiet again for a couple of minutes. I thought maybe that was it, that no one else would speak.

But Jerry picked up where Lee left off. "I'm on the same page as you, Lee. I think you and Leslie are actually doing better than me and Joy. I know there are tons of people out there who are in need. And I want the government to have programs for them. However, if people just want a free ride, if they don't want to work, somebody needs to give them a little tough medicine. The average American who has worked all his whole life wants someone in their corner for a change."

Jerry gave a big sigh. But he had more to say. "My son got laid off by his construction company last spring. He didn't go on welfare or unemployment."

Jerry paused and looked around the table, then added, "He certainly could have. He's working at a Walmart right now. Jimmy is bagging groceries. Is Biden going to do anything to improve his situation? Will he do more than tell Jimmy that things are going good? I doubt it."

Jerry stopped again, shook his head, and looked down at the table.

When he looked up, he said, "Trump is a blowhard. I know that. But Trump's biggest policy promises weren't for someone from some Latin American country. And they weren't for some spoiled American who has decided to change their sex. Trump was creating noise on issues important to those of us trying to figure out how to survive. He asked questions that needed to be asked— questions that no one else was asking. OK. He's a bit of a narcissist. I'm not dumb. But Trump spoke clearly to those of us who are just trying to get by. He wasn't obligated to the fancy bureaucrats who live in big homes or who spend all of their time and energy creating rules and regulations that make it harder for common folk. We voted for Trump because we wanted someone who would prioritize the rest of us who are frustrated with the bullshit that Washington creates every day."

Again, silence for a moment. Then Jack spoke up.

"You've heard it from me before," he said, "so I won't give another speech on it today. My main issue is that the abortion battle is not over. Biden speaks about being fair to everyone. But how about the unborn? Biden doesn't believe they exist."

Jack paused and might have continued, but Tom Benson, the other Roundtable member who joined after me, spoke up.

"Farmers and ranchers," said Tom, "those of us who own small spreads all over this country— we're being destroyed by the government's ecological rules. I'm not saying we shouldn't take care of the environment. Of course, we should. But the Democrats— and Biden— want the little guys to make all of the sacrifices. You can only make so many sacrifices, and then you're out of business. Hell, if the elites want to save the world, why don't they make a few sacrifices themselves? What Lee and Jerry said goes double for me. Ten years ago, I owned my ranch free and clear. But I've had to mortgage it to stay on the property."

Tom looked around the table. He clearly had everyone's attention.

Tom shook his head sadly from side to side before saying, "Each year, my mortgage grows as my bottom line shrinks. I'm caught between a rock and a hard place. The cost to feed my cattle increases, and the markets pay me less for my beef. How do you think that works? Big spreads— they buy feed at a discount. They sell their cattle directly to chains— eliminating the middleman. They make out. Not us little guys. And on top of that, I have to invest more and more every year to cut down my herd's impact on rivers and streams. I'm losing the battle, Doc. The math just doesn't work. We need someone to do something radical because the way things have been— it just ain't fair. When Trump spoke about tough times, he was telling the truth. Biden just pays more lip service."

Jim and I said nothing. I am not sure how Jim felt about Biden winning, but I sure hope Biden will do something for these guys. However, I would be lying if I said I was confident.

After Doc got his feedback, I figured he would challenge the statements that Lee, Jerry, and Tom made about the Democrats— speak about why Biden was the better choice. But I was wrong, he didn't. Doc deserved more credit than I had given him. Instead of disagreeing with what they said, Doc just thanked Lee, Jerry, Jack, and Tom for their willingness to be open.

Then Jim made a comment about the Green Bay Packers, and the conversation changed, I am sure to everyone's relief, to the upcoming NCAA and NFL football playoffs.

Today's Coffee Roundtable turned out to be pretty interesting. As we headed out of the Electric City Coffee House, I looked at the others. It seemed that each of them felt as good about the morning's discussion as I did.

1/7/2021— The Attack on the Capitol

Yesterday, January 6th, I woke up at eight, went into the kitchen, started a pot of coffee, filled a bowl with Wheaties, and turned on the TV.

The newscasters on both Fox and CNN were intense. Of course, that's nothing new in and of itself. But my attention increased when I heard what they were saying about an election protest taking place near the United States Capitol Building.

Over the past few weeks, I've heard Trump encourage supporters to attend a big *Save America March* at the capital. The protest was aimed at supporting his claim that the 2020 presidential election had been stolen from him.

The House and Senate were scheduled to vote yesterday on whether to accept state-certified presidential election results. That would finalize Biden's election. But Trump wanted the vice president to stop the Senate hearing. Trump wanted him to direct states to do some sort of a recount of their ballots. Trump believed that if that happened, he would win.

As I watched things unfold, the crowd at his rally kept getting bigger and bigger. At 10 AM, Trump began a speech in which he told his supporters to go to the Capitol Building and make their voices heard. Some took off for the Capitol Building as soon as he said that. Others, in particular a right-wing militia group named The Proud Boys, were already beginning a protest at the Capitol Building.

CNN panned the crowd while Trump spoke. Signs supported Trump's contention that he had won the election. Some attendees carried weapons. A Confederate flag was being waved in the audience. When Trump finished his speech, most of the remaining crowd headed to the Capitol.

Meanwhile, at the Capitol Building, some of the crowd started marching toward a police barrier. The police tried to stop the marchers. They were not successful. The crowd started chanting "Fight for Trump."

I watched the demonstration in amazement. Was I watching an American coup live on television? Was I seeing the end of our democracy?

I fixed myself lunch, a ham and cheese sandwich, while I stayed glued to the TV. If this wasn't really happening, it would qualify as an entertaining movie. A little after noon, the networks announced that the Capitol police had labeled this a *riot*.

Then the mob broke into the Capitol Building, and the Secret Service evacuated Vice President Pence from the Senate. Police were getting beaten up. Rioters were searching for the House Speaker, Nancy Pelosi, chanting, "Where are you, Nancy?" Senators and Representatives of both parties were calling the White House to ask Trump to tell the rioters to leave and asking for National Guard support for those still in the Capitol. After Trump tweeted that Mike Pence didn't have the courage to protect the country, the rioters began to chant, "Hang Mike Pence."

It was like watching a revolution in some banana republic.

A little after I finished my sandwich, Trump sent out a tweet asking supporters at the Capitol to remain peaceful. Remain peaceful? If that was peaceful, I'd hate to see violent. For the first time, I realized how dangerous Trump is.

At 1:30, our time, the White House press officer announced Trump was asking the National Guard to come to the Capitol.

At two, Biden addressed the nation and called on Trump to "demand an end to the siege." A little while later, Trump sent out a video that asked his mob to go home. He didn't call them a mob. Instead, he said, "We love you. You're very special."

At nine-thirty in the evening, the House and the Senate continued their joint session, and I went to bed. When I awoke this morning, I went into the kitchen and turned on the TV.

I learned that in the middle of the night, the vice president announced that a majority of the electoral college votes were cast for Biden. That officially confirmed Biden's election.

The day's chaos had ended.

A Dream, 1/9/2021— The Night of the Broken Glass

When I woke up this morning, my heart was beating rapidly. For a little while, I sat on the side of my bed visualizing the dream I had just had. Suddenly, I realized it was the first Berlin dream I'd had since moving to Great Falls. It was about Kristallnacht— the Night of the Broken Glass. I picked up my journal and headed to the kitchen, where I started a pot of coffee. I will write the dream up in German as I have in the past. Then afterwards, I'll translate it into English for my book.

In the dream, Greta was sitting in their apartment kitchen listening to the radio. The announcer was speaking about a Polish refugee who had shot an official from the German embassy in Paris. The radio announcer quoted Joseph Goebbels as saying that every German Jew would pay dearly for this assassination. He reported that attacks were happening to German Jews, their houses of worship, their homes, their property, and their businesses. The announcer said these attacks were a spontaneous reaction of the German people.

Greta kept looking up at a wall clock as she continued to listen to the radio reports. She had a worried look on her face. The apartment door opened. It was Karl. Greta stood up and went to him. They embraced, and she wept.

"When I heard," she said through sobs, "about all of the violence in the streets, I feared for you, coming home through these riots. I was afraid for myself as well, sitting here at home, a woman whose mother was raised Jewish. Oh Karl. I am so frightened."

Karl wore the most serious look I had seen on him in any of my dreams.

"It was awful," he responded. "I generally walk home past the Prinzregenten Strasse Synagogue. As I approached it this evening, I saw the house of worship was on fire. Dozens of Hitler Youth armed with clubs and stones stood by as crowds of people watched the synagogue burn. Many cheered, and no one tried to stop it. I avoided going in front of it by turning onto Bundesalee, but that route was no better. I saw Jewish shop windows being smashed by Hitler Youth with clubs, viewed merchants being beaten by the Brownshirts, and stores being emptied of their contents, stolen by hordes of people of all ages. It was chaos, Greta, horrible, awful, hateful chaos. I watched an old Jew being thrown to the ground, beaten by teenagers. I saw furniture being tossed out of apartment windows onto the street. It was so frightening, Greta. How can this be happening in our Germany?"

Suddenly, it was Karl who broke down weeping. I was shocked to see their roles reversed. Greta consoled a distraught Karl.

Historical Note, 1/9/2021— Kristallnacht

I am willing to bet that this week's Capitol Building riot prompted my dream about Kristallnacht.

I have been sitting in my kitchen, remembering when I first learned about the Night of the Broken Glass. It was 1988. I attended an assembly at Jeannie's school memorializing the horrid event on its fiftieth anniversary. A Jewish man who had seen the violence spoke to Jeannie's middle school students, describing the viciousness he'd seen.

A few days after the assembly, Jeannie's teacher wrote to the speaker. She thanked him for his presentation and asked if he would share a copy of his comments so that she could share his talk with her class.

Jeannie gave me a copy of the talk she received from her teacher. I folded it over and placed it in my journal next to the entry that described my attending the talk.

I read it through today. His talk seems relevant to my Weimar analysis and to what happened earlier this week in Washington, DC.

I Googled the Jewish man who gave the talk to the middle school students. I learned he passed away in 2016. As a means of more fully describing what Karl and Greta experienced on that night in 1938 and in honor of the Jewish man who addressed the students, I've included his presentation below.

Memories of Kristallnacht See Note 1
*It is difficult to speak about the ghastly
pogrom, known by the German euphemism,*

Kristallnacht, the Night of the Broken Glass, when open season was declared on Jews and tens of thousands of windows were broken throughout Germany. It was, of course, more difficult to live through it. Some of the hard questions are: "How are we connected to Kristallnacht and the Holocaust that followed it? How are we to interpret that tragic history? What can we do about it in terms of the future? And who is 'we'?

If remembrance and concern are confined to us alone, or to only a tiny minority of the Jewish minority, what can be the outlook for the future? The point is that there is more than one "we". The "we" is humanity, the human community, though to speak of a human community remains only an ideal, as is evident from the ugly reality of our still dangerously fragmented and strife-torn world, East and West, North and South, in the Middle East, and in our own country. Not only are there differences between the diverse 'we's' that we belong to, but within these 'we's', people think and react differently, just as the victims of the Holocaust consisted of different 'we's' and differing individual human beings. Clearly, none of us can speak for all the victims or for all survivors or for all who care and remember. But speak we must.

In November of 1938, I had just turned 17, a few months younger than Herschel Grynszpan. That summer, I had returned to my home in Frankfurt am Main, from Italy, where I had studied at a business school near Milan and worked as an interpreter in San Remo. In San

Remo, by the way, there was an incident that will give you a flavor of the times. When my mother visited me there in the spring of 1938, it was announced by the authorities that since Herman Göring, Hitler's Reichsmarshall, was vacationing there, all visiting German Jews would have either to go back to Germany or go to prison. Mother chose to go back to that larger prison, Nazi Germany.

During that fall of 1938, I was waiting in Frankfurt for my U.S. immigration visa, though it was not until 1940 that my quota number "13,204" came up. The U.S. quota for Germans was relatively small, as you know. While the Nazis denied that Jews were Germans, the United States treated them as Germans. Even those of us with close American relatives and affidavits of financial support found it very difficult to come to this country. On the 7th of November, 1938, we heard on the Frankfurt radio that a Polish refugee from Hanover by the name of Herschel Grynszpan had shot Ernst vom Rath, the Third Secretary of the German Embassy in Paris. Apparently, the act was a desperate gesture of revenge to call the world's attention to the inhuman treatment of Jews, including Grynszpan's family, which had just been deported from Germany back to Poland under the cruelest conditions. Of course, we did not hear that explanation until later, since the Nazi propaganda talked only about the 'typically criminal behavior of the Jew Grynspan.' Many Jews were fervently hoping that vom Rath would not die since it was feared that his death would make the persecution of Jews in Germany only worse. But few could have anticipated the horror that unfolded on the night of the 9th to the 10th of November, after it was reported that vom Rath had expired.

My parents and I were gathered around the radio, listening to the vicious Nazi propaganda with its threats that every German Jew would have to pay dearly for the deed of Grynszpan. Joseph Goebbels, Hitler's Minister for Propaganda and Popular Enlightenment had given free rein to what was to happen, and in line with the Hitlerian technique of the big lie, he and the controlled media repeated again and again that the brutal attacks on German Jews, their houses of worship, their homes, their property, and their businesses, were a result of the spontaneous reaction of the German people. Actually, it was the stormtroopers of the S.A. (Sturmabteilung) and later the S.S. (Schutzstaffel) who led the orchestrated assaults. Most of what we learned about what was going on came from foreign shortwave stations like London and Radio Luxembourg. To this day, I remember the announcement advising of the regular newscasts in German: "Ici Radio Luxembourg, Vous allez entendre dans un instant les communications en langue Allemande." Naturally, the Nazis threatened severe punishment for listening to foreign newscasts.

Our apartment in Frankfurt was on the third floor, at a corner location. How well I remember gazing in horror from a window in my mother's music room as flames shot up from the roof of the synagogue, half a block down the street. The large and beautiful building, in Byzantine style, was a well-known landmark of the Westend. It was shortly after midnight that I called my parents and we stared in disbelief. Later, I learned that the firetrucks and firemen had simply stood by, only making sure that the adjoining buildings would not catch fire. Unlike many of the 270 synagogues put to flame that night in Germany, ours was not totally destroyed, although the inside was largely burned out.

Two or three houses away from us lived the mayor of Frankfurt, a Nazi by the name of Krebs. That circumstance may have been the reason that our home was not attacked. In the Old City of central Frankfurt, where the more conservative and orthodox segments of the Jewish community were located, many apartments were ransacked, furniture thrown from windows and balconies, and Jewish citizens beaten up.

On the morning of Thursday, November 10, I decided to go downtown to see what was happening to my mother's grave dismay. I assured her that I would be careful, and in youthful innocence, or perhaps ignorance, off I went. Unlike me, who had blue eyes and, at that time, blond hair. The Zeil, the main shopping street, was littered with glass from the store windows. S.A. men congregated before the shops, carrying abusive signs, warning people not to buy from

Jews. Near the Opernplatz, the opera square, I saw a crowd assembled in front of a shoe store (called "Speyer", as I recall). Some young men climbed over the jagged glass of the shop window and threw shoes and shoeboxes out onto the pavement. Shouting expletives and slogans like "Juda verrecke" (Juda croak), others would throw the shoes back into the shop, to the amusement of some of the onlookers.

What particularly struck me was a policeman who, once in a while, would kick some of the shoes out of the way so that pedestrians could continue to walk by. "Ordnung muss sein" order, if not law, must be preserved). The police behavior, like that of the fire brigades, was in line with Nazi directives from Berlin.

During that day, my parents and I learned that many of the men of families with whom we were acquainted had been picked up and sent to concentration camps.

On Friday morning, the 11th, a man in civilian clothing came to our door and explained that he had been delegated by the Gestapo (the Geheime Staatspolizei - the secret police) to pick up my father. My recollection is that my mother tried vainly to convince the man that I should go instead, since I was younger and my father was 64. The man turned out to be an attorney who, like my father, had lived many years in Strasbourg. They had known each other by reputation. (My father had been an importer and exporter in Strasburg before World War I, when it was still a

*part of Germany). The attorney expressed
embarrassment and shame, explaining that unless
he followed orders, he would endanger himself and
his family.*

*My father was taken to the Festhalle, where he
was held with hundreds of other Jews who were to
be transported from there to concentration camps
like Dachau, Buchenwald, and Sachsenhausen. The
men had to engage in gymnastic exercises,
although those over 60 were excused (one man
had died from exhaustion the previous day). My
father, typically, insisted on taking part. In
principle, he didn't like being exempted. I still
recall how outraged he had been in April 1933
when we saw on the Zeil the first organized
boycott of Jewish shops and department stores.
Having served as a frontline Unteroffizier for over
4 years in World War I, and before that, two years
in the Kaiser's army, he deeply resented the
accusations of Hitler's and Goebbels' propaganda
machine that Jews were cowards and betrayers of
Germany.*

*To go back to my story, my mother began to
call around to other Jewish families whose men
had been picked up and sent to concentration
camps on the preceding day. She was told that it
was best to hire an attorney, and she promptly
made an appointment. At about 10 p.m. that
evening, the doorbell rang, and my mother,
leaning out the window, heard the voice of my
father. I will never forget how she jumped for joy
and how we celebrated his homecoming.*

It turned out that he had been released almost by happenstance. He had been picked up on Friday, the day the Nazi regulation went into effect that only Jewish men between 18 and 60 were to be sent to concentration camps.

The rounding up of Jewish men on the first day, the 10th, was more disorganized, and we were told of a Jewish boy of 14 and a senior of 84 who had been taken. The camps were not prepared for the many Jews who were being imprisoned from all over Germany. There were not enough toilets, kitchen facilities, bunks, and so forth. Some men's limbs froze during the bitter cold to which they were exposed without blankets, and of course, the stench in the overcrowded barracks was unbearable. The number of Jews who died as a direct or indirect result of Kristallnacht has been estimated to be between 2,000 and 2,500. Most of the 30,000 who were taken to concentration camps during the Kristallnacht period were eventually returned to their homes, though they had to wait weeks or months for their release. An earlier release was granted to those who could show they had an entrance visa for another country. But as you know, most countries were reluctant to accept Jews, especially after Hitler prohibited people from taking more than 10 marks ($4) with them when they emigrated.

There is no time this evening for the horror stories which I could tell about my relatives, school chums, and friends and acquaintances of my parents. Let me mention here only the experience of a business friend of my father whose last name was, symbolically, Dreyfus. He was one of the few German veterans honored with the Pour Le Nérft, the highest German World War I decoration for bravery in action. When he visited us, his hair had turned completely white. Later, we found out that at least at that time, veterans with the Pour 2e Nérft were exempt. Obviously, this incident cannot be compared with the brutal murders and other atrocities like being forced to clean streets with toothbrushes, being assaulted by S.A. men and other rowdies, being forced to flee in the middle of the night, or being deprived of home and livelihood.

In January of 1940, my father was able to leave for the United States on a non-quota immigration visa obtained thanks to his son in America, my half-brother.

However, the U.S. Consul in Stuttgart, a reputed antisemite, refused to issue a non-quota visa to my mother because she was not my half-brother's mother, but only the wife of my father. To the obvious concern of my father, the Consul asserted brusquely that the United States was not ruled only by Mr. Roosevelt but also had a Congress. And it was their immigration laws that applied in this case. He apparently did not know that even Mr. Roosevelt (with not a little assistance from his Secretary of State, Cordell Hull) was very cautious in providing the help that might have rescued so many of German and other European Jews. As a result of all this, my mother received a quota number which was much higher than mine. Hers was in the 23,000 range. When her number came up, the ship passage which my father had booked for her in New York had been sold to the highest bidder.

My Viennese-born mother had been a popular opera star. Her last opera engagement had been as the first contralto at the Frankfurt opera, where she sang Carmen in Carmen, Queen Amneris in Aida, and other leading roles. (Four trunks of some of her personal belongings, including some recordings of her singing, reached me after the end of the war.) In June of 1942, she consulted in her home with a Frankfurt banker about her precarious financial situation, the Nazis having by then confiscated almost all of my father's property.

Their meeting together was denounced by someone in the neighborhood as violating Nazi laws regarding relations between Aryans and Jews. The Gestapo took the banker to their headquarters. My mother was so concerned with the fate of this man, a Catholic with a large family, that she decided to go to the Gestapo headquarters to explain the completely innocent meeting she had with the banker. Years later, from a letter of a Christian acquaintance who was allowed to bring her a suitcase with clothing and toilet articles, I found out that on that same night my mother was put in a box car like the one you may have seen at the Holocaust Museum in Washington DC, and that it was believed that this shipment of Jews was sent to Lublin.

I did not find out until 1987, through a German memorial book commemorating the German Jewish victims of National Socialism, that my mother was killed at Lublin's Majdanek concentration camp. The book recorded no date, but only the entry verschollen (disappeared). I must add that several of my uncles, aunts, and cousins in Germany and Austria were also victims of the Holocaust.

There is no time here to relate my own escape in March 1939 to England where I stayed on a farm with English friends until I was able to immigrate to this country in May of 1940, except to mention that after the war broke out, on the 1st of September 1939, the British government declared Jewish refugees from Germany, like myself, to be enemy aliens. We had to report regularly to the British police. Still, I was very grateful to find temporary refuge in England.

In concluding this remembrance, I want to reiterate that, like everyone else, I cannot speak for all, not even for my beloved mother, to whom I was very close. But like others, I must speak up, for unless we humans find a way to truly care for each other, the world will learn nothing from the bitter lessons of the past.

So, I pose the question— the answer to which must transcend this worthy memorial occasion — what has the world learned and what have we learned? I say the 'world', for despite ethnic, national, religious, and other diverse heritages, needs, and strivings which all too often put the stress on human apartness (in South Africa they call it apartheid), we are all part of humanity - and therefore the question concerns us all.

The difficulty is that to really understand and learn from Kristallnacht and the Holocaust, we need to understand more of human history. We need to understand the social, moral, political, and even economic contexts that make possible a Kristallnacht and extermination camps - genocide, slavery, apartheid, ethnic cleansing, massive rape, racism, antisemitism, oppression, heartless exploitation, in short, the continuing injustice and inequities we see in so many parts of the world, even in our own society.

For me, such contexts and conditions of understanding lead to a rejection of the exceptionalism thesis that is frequently applied to groups such as Germans, Americans, and, of course, Jews. I reject the idea of Deutschland, Deutschland uber alles, uber alles in der Welt (Germany over everything in the world), or Amerika uber alles, or that Jews as a group are genetically inferior or superior to other human beings. One can be proud of one's cultural, religious, or other traditions and heritage without denigrating the intrinsic worth of other human beings.

Yes, the Holocaust, the industrialized, mechanized slaughter of two-thirds of Europe's (one-third of the world's) Jews was unique. But to compare the moral significance of its uniqueness with the unique tragedies that have befallen other groups, including American native peoples, African and Asian peoples, Armenians, Gypsies, the vast majority of Haitians, and the millions of women who have been raped over the centuries would be both morally and politically counterproductive.

So, I profess after all that I have witnessed, that to me being Jewish is, first of all, a way of being human. That is, it means embracing others who seek to be human through a different cultural or religious heritage. The struggle for human justice and freedom from fear and want may take centuries to win. But it is a struggle that must continue. Since I was born as a Jew, perhaps fate has chosen me to survive so I could do my part to help my fellow humans live in dignity and mutual understanding. This is an almost overwhelming task, indeed, but then I am not alone.

9/15/2019— Note about Grandma's Newspaper Clippings

Note: Included with Grandma's letters from Ilse were two yellowed newspaper clippings that Grandma had cut out from the newspaper. I have included those news articles below. They represent important elements of my story.

FLASH: GERMANS SURRENDER UNCONDITIONALLY
REIMS, France, May 7, 1945 (Delayed)
The Associated Press

———————————————

Through an iron-faced Prussian general, speaking after he had finished signing the unconditional surrender of the Nazis, Germany today pleaded for mercy for the German people. On the wall behind his back was a huge chart tabulating Allied casualties.

He was Col-Gen. (Alfred) Jodl, chief of staff of the German Army. He was standing in a room of a red schoolhouse in Reims, where Gen. Eisenhower had his advanced headquarters.

On a big wooden table in front of him lay four identical documents to which he had just affixed his signature—one each for the United States, Britain, France, and Russia. … Seventeen correspondents were present at the signing and heard Jodl's plea. After he had signed the four instruments of surrender, and after the military representatives of the four Powers had signed them, Jodl asked for permission to speak. He was told that he might.

He held himself stiffly erect. His voice was low and soft. He said: "With this signature, the German people and armed forces are, for better or worse, delivered in the victors' hands. In this war which has lasted more than five years, both have achieved and suffered more than perhaps any other people in the world. I express the hope that the victor will treat generously with them." His face was expressionless.

So were the faces of the American, British, Russian and French generals who represented the Allies. All had seen the German murder camps and all knew the furious cruelty of German occupying forces.

Jodl finished speaking and sat down. A moment passed in dead silence. Then the German representatives were taken down the hall to meet Gen. Eisenhower.

… Again, there was a moment of heavy silence.

Then Eisenhower spoke. He was brief and terse as always. His voice was cold and stern. His steel blue eyes were hard. In a few clipped sentences, he made it plain that Germany was a defeated nation and that henceforth all orders to the German people would come from the Allies. He said they would be obeyed.

Then the Germans filed out. It was over. Nazi Germany has ceased to exist. The war had ended.

BERLIN UPDATE
BERLIN, MAY 10, 1945:
By HAROLD KING, Associated Press, AP Moscow bureau chief

This town is a city of the dead. As a metropolis, it has simply ceased to exist. Every house within miles of the center seems to have had its own bomb. . . . The scene beggars description.

I have seen Stalingrad; I have lived through the entire London blitz. I have seen a dozen badly damaged Russian towns, but the scene of utter destruction, desolation and death which meets the eye in Berlin as far as the eye can rove in all directions is something that almost baffles description.

Dozens of well-known thoroughfares, including the entire Unter den Linden from one end to the other, are wrecked beyond repair. The town is literally unrecognizable.

The Alexander Platz, in the east end, where the Gestapo headquarters were, is a weird desert of rubble and gaping, smoke blackened walls. From the Brandenberg Gate, everything within a radius of two to five miles is destroyed. There does not appear to be one house in hundred which is even useful as a shelter. . . . The only people who look like human beings in the streets of what was Berlin are the Russian soldiers. There are two million inhabitants in this town, the Russian authorities told me, but they are mostly in the remoter suburbs. In the center part of the town, you only see a few ghostlike figures of women and children—few men—queuing up to pump water.

If Stalingrad, London, Guernica, Rotterdam, Coventry wanted avenging, they have had it, and no mistake about it. The Red flag, or rather several red flags, fly on top of the Reichstag which is burned hollow. The Tiergarten opposite the Reichstag looks like a forest after a big fire. There was heavy street fighting here. . . . The population and the Red Army soldiers are attempting to clear some of the main streets.

The Russian command has already erected at all main squares and crossings huge sketch maps without which it would be impossible to

find   one's   way   about.
Except for an occasional Russian army car or horses drawing Russian army carts, there is a complete silence over the city, and the air filled with rubble dust.

One sign of life, however, are the interminable columns of displaced persons of all European nationalities who seem to be marching through Berlin in various directions, carried forward by a homing instinct more than any clear idea where they are going.

These columns of freed slaves are sometimes a mile long.

Ilse's Letter, 8/12/1945— Update After War

Dearest Sister,

My life has turned into a nightmare. I hope you understand why I was unable to write to you for such a long time. There is so much that has happened— so many things I need to share with you after all of these years. I now have the opportunity to share with you what has happened to me, what I have witnessed. Our beautiful Berlin has been destroyed. My life has been ruined along with this city that I love.

The last time I was able to write to you was in 1937. I was on a brief holiday and sent you a postcard from Magdeburg. Times were already difficult. Suspicions of one another in Berlin had grown. People who were viewed as suspicious often disappeared.

At the time, I had no idea what was happening. I had heard that those who were disloyal to the Reich or dishonest in their business dealings were taken from our community to be reeducated. I have since learned that these camps were not about reeducation— they were scenes of horror. I have also learned that Jürgen was part of the Nazi machine that created the terror in those camps.

Gisa, I have loved my country, and I don't think that was wrong. I listened to our leaders and trusted them. I read the daily newspapers and felt certain that they would only tell me things that were actually happening. The regular radio broadcasts told me how awful England and France were— how the United States and Russia were threats to the fatherland. I listened. I still love my country. Germany is not and never was the Nazi Party. But the Nazi Party controlled it.

I now know that we were misled. I understand now that innocent people were imprisoned under horrible conditions, that many of them died in those camps— they were murdered. And worst of all, I learned that my husband Jürgen, who I once believed to be so wise and so good, and who I loved so much, was an active participant in those horrid acts.

When I sent you the postcard in 1937, I was fearful that I could be accused of disloyalty to the Reich by communicating with those in other lands who were loyal to other powers. I was afraid of my husband Jürgen, who had been so sweet and loving when I first met him, but had turned into a tyrant. By the time I sent you the postcard, I rarely saw Jürgen. When he was not on duty at the Sachsenhausen re-education camp, I learned he was spending his time with another woman.

In the fall of 1938, Jürgen left Berlin, assigned to a post in Poland. Jürgen said he could not tell me more. I now believe what he did there was no less awful than what I have since learned he did at the death camps of Dachau and Sachsenhausen.

Before the war, I saw Jewish families being marched to the trains. Jürgen told me they had committed crimes against the Fatherland or against other Germans.

Shortly before Jürgen went to Poland, I was shocked to learn that not all of these supposed criminals were evil. Do you remember Mutti's dear friend Clara? I used to play with Clara's daughter, Judith. One day, as I waited for a tram to take me to the market, I saw a group of Jews being escorted to the Grunewald S-Bahn train station to be transported to the work camps. One of these Jews was Clara's daughter Judith. Next to her were her three children. Each of them was lugging a suitcase.

I was shocked. I wanted to speak to Judith. But the guards who were marching alongside them pushed me aside. I could see that she recognized me as well.

Judith wept. And I wept.

I returned home. It was one of those rare occasions when Jürgen had come home for an evening. I told him about what I had seen. I asked if there was any way I could testify that Judith is a good person. Jürgen cursed me. He told me that I was a stupid woman, that all Jews needed to be eradicated.

After Jürgen left for Poland, I found work in a factory producing uniforms for our soldiers. The days were long, the work hard, and our supervisors unkind. I made friends in the factory— other women whose husbands were fighting for the Führer.

On Fridays, after I received my pay, I went to the market to purchase food supplies. The quality and amount of goods on the shelves had continuously declined during the last decade. What I was able to buy reminded me of the years I took care of our father after you and Dieter left for Montana.

As time passed, the workers in our factory began to understand what was happening. Our Germany was being destroyed. You cannot imagine how frightening those nights were when anti-aircraft fire signaled that Allied bombers were coming. I heard and felt bombs land, then listened to the fire engines race to extinguish the fires.

Each morning as I walked to work, I would pass devastation from the previous night's bombing. Gisa, you cannot imagine the destruction and would not recognize our city center. So many beautiful structures have been destroyed. Our Berlin has become a wasteland. As the end of the war approached, all of us in our factory knew Germany had lost. We prayed for it all to end as soon as possible.

In May, after the Russians arrived and were soon followed by the Americans and the British, our lives were about to change. We were afraid. We had no idea of what to expect. Along with all other physically able women, I was directed to work on cleaning up the damage and waste left by the bombs.

We work hard separating bricks and other salvage from the waste. It is heavy physical labor for which we are paid a very small wage. We are always hungry, and while the Russians have set up kitchens to feed us, each meal offers so little soup, Gisa— and that soup is so thin.

Pamphlets have been distributed to all German citizens. I have learned of the horrid murders Germany committed— about the atrocities to Jews, to intellectuals, to anyone who questioned the power of the Nazis. Gisa— I have such shame. What our nation has done is so awful! I just didn't understand it as it happened. I just didn't know.

Since the war's end, most women I know have learned their husbands' fate— whether they died or became prisoners of war. I am ashamed to say this, but when I learned that Jürgen had died, I thanked God. I don't know how he died, and I don't care. I am just glad I will never see his ugly, hateful face again.

The beautiful apartment I loved so much has been taken from me. The flat with all of the elegant furniture, as well as my personal possessions, was given to Russian officers.

Before I moved out, I learned that the family that had lived in the building before me— a husband, wife, and two children— had escaped to France. I have since learned that that family was later placed in a French prison camp where they perished.

I live now in a small room in a flat which I share with three other women and their children. It has no heat and no water.

Since I was a small child, my goal has been to try to live a good life. I dreamed that someday I would find a kind husband and give birth to three beautiful children. This wasn't to be. Gisa— when you left, we had no idea of the future terror you were escaping. My life has become hell.

I was interrogated regarding my behavior during the Third Reich in a brief interview. Three men, a Russian, a Brit, and an American, wanted to determine what crimes I might have committed as a part of the Nazi regime. At the end of that interview, I asked the American how I could send a letter to you. He told me that if I brought him the letter, he would post it for me. When and if you receive this letter, know that it was sent with the assistance of George Thompson of the State of Illinois.

When the Führer came to power, I felt as if someone had finally come to save the fatherland. He told us how much he loved our land. He promised us so much. As I look back at the awe I felt so deeply, I now recognize this man was deranged. Adolph Hitler did more to destroy this land we love than anyone has in German history. It is our disgrace that we allowed him to come to power. That is now the past, and we must live with its horror. We allowed it to happen. I will eventually die with that shame upon my soul.

I will write again soon. I miss hearing from you and hope that you and your family are well. The return address shown on this envelope should find me.

Gisa, if you can send me any dollars, they will help me feed myself. Any amount you can afford will make a great difference.

Finally, more important than any of the sad words that are written on this page is my love for you.

As always,
Your loving sister, Ilse

Ilse's Letter 9/21/1950— Touching Base

Dearest sister,
I received your letter yesterday. My highlight each month is hearing from you and the love and generosity that accompany your messages.

Today is the anniversary of your loving generosity. Five years ago, I was blessed when I received that first Western Union money order for forty dollars. What a godsend that was! It seemed like you and Dieter were giving me a fortune. I remember laughing after converting your gift into Reichsmarks. Afterwards, I experienced the joy of my new wealth at the meat market where I purchased a lovely bratwurst, at the baker's where I bought a large loaf of black bread, at the cheese shop where I bought a lovely chunk of Emmenthaler, and at the farmer's market where I indulged myself with a purchase of carrots, cabbage, and potatoes. I grimace as I recall the stomachache I had for a week after consuming too much of the soup I made from those beautiful foods from my loving sister!

Five years later, I still receive your monthly money orders. They allow me to continue renting my room and purchase foodstuffs for wonderful meals. You and Dieter are my special angels. Thank you so much!

Life in West Berlin has improved since the blockade ended. There are more goods on the shelves. And yes, in answer to the question from your last letter, I do worry less. Yet the conflict between the Russians and the Americans continues almost daily. Uncertainty about what the future will bring has not declined. Each Sunday, as I walk to mass, I pray that God will see us through the political hate that has dominated my life.

I am feeling better than I was when I wrote to you last month. While my cough persists, I am hopeful that it will go away before winter comes. However, as we all know, the aging process is full of challenges.

I continue to work part-time at the bakery. The proprietor graciously allows me to take a day off when my cough becomes particularly bad. Even then, he brings me a small sack of fresh, warm brotchen since the bakery is so near to my room.

My rooming house landlady complimented me yesterday on how young I look. I have lost much of that extra weight I had complained to you about.

You must send me more photos of your beautiful grandbaby, Hans. He has grown so big! You and Dieter should be proud of Mathew and Nancy for giving you your beautiful grandson, Hansi.

As always,
Ilse

2/10/2021— COVID

I received a call last night from Anne Brennan, Doc's wife.

I congratulated her on beating COVID and told her it was wonderful to hear from her. She thanked me but said that her being cured had come at a price. Just as she was beginning to feel better, Doc came down with the virus.

She told me Doc has had COVID for over a week now. Anne is worried because Doc smoked a lot when he was younger. She said his coughing is coming from deep in his chest. His breathing has become difficult.

I asked her if I could stop by to wish him well. She said that would be nice. She recommended I wear my mask. She would set us up in their living room and would definitely seat me across the room from Doc.

This morning, I picked up some red roses at the grocery store and drove over to Doc's home. I had never been there before. The house is on a large landscaped lot overlooking the Missouri River. It is a single-story home with cedar siding and a modern flat roof. The house was probably built in the 1980s.

Anne greeted me at the door. She looked tired— and worried. She is of medium height, slight build, wears wire-rim glasses, and has short gray hair. I handed Anne the roses. She thanked me— for both the flowers and the visit— and led me into a large, high-ceilinged living room.

Doc was reclining on a long couch. Anne suggested I take a seat across the room from him, next to an open window. Anne helped Doc sit up. Then she left the room.

I could see how difficult it had been for Doc to sit up.

Once he was upright, he gave a few deep coughs, then he said in a hoarse voice, "Sorry, Hans. This is not the ideal circumstance for you to meet Anne, and I certainly can't give you a grand tour of our home. But I appreciate you stopping by, and thank you for the roses."

Doc coughed for a moment. It sounded really bad.

Doc spoke slowly, with great effort, "COVID has been hell. It was tough seeing Anne go through it. And just when I was starting to relax because she was feeling better, it hit me like a ton of bricks. Hopefully, I'll feel better in a couple of days. I'm downing all the vitamins I can find. It's rotten that the vaccination became available at the same time as I got the virus. What a bummer."

I didn't know what to say. I just said, "Yeah. What a bummer."

Then I added, "Your home is sure beautiful, Doc."

He half coughed and half laughed before saying, "Thanks. We'll have to have you over here sometime when I'm not an invalid."

Again, I didn't know what to say.

"How's the book going?" he asked.

I had to think about it for a second before responding. I was so focused on how hard it was for him to sit up and speak that I couldn't remember the last time I'd worked on it.

"It's going OK," I said. "I focus on one section at a time— going back to the history books, making sure I got it right, cleaning up the language and stuff— and hoping the whole thing comes together. We're almost done, I think. But you got to get better, Doc, because you're the one who's going to tell me whether it's working or not— and what I have to change in order to improve it."

Doc laughed. But the laugh turned into a coarse cough.

A moment later, Anne came into the room and gave Doc a look full of worry.

"I think Doc has got to get some sleep," she said. "Hans, I'm glad you came today. But he needs to rest now. Maybe you could stop by in a few days, you know, when Doc's feeling better?"

Doc, a gray, serious look on his face, smiled and said, "Anne used to be a charge nurse, Hans. She's the boss in this here hospital. Gotta do whatever she says."

I stood up and thanked them both for allowing me to visit. Then I headed out. As I left the room, Doc slid back into a horizontal position and closed his eyes.

Anne saw me to the door.

"Thanks," she said, "for coming over. Doc likes you so much. This project with you has been the most satisfying thing he's worked on since he retired. It's meant the world to him. I enjoyed meeting you and hope to see you soon."

As I drove home, I was concerned.

4/4/1951— Notification from Berlin

Grandma's papers also included the following letter.

4 April, 1951

Frau Gisa Braun,

It is my solemn duty to inform you that your sister Ilse passed into the arms of our Savior on the second day of April in this year of our Lord, 1951. Ilse, leased a chamber in my rooming house for the past six years. She was a quiet, good person who always showed respect to me and others in this building.

I believe Ilse kept you well informed of her battle against lung disease. In the past few weeks, her condition worsened. She became bedridden. I sat by her bedside during much of this time. Ilse often spoke to me of her love for you. She asked that I write to you upon her passing and thank you for all of the generous love and gifts you have given her throughout her life.

For most of her life, your sister worshipped at St. Nicholas Church before it was badly damaged toward the end of the war. Since then, she worshipped at nearby Lutheran Churches. Father Gustav, who provided spiritual direction to Ilse since the devastation of St. Nicholas, sat at Ilse's bedside as she passed to Jesus. He assured Ilse that her remains will receive a Christian burial in consecrated ground. Should you wish to contact Father Gustav to learn more about Ilse's final moments and the location of her interment, I have enclosed his card with this letter. Ilse asked Father Gustave to donate her few possessions to the Archdiocese of Berlin.

Ilse often spoke about her happy memories of childhood with you and her loving parents. I know that while this letter will prompt a great deal of sadness for you, it should also bring some level of thankfulness that your loving sister has been released from the pain she endured throughout much of her life.

I wish you peace that hopefully will accompany the memory of your sister's love,

Olga Dietrich

Note: I searched through Grandma's papers but was unable to locate Father Gustav's card or any additional information about him.

2/14/2021— Terrible News

This morning, I was drinking a cup of coffee while watching a CNN panel discussing Trump's second impeachment trial.

The phone rang. I hoped it would be Doc letting me know he was feeling better, that he would say something like, *I am feeling better. Let's meet for coffee at Electric City tomorrow. I'd like to hear how you are going to address January 6 in your book.*

But it wasn't Doc. It was Anne, his wife. The moment I heard her voice, I knew what was coming.

"I'm sorry, I have to pass on terrible news, Hans." Her words confirmed my fear.

"Last night," she stopped speaking for a long moment, "last night, Doc passed away. He was so sick at the end, Hans. It was a release. I.... well, there is not much more I can say. Doc cared for you a lot, Hans. He would come home after having coffee with you— he would be speaking excitedly about the history of the Weimar Republic— about your Berlin dreams— about your family's history. He couldn't stop talking about your project and......"

There was another long silence. I waited.

Anne continued, "Doc is gone now— hopefully to some sort of better place."

I was caught off guard. Doc had become family for me. I am ashamed to say that my feelings were entirely focused on my loss. All of a sudden, I realized Anne must be hurting. I tried to say something thoughtful to her. I think it came out empty. The conversation was short. I thanked her for calling. She thanked me for being such a good friend to Doc. That was it.

After I hung up the phone, I felt lost, utterly empty and lost.

2/21/2021— So Very Sad

I just came back from Doc's graveside service at Highland Cemetery. There were hundreds of people there— folks of all ages— all standing in sad silence in the cold, blowing snow. I realized Doc was loved by a lot of people. I listened while friends and former patients spoke about how important Doc had been to them— to their families. It made me feel sort of small— sort of like my life has been nothing.

Anne was there. We briefly exchanged kind, polite, empty greetings. Anne told me she hoped we could become friends someday. She looked so tired, so sad.

The sense of great loss appeared to be a common theme for all of the mourners.

Ronnie and Sandy were there. Ronnie's eyes were red. He'd obviously been crying. Doc and Ronnie may not have agreed on anything political. But the look on Ronnie's face showed me how much Doc had meant to him.

It was lonely driving home. This evening, Jeannie invited me to join her family for dinner. I told her how sad I was. Then I wept. Jeannie was sweet. She really tried to make me feel better. But on a day like this, there isn't too much anyone could say.

I was awfully fortunate to have gotten to know Doc.

3/8/2021— Done with the Weimar Project

It has been almost two months now since Doc passed away. In that time, I haven't turned my laptop on once.

Working on *The Weimar Journals* was satisfying. It gave me a lot of stimulation during a period in my life that was otherwise empty. I learned a lot as I researched German history, family letters, and looked back at my personal history through my journals. That learning can never be taken from me.

But I have run out of gas.

Trump is pretty much history. Hopefully, this country will recover from COVID. And I can only hope that the partisanship that has dominated our lives will diminish.

But I am done working on *The Weimar Journals*. I need to start figuring out where to put my energies.

A phrase I have heard often recently comes to mind: *It is what it is.*

4/15/2021— Personal Projects

I am going nuts without anything to work on. When I had the auto shop, the next customer's car was always there, requiring total attention. After I moved to Great Falls, my century-old fixer-upper house offered me a basket of projects. As I got close to finishing all of those home projects, I was introduced to the Bison Coffee Roundtable. Those meetings brought relief to my isolation. But Doc's suggestion that I work on the *Weimar Journals* is what made the big difference.

The past few months have been empty. Losing Doc was a blow that will never totally heal. It's been over a year now that everyone has been struggling against COVID. There is no real end in sight. I don't feel as vulnerable to the disease as I did before. Receiving my COVID vaccination was a big deal. But time is moving slowly.

1/20/22— I find a Project

Before I jumped into *The Weimar Journals*, I had been playing with the idea of building a garage off the alley. My backyard is large enough to absorb a good-sized double garage.

I've been doing a little research on the web. A twenty-four-by-twenty-four-foot garage would let me park my truck and leave a second parking space for me to rebuild an old classic car. I'm also thinking of having a workbench go across the back of the garage. The cost of construction would probably be less than fifteen grand, which I would fund with the remaining proceeds from the sale of my Billings home.

I ordered blueprints online. They include a materials list. I plan to go into the city this week and apply for the necessary permits. I should be going whole hog on the project by the time the weather warms up and have the garage completed by the first snow.

10/30/2022— My Garage is Complete

The most satisfying moment in any project should always be when you can say *I'm done.* I can say that today. My garage is complete! The City gave me a final permit approval this morning. Building it was a back-breaker, but the garage looks fantastic and came in on budget (almost).

I didn't do it all by myself. George, a cement mason who lives a couple of doors down, finished the floor, and his buddy, an electrician, hooked up the electrical to the main box. Other than that, I did do it all.

The space is perfect for my pickup, and there is plenty of space for me to work on a project car. Yesterday, I brought up my set of mechanics' tools from the basement and started looking online for a classic fifties car to tear apart and rebuild.

1/30/2023— A '56 Ford Fairlane

Today, after regularly searching through a half-dozen classic cars-for-sale websites and checking out about twenty different possible vehicles in person, I purchased my project car, a '56 Ford Fairlane sedan. I bought it from a rancher near Raynesford.

After looking at a bunch of photos of the car on the internet and speaking with the rancher on the phone, I drove over yesterday to inspect it. The car has only ninety-eight thousand miles on it— at least that's what the odometer says. Before going to look at it, I went over to the NAPA Auto Parts Store. They confirmed that parts for the car will be easily available. This Fairlane is exactly what I was looking for. I paid cash on the spot. It hitched up nicely behind my pickup. I hauled it home, and it's now sitting in the garage.

My Fairlane was sitting in the rancher's dusty old garage, undriven, for at least a couple of decades. Its two-tone blue paint is super-faded and there's rust on the engine hood. But its chrome accents look sharp, and the body is straight and solid. Rebuilding the three-speed automatic will be a piece of cake. But I'll have a local machine shop help me rebuild the block.

This beautiful sedan hits a sweet spot for me. Grandpa had a two-tone green '56 Fairlane. He loved it. I have memories of him and Grandma taking me to the Dairy Queen in that car. I would always get a Dilly Bar.

I'm jazzed. This sedan is exactly what I was searching for. I'm ready to begin work on it on Monday morning.

9/16/2023— **The Beautiful Fairlane**

After one of my auto shop customers gave me the go-ahead on a complex repair, I'd roll up my sleeves and tear into their car. I would always try to exceed my customers' expectations. When the repair was completed, if it had met my standard of quality, I was always satisfied, and they were always happy.

That's how I feel about my rebuild of the Fairlane— happy and satisfied. I enjoyed working on this 1956 classic, but I'm thrilled to say *I'm done*. The two-tone blue paint job was the last detail. I hadn't painted a car since the sixties, and almost had a nearby body shop do it for me. But I figured I might as well go for it, and it wasn't a mistake. Once the paint was dry and the trim back in place, I stood there and admired my new old car for half an hour. It looks so nice. My Ford Fairlane is an absolute beauty.

When I had it idling during the final tune-up, the car didn't vibrate or make a sound. Standing next to it with the hood down, you couldn't tell if it was running or not. I doubt it ran that nicely when it was new.

I drove over to Jeannie's today to show it off. She hadn't seen the car since the seats were reupholstered. I took her and her daughters out for a spin around town, up Second Avenue, and back down First. I repeated that loop a couple of times and received several thumbs-up from pedestrians.

Then we headed over to Ford's drive-in (where else in a Fairlane?). I treated Jeannie and the kids to chocolate shakes, cheeseburgers, and onion rings. Sitting there in the Fairlane, eating that classic lunch, it was like old times.

I am so glad I took on this project— and now, I am so pleased that it is complete.

9/20/2023— Dream Inquiry, "Where Is She?"

I stopped working on *The Weimar Journals* more than two years ago. It never occurred to me that I would have another Berlin dream.

This afternoon was cold and rainy. I was sleepy and decided to take a nap. I went to my bedroom and quickly fell asleep. When I woke up, it was dark outside. I felt panicky and disoriented. I'd just had another dream about Karl and Greta. I headed to the kitchen, stuck a cup of coffee in the microwave, and started writing the dream up in my journal.

*****

The dream took place in a sterile office lobby. There was no one there except for a clerk working behind a counter. The thing that stood out was the uniform the clerk wore. It was grey-green, had a black belt with a round silver buckle, silver buttons, a black buttoned-up collar, and black shoulder markings. Silver eagles were sewn onto the uniform's left sleeve and above the right jacket pocket. I recognized the uniform immediately and, from it, understood my location. I was in a Gestapo headquarters.

A man came into the lobby from the street and approached the clerk. I recognized him. It was Karl.

"Heil Hitler," Karl said to the clerk while raising his right arm in the fascist salute. "Would you be so kind as to assist me? My fiancé has disappeared. I was told your office might have information about her whereabouts. If, by some chance, she has been detained by your office, I will be able to share information with you that should result in her release."

The clerk looked Karl up and down. Then he handed Karl a paper form and said, "I am not certain that the Gestapo will be able to assist you. But I will check our records to determine what information we have once you have given me your name, address, and the vital information about the person you are seeking."

Karl took the form to a wooden standing desk in the back of the lobby. He wrote on the form for several minutes, then handed the completed form to the clerk.

"Please wait here, sir," said the clerk. He raised his arm and said *Heil Hitler*. Karl returned the salute. The clerk disappeared through a side door in the lobby.

Minutes later, the clerk returned and said to Karl, "We may have some information for you, Herr Becker. Kindly follow me back to our interview room. Lieutenant Mueller will inform you of the facts related to your Fräulein Bauer."

Karl followed the clerk through the side door and out of the lobby.

My dream ended. That was when I woke up in a panic.

9/23/2023— A Conversation at Electric City Coffee

This morning, I was drinking a cup of coffee at the Electric City Coffee House when Anne Brennan walked into the coffee shop. I hadn't seen her since the graveside service two and a half years ago. She gave me a big smile and waved. I waved back. While she was in line to order, she turned toward me and asked if she could join me.

A few minutes later, Anne sat down. We had the somewhat uncomfortable conversation you sometimes have when you don't know someone so well and haven't seen them for a considerable period of time. We each struggled to say a few things about how we had spent the last couple of years. Then Anne talked about how much she missed Doc. I told her I missed him as well, and things loosened up. I sympathized with how tough it is to lose a mate— I told her I had been there and explained how empty my life had become after losing Mary.

The barista brought Anne her cappuccino, and we continued to chat.

Anne said, "I am aware how tough it was for you to lose your wife."

She paused, then added, "I have an admission to make, Hans. I know a lot more about you than you know about me. Doc wasn't totally up front with you in the beginning of your relationship with him. Doc and I always worked closely together on projects. Pretty much from the outset, when the two of you started working together, Doc shared your materials with me about your project— including your journals."

I laughed and said, "I think it would be a little absurd for me to get too mad at Doc for sharing my stuff with you after all this time. If I did get mad at him, it wouldn't make a whole hell of a lot of difference to him. Would it?"

Anne joined in the laughter and replied, "I'm relieved."

She asked me how my book was coming.

I told her, "It isn't. I dropped *The Weimar Journals* project shortly after Doc passed away. The fire was gone."

Anne responded, "That's a real shame."

Then she totally surprised me.

"The suggestion," she said, "to write the book from your journals, dreams, family history, and Weimar Republic research. It was my idea. I suggested it to Doc after reading your journals. He immediately liked the idea. I always worked with Doc on his writing projects and edited all of his drafts. I did the same for your project. Many of the suggestions Doc gave you after reviewing your materials— they were mine."

I was gobsmacked. She could see that and began to laugh. I started to get embarrassed— I think my face turned red. Then I realized how weird the whole situation was and joined her in laughter. What else could I do?

Once we stopped laughing, I asked her, "What have you been doing with your time?"

"Oh, I've been volunteering at the free clinic," Anne responded, "at the food bank, and…"

She was quiet for a moment, then said, "And I've been doing a lot of reading."

She was silent again for half a minute before finishing her thought. "To tell you the truth, Hans, life has been fairly empty. Not being able to have children was never a problem for Doc and me. We were always so busy. Living with Doc was an adventure. He was always having a new idea or willing to try something new, or talking about some interesting news issue, or telling me about a book he'd just read, or one he'd heard about. But now, well, I really envy you— I mean, having your daughter's family here in Great Falls."

Then Anne asked me what I'd been doing.

I replied, "When I took up the *Weimar Journals* project, I decided to forget about other projects I had considered taking on."

"Yes," she said and chuckled. "I remember them too."

"Anyway," I said, "a few months after I dropped the book project, I decided to go ahead and build that garage. I got it done. My other idea, if you recall, was to buy an old car and restore it. That's what I've been working on. I now have a really nice two-car garage. Sitting in it is a shiny, almost new-looking, 1956 Ford Fairlane. I completed the restoration a few days ago. For a test run, I am thinking about taking it out on a day trip to Glacier National Park."

I paused before adding, "Got any plans tomorrow?"

"I'll have to check with my social secretary," Anne responded with a chuckle.

After saying that, she smiled and said, "Why, how nice! My calendar is clear."

9/29/2023— A Day Trip to Glacier

Yesterday, Anne and I drove to Glacier National Park (and back) in my '56 Fairlane.

It was a clear, cool day. I picked Anne up at her home at eight, and we were on the road. The Fairlane was running beautifully. We didn't talk a whole lot as I turned onto I-15 going north out of Great Falls. We followed that for about seventy miles until reaching State Highway 44. I left the interstate there and traveled on a two-lane road heading west.

Fifteen minutes after leaving the interstate, we were riding through Valier, a small town along the way, and were passing a coffee shop in a building that looked like an old bank from the 1920s.

"Would you like a cup of coffee?" I asked.

"I was going to suggest it if you hadn't," replied Anne.

I pulled into a parking lot behind the little coffee shop.

We went in. The coffee shop was called *Folklore Coffee*. There were no other customers. A young female barista with blue-green hair and a long ponytail asked us what she could fix for us. I ordered a coffee latte and a piece of cherry pie. Anne ordered a cappuccino and an apple tart.

"My treat," she said as she pulled a credit card out from her wallet.

We sat down at a small table while the barista fixed our drinks and heated our baked treats in a microwave.

"Look at that," Anne said, pointing behind me.

I turned around and looked. There, on the brick wall behind me, was a large reinforced metal door— maybe six feet tall by three feet wide. It appeared to be the armored entrance to an old bank vault.

The barista with the colorful hair was setting our drinks and treats down on our table.

Anne asked her, "Is that a bank vault?"

"Yup, she said. "It sure was. This little building dates back to 1910. It's been a lot of things over the years. It was originally the First National Bank for this thriving little town. They shut the bank down at the beginning of the Depression. I think they shut it down after it got robbed too often rather than because it ran out of money."

"I've always wondered," said Ann, "what politics are like in a town like this?"

I was embarrassed by the directness of her question.

The barista, however, did not seem to be offended. She gave a smile and replied, "Politics? You mean local politics, or do you mean national politics?"

"National politics," replied Anne with a twinkle in her eye.

"That's a good question," the barista said. "The politics around here are pretty interesting— but I don't think they're too unique. I was raised near here, and went to high school twenty miles away. People in this part of the State have seen a lot of change. Jobs are going away. Prices are going up. And wages are staying low. Locals watch their TVs and see all the money being made in this country, and they know they aren't the ones making it. It's frightening for them."

She paused, checked over his shoulder to make sure she had no customers waiting, then continued, "Attitudes around here toward national politics are governed by people's fears. They read about people of color rioting and immigrants coming into this country. They're afraid that things are going to get worse instead of better. When I was in high school, I got to know a few immigrants, some gay kids, a bunch of Native Americans, and a slew of others who weren't mainstream white Christians. They were cool people. So, I'm not full of fear. But people who grew up around here— they see this country change and they're uncertain what it means for their futures."

The door in the front of the coffee shop opened. A Native American woman walked into the coffee shop.

The barista turned around and headed toward the front counter while saying, "Hi Shirley. How's it going?"

Anne and I watched as the barista and her customer chatted while the barista fixed a large, cold coffee drink to go.

After the customer left the shop, the barista returned to our table and continued her response to Anne's question.

"The people around here are straightforward and honest," she said. "They just want to have a life for themselves— and for their kids. But things are changing. They're afraid. Even if they have a job and a home, even if their farm is doing OK, they wonder what is going to happen to their kids. They hear about more immigrants coming into this country from faraway places— immigrants with different colored skin and different religions who speak different languages. They are afraid these people will steal their place in society. That frightens them. These are God fearing people who have worked hard. They wonder, 'What can we do?' Then somebody comes along and tells them he can solve their problem, while the Democrat candidate won't even admit that there is a problem. Guess who they vote for?"

She stopped speaking and looked over her shoulder at a couple who had just entered the coffee shop.

Before leaving us to take their order, the barista added, "The politics here in Montana are the politics of fear. These are good people. They are happy to have a simple life. They just want some security for themselves—and for their kids. Change can be awfully hard."

Anne and I had finished our coffees and our treats. We thanked the barista as we left the shop and headed out to my shiny, two-tone blue Ford Fairlane.

As we got out onto the road, I said something to Anne that had been troubling me. "You know, Anne, I've been feeling pretty guilty. After my wife passed away, my life became pretty empty. Nobody really touched base with me. I was by myself. I sold my business and moved up here to Great Falls. I kept busy by working on the house. But my life was pretty empty. When my next-door neighbor, Ronnie, invited me to join the Bison Coffee Roundtable, I was thrilled. Shortly after that, Doc reached out to me. He was so welcoming, so open. Then he suggested this project— a book based on my journals. I seized upon that opportunity because my life was so empty. Doc really helped get my life back on track."

I said nothing for a couple of minutes, just letting the scenery pass us by.

Then I finished my thought. "Doc was my only friend. When I came over to your home after Doc got ill, I could see the pain you were going through. After you called to say that he had passed away, I was devastated. I went to the burial and saw all of the people who had been his friends. It was humbling. That was two and a half years ago. I never checked in on you, never gave you a call, or stopped by to see how you were doing. I assumed that with all of those people, you wouldn't be alone like I was. Now, I realize what a selfish and self-centered perspective I had. I apologize to you."

Anne just looked ahead at the road. We could see the snowcapped mountains in the distance. She was silent for about five minutes before responding. In the corner of my eye, I saw her brush away a couple of tears.

"Thank you for those thoughtful words, Hans," she finally said. "It did get pretty lonely after Doc passed away. All of the other couples who were friends to Doc and me— well, they sort of disappeared. I don't think any hard feelings were intended or that things would have been that much different for Doc— I mean, if I had passed away and he was the one who was left alone. But yes, it was pretty lonely. I don't think you and I are so unique in that regard. I just think that's what happens when a couple is separated by death— or probably even by divorce, for that matter. People just don't know how to approach the survivor."

The Ford Fairlane continued to carry us toward those beautiful snow-peaked mountains as we enjoyed a comfortable silence.

After a few minutes, Anne continued. "Most of the people at Doc's funeral had been his patients, were his coworkers, or knew him from when he was a kid. I met Doc in college. I grew up in Missoula and was attending the university there to get my nursing degree. I was finishing that up when I met Doc. He was on rotation at the University Hospital. It was not quite love at first sight— at least not for me. Doc got there before me. But we were married within a year. When Doc told me he wanted to return to Great Falls, I had some trepidation. I knew that Great Falls was not as culturally up to snuff as Missoula. But I went along with it. During all these years I lived in Great Falls, I never made that many close friends. Life was either work or having fun with my husband. I didn't make other close connections."

She paused before adding, "That's how it goes, I guess."

The rest of the ride was beautiful. We got to Glacier National Park, drove in a way, and went for a hike, enjoying the breathtaking views. Then we turned around, headed back to the car, and drove back towards Great Falls. We stopped for an excellent burger and milkshake in Browning. We also broke the trip up a couple more times just to get out of the car and stretch our legs. My Ford Fairlane behaved beautifully the whole trip.

When I drove up the driveway to her home later in the afternoon, Anne told me we should become friends. She said she hoped I would give her a call soon. She would like to do something with me again.

I promised to give her that call.

A Dream, 2/5/2024— The Nightmare

When I went to bed last night, the wind was howling. I could feel cold creeping into my room.

When I woke up in the middle of the night, my heart was pounding and I was confused, unsure of where I was. It took me a minute to realize I was in my bedroom in Great Falls. I had just had another Berlin dream.

I looked at the clock. It was 3:50 in the morning. The sound of the wind had disappeared. But it was awfully cold in my bedroom. I knew I needed to write my dream down. So, I threw on my robe and slippers, grabbed my journal and pen, and headed to the kitchen. After turning up the thermostat, I began to write.

This dream was different. Though it was clearly Berlin, I saw none of the other folks I'd become familiar with from my previous Berlin dreams.

In the beginning, I was standing in front of the Brandenburg Gate. I was in a panic— crying out to assorted people as they walked past me, "What happened to Karl Becker? Where is Greta Bauer? Please, can you help me find my friends?"

I was walking through a constant flow of men and women dressed in old-fashioned clothing, German soldiers in green or brown uniforms, and officers in grey uniforms with SS insignias or red armbands with black swastikas. I passed under the Brandenburg Gate, heading along Unter den Linden. All the while, I kept asking those I saw, "What happened to Karl and Greta? Where are they? Can you help me, please?"

No one responded in any way. They didn't even look at me. It seemed as if I was invisible to them. In the dream, my sense of urgency was different from any feeling I remember having from any of the other dreams. It was a feeling of being lost— of extreme emptiness— of complete and absolute worthlessness.

As I reached the end of Unter den Linden, instead of seeing monumental buildings, I stood in front of a huge mound of horribly thin, naked, lifeless bodies. This mountain of death was reminiscent of photographs I've seen taken by GIs immediately after the Allies entered the Third Reich's concentration camps.

And that was the dream.

I just looked up at the kitchen clock. It is 4:30 in the morning. I feel like calling Doc. But of course, that is crazy. Doc is gone. Anyway, it is too early in the morning to call anyone. But I realize that even if it wasn't so early, there is no one whom I can call. No one who wouldn't think I had just lost my sanity.

I feel so alone.

I am going back to bed. Hopefully, I'll be able to get some sleep.

2/5/2024— Several Hours Later

I was groggy when I woke up at nine this morning. I found my way into the kitchen and made a pot of coffee. A little while later, I sat there, sipping the coffee, realizing that I needed to speak with someone about my dream. But there was no one to speak with.

I have not mentioned any of my Berlin dreams to Jeannie. While I should probably do that sometime, today is not the day. Jeannie is too busy and doesn't need the worry— and she would probably think the whole thing is more than a little weird.

The only person who would understand what the dream means is Anne. I haven't called or touched base with her since our drive to Glacier National Park last fall.

But if I do want to speak with someone, Anne would be the one to contact.

(Half an hour later). I broke down and called Anne. She responded warmly, asking how I had been. I asked her the same. Then, I got to the issue at hand. Would she meet me at the Electric City Coffee Company in about an hour? Anne told me she would.

She hesitated, then asked, "Could you tell me what this is about?"

I told her, "I had another Berlin dream."

I heard a brief, light laugh on the other end of the line before Anne said, "See you in an hour."

2/5/2024— Coffee with Anne

I just returned home from my get-together with Anne at the Electric City Coffee House. I generally walk there, but it was too damn cold this morning. I'm at home now, sitting at my kitchen table, journal in front of me, writing a description of my get-together with my good friend's widow.

I arrived at the coffee shop a little early. Anne arrived a little late. By the time she got there, I was sitting at a table in the back, enjoying my latte and twice-baked almond croissant. When Anne arrived, she was heavily bundled against the cold in a thick down parka with a red wool scarf wrapped around her neck. As she unwrapped herself, she scanned the coffee shop. When she saw me, she gave a big smile, a wave, and walked over to the table. I stood up and she gave me a big hug, put her jacket on the back of a chair before returning to the coffee counter to order a drink and a pastry.

A few minutes later, as she sat down, she gave another warm smile and said, "I am absolutely on pins and needles. I cannot wait to hear your dream."

I held off on beginning my description and asked her how she'd been.

She smiled and said, "Oh, I hate cold weather, Hans— always have. When Doc decided to retire, I told him we ought to move somewhere where the sun shines a lot and it gets uncomfortably warm— all year round. Doc wouldn't consider that. His compromise— which I accepted— was that every winter, we would travel to some tropical paradise for a few weeks. Now that Doc is gone, I have discovered that I am just too old and settled in my patterns to make such a big move. But I still take an annual trip to some sort of paradise. I just got back a couple of weeks ago from the hotel in Cabo that Doc and I used to visit. While I was there, I slowed down, soaked in the sunshine, drank some Margaritas, and read a good book. When I returned to Great Falls, I was fully prepared to freeze my butt off."

The barista placed Anne's cappuccino and lemon bar in front of her. Anne thanked him and took a sip of her drink.

After a small bite from the lemon bar, Anne looked up and gave me another big smile before saying, "I am all ears, Hans. I cannot wait to hear about your Berlin dream."

I had my journal with me. I had decided that reading my journal entry describing the dream was the way to go.

A few minutes later, after I finished reading it to her, I realized my hands were shaking.

Anne had watched me closely as I read. Then, she took another sip of her drink and silently looked out the coffee shop window. We sat there without a single word being said for maybe five minutes.

"Well," she finally said, "that was intense."

I waited for more.

"I could ask you what you think the dream meant," she said. "But that would not make a whole hell of a lot of sense. What your dream means is self-evident. The symbolism is so bold and clear. Wherever your series of Berlin dreams is coming from— whether it's from your subconscious psyche or from some sort of surreal communication from the past, the conflicts presented to you are quite apparent. I don't need to tell you that there's no one out there— not me— not Doc— if he were alive— and not any ghosts from Germany. No one else can respond to your question about those two characters, which I believe were totally invented by you for your dreams."

I chewed on what she had said, but didn't respond. Her words were interesting. But what was I going to do? Somehow, there had to be more.

"I have a question for you," she said. "I know you were talking about taking a trip to Berlin. You haven't mentioned taking that trip to me. Did you ever go on it?"

I replied, "I made plans to go there in early 2020. But after COVID hit, I dropped the plan. Then, once I decided to stop work on the book, I didn't give it any more thought, even after COVID was no longer an issue."

Anne appeared to ponder my response.

Then, she looked directly at me and said, "I know that Doc gave you a lot of advice about writing the book and feedback on what you had written. I know this because, as I told you before, a lot of that feedback and advice came from me. But I don't think Doc ever analyzed your dreams— I don't think he ever told you what this whole thing means. I think he thought it was an incredible collection of related perspectives that fit together— like a jigsaw puzzle. I am sure he had his psychological insights— in fact, I know he had those insights. But I don't think he would ever have told you his conclusions or beliefs about what was going on in your dreams."

She paused, took a deep breath, blew it out, then continued. "This all is obviously very important to you, Hans. The reason you had the dream last night is that there is something inside of you that is pushing you to put the pieces of this whole thing together. What is this whole thing? Is it the history of your family? Is it your heritage? Is it your intellectual curiosity about the Germany of the past? Or maybe your questions are about dangers the United States is facing today— dangers reminiscent of those in the Weimar Republic. Whatever it is will continue to lurk inside of you until you somehow address it— whatever *it* is. If I were you, Hans— if I were you, I would be curious about what I would learn if I traveled to Berlin. The whole *Weimar Journals* project was never about a book. The project was about you answering questions about yourself, your history, and what's going on in the world. I think you need to try to answer those questions, Hans. If I were you, I'd be making reservations to go to Berlin."

It was my turn to be speechless. She was coming at this much differently than I had anticipated.

Anne waited for some sort of response.

When I didn't offer one, she had more to say. "And I will be totally upfront with you. While I believe those things I just said about the value of a trip to Berlin, about it being important for you to understand what is going on in your dreams, I want to throw out one more idea. If you really want to figure out that dream (and all of the stuff behind it), you need to go ahead and finish your *Weimar Journals* book."

She looked at me. I could tell she was studying me—trying to gauge my reaction.

When I didn't give a reaction, or at least didn't think I had, she said, "I would love to take on Doc's role— be your project advisor. Completing that project represents a huge opportunity for you to reconcile a lot of things in your life. And I'll admit that my perspectives may be a bit selfish. I am intrigued with all the elements you shared with Doc— and with the rough drafts I have seen of what you have written— and now, add to all of that, I am intrigued with this dream."

She stopped speaking.

I waited a couple of minutes.

"Even if you leave this project dropped for good," she continued, "I would love the opportunity to read through your most recent draft of the book— if you would be willing to share a copy with me."

I had listened to her. I could almost hear Doc saying many of those same things to me. But when Doc offered me a suggestion, I never gave him an answer on the spot. And this morning, I sure as hell wasn't about to change that practice. I would think about what Anne had suggested. But my gut check was that I didn't like either idea. No. I didn't like them at all.

Anne continued, "I know I am not you, Hans. But if I were you, I would want to finish that project. That being said, I'm just throwing the idea for you to chew on. Maybe finishing the book isn't your cup of tea? But as far as going back to Berlin? I am certain you will not be satisfied with all you put into this project unless you find a way to pull it all together. And the best way I can think of to accomplish that is by making that journey to Berlin."

I took a deep breath and blew it out before saying anything. It was my turn to take some time in silence.

When I did respond, I began by saying, "You have confirmed that it was a good idea for me to call you up this morning, to meet with you to share my dream— and to ask for your thoughts."

I took a deep breath and said, "Your ideas about the trip to Berlin make sense. I might go. But I need to think about it a little bit more before reaching a final decision. As you may have figured out, I tend to make decisions slowly. But as far as finishing the book? Boy, Anne, did you catch me off guard on that one. I don't know. Yes, I have finished my garage and gotten my beautiful Fairlane running like a top. And yes, I am not sure what's next. And another *yes*, a lot is going on inside me that I don't understand. I will try to be open— I will try to digest your ideas— and I will also at least consider going back to the journal project."

I thought I had said enough. But Anne wanted more.

"And?" she said.

I chuckled before saying, "And I'll probably be able to tell you what I think in a couple of weeks. But right now, Anne? Right now, I just need to chew on what you've said— and on what I've dreamt. In any case, thank you. Your suggestions were thoughtful— and they are very much appreciated."

I paused and added, "Doc was fortunate to have you in his life."

We made small talk for a few more minutes before getting up and leaving the Electric City Coffee House.

As we walked out of the coffee shop, Anne asked, "How about coming over and having dinner at my place on the fifteenth? I make some pretty mean Wiener Schnitzel. If you are ready and willing, you can share your thoughts about going on an adventure to Berlin. And Hans, I also appreciate having you as a friend. I hope we can continue to get to know one another better."

2/8/2024— A Political Roundtable Discussion

This morning, the Coffee Roundtable had its first lengthy political discussion since January of 2021. I think that part of the reason why Ronnie hasn't put political conversations on the agenda is that once Doc passed away, the joy he found in having these debates was gone.

The other reason is that Trump's presidency ended in chaos and negativism. It seemed like MAGA was over— at least to some of us.

But now, the 2024 election is almost here. Trump has been able to resurrect his image, to portray himself— at least somewhat accurately— as being the constant target of the government machine. Trump has fought back. And Ronnie led off the discussion today by saying that it will play well to most Americans.

I have to admit that Trump has been resilient. He accused those who tried to prosecute him of being part of a plot to destroy America. Many Americans, including some from our Coffee Roundtable, think that statement is the absolute truth.

Jerry must have been listening to a lot of Trump's speeches. Hearing him talk about all of the evil people coming across the border was like listening to a Trump speech. But Jerry does have a point. Biden has done nothing to shut down the flow of illegal immigrants. And while unemployment is low, how long will it stay low if people keep flooding into our country?

Steve criticized Biden's blah-blah-blah on how good the economy is. Steve said that when he goes to the grocery store, he has to buy less food on each trip to stay within budget.

Tom told us that the amount he received when he sold his cattle hasn't increased. But, he said, the cost of feed, electricity, fuel, and almost every agricultural supply has. He said his farm is being squeezed out of business. He is tired of Biden telling him the economy is so good when it isn't. The Democrats, Tom said, are just out of touch.

Jack spoke angrily about how the federal government was doing everything they could to facilitate abortions. He told us that if we want to see abortions end, we are going to have to get the Democrats out of office.

Jim offered a different take. He spoke about how the communications between his tribe and the federal government have improved, and that the management of both health care and the amount of respect paid to Native Americans by the federal government have reached new highs.

Ronnie was pretty silent. I am not sure where that came from. It may be that he was haunted by Doc not being present.

No one in the group knew I had voted for Biden in 2020. I think Jim and Steve also voted for Biden. But since nobody asked how I voted, I decided it was better to just keep quiet.

Of course, as the discussion went on, I couldn't stop thinking about what Doc would be saying if he were with us.

We only talked politics for about twenty or thirty minutes. Energy at the table picked up when we started speaking about the Super Bowl. Ronnie said there was no way San Francisco could lose the Super Bowl. Lee Thomsen, who had been pretty quiet through the whole political discussion, told Ronnie he was full of shit. Kansas City would win.

As I walked home, I thought about all that had been said. I know Trump is volatile and a royal wild card. But Biden? He listens to himself too damn much. And at least Trump talks about real problems.

2/12/2024— Considering my Options

I've been thinking about the two suggestions Anne made after I described my nightmare to her. She recommended I take a trip to Berlin. Such a trip, she reasoned, would help me pull together my different emotions and thoughts. It would also give me a chance to confirm the historical notes I assembled while working on the *Weimar Journals*.

I'm feeling like that suggestion makes a lot of sense. In addition to giving me a chance to think through those elements, I've never been to Europe. The trip would be an exciting vacation even if it didn't result in any new insights into my dreams.

Her other suggestion— that I start working on the book again— is not so welcome. Working on *The Weimar Journals* was great when I was stuck in the emotional mud of being recently retired, losing my wife, and moving to a new city where I knew no one. It turned into a wonderful means of getting to know Doc. And when the isolation of COVID hit, it was a real lifesaver.

While I don't have a project to work on right now, I'm not sure I have the energy or desire to come back up to speed on all the pieces that fit into the book draft. Doc is gone, and while I have learned how important Anne was for my project, I'm not sure it would be appropriate for me to be working on writing a book with my dead friend's widow.

Anne invited me over for dinner this week. I will tell her I like the idea of going to Berlin, but that I am not ready to take on *The Weimar Journals* again.

Anne said she'd like to read through my most recent book draft. That's fair. I'll print a copy of *The Weimar Journals* for her— and I will probably print one off for myself as well.

2/16/2024— My Dinner with Anne

Yesterday, Anne had me over for dinner. I arrived at her place at about six. When she welcomed me at the door, I handed her the draft of *The Weimar Journals* and followed her into her large and impressive kitchen. I sat down on a barstool next to a kitchen island, and Anne poured each of us a glass of dry white wine. Then she turned to a large wooden cutting board and began to pound pieces of veal with a large wooden mallet.

After she finished pounding the small cuts of veal into thin pieces, she dipped each piece in flour, bathed it in an egg mixture, coated it with bread crumbs, and placed it onto a sizzling hot cast-iron skillet. This all brought back warm memories of Grandma fixing what used to be my favorite dinner.

While the Wiener Schnitzel sizzled in the pan, Anne dished up potato dumplings from a pot on her large gas range and removed a bowl of cucumber salad from the refrigerator. She finished up her meal prep by pouring brown gravy from a small pot into a blue and white pitcher.

Minutes later, we were sitting at her dining room table. I raised my glass of wine and said, "To Doc."

"To Doc," she repeated. We touched glasses.

The dinner was fabulous.

"You seem as skilled in fixing Wiener Schnitzel and dumplings as my grandma used to be. Where did you learn to cook in the *Deutschen stil?*" I asked.

Anne laughed and replied, "You aren't the only one who had a parent who immigrated from Germany. My mom left Stuttgart in 1932. That may be part of why I have found *The Weimar Journals* so fascinating.

"I'd like to hear more about that," I said.

She smiled and said, "I'll tell you about my mom someday."

As I ate, I thought about Doc and Anne. The two of them had been a couple for over forty years. I wondered how they'd met. I asked Anne.

She smiled before saying, "I had just been hired at the University Hospital— fresh out of nursing school. Doc was an intern. Each time I saw Doc, he'd start a conversation with me, asking questions like *What did I think of Nixon?* or *Did I like to hike in the mountains?* He always closed out our brief conversations by asking if I would go out on a date with him. I would give a brief response to each of his questions. Then I'd tell him something like, 'No, Doctor. Nursing happens to be my profession. I'm not here to participate in any dating games.'"

Anne took a sip of wine, savored it, and took a deep breath before continuing. "I had a little bit too much to drink at that year's University Hospital Christmas party. What can I say? The rest is history. We got married within a year in a civil ceremony. Our parents were aghast. But I guess it all turned out pretty good."

"I have you at a disadvantage, Hans. I've read your journals and know your history," she said with a smile. "I know it almost as well as I remember my own. Mary seemed like a wonderful person. It's tough losing someone who is that close to you, isn't it?"

I sighed and replied, "Yes. It is."

Anne changed the subject. "Now I think I did my part, I cooked you a good German meal. You said you needed time to respond to my suggestions. What are your thoughts?"

"I considered both of your suggestions," I replied. "One made a lot of sense. I've never been to Europe and always have been curious about Berlin— you know, family connections. And even without considering the book or my dreams, it makes a lot of sense for me to go to Berlin. It will be fascinating. I've made a reservation to go there in April. That serves to prove that I've got an open mind."

"OK," Anne said. "That sounds like you're giving me the good news. What's the bad news?"

I laughed. Anne was reading me like a book.

"You studied nursing, right?" I said.

"Yes," she responded. "With a minor in history."

"I didn't go to college," I replied. "Researching the Weimar Republic was a totally new experience. Analyzing the politics and history—present and past— turned out to be fascinating. It was satisfying going through my journals. The writing and research project turned into an excellent way to pass the time during COVID. And getting to know Doc was the best part of it all."

She said, "But?"

"But I don't see myself as a writer," I said. "I'm an auto mechanic who no longer has a job. I'll find some other project that's satisfying. But I'm not trained to be a writer and am not planning on getting trained."

Anne said, "Let me open another bottle of Moselle."

She didn't wait for my response. She just stood up, went into the kitchen, and returned a moment later with another bottle of wine.

As she removed the cork from the bottle and filled our glasses, she said, "I want to talk about some tangential stuff. I love shooting the breeze about philosophy, history, and questions about where we all fit into this world. After we've finished a couple more glasses of wine and exhausted discussions of history and the meaning of life, I'll try to talk you into working on the book. But before I do, I need to let you know that if you ever decide to change your mind— if you do become that writer— I want to be Doc's replacement advisor— your assistant on this project."

She took a sip of wine. I did the same. That wine was really good.

Anne continued, "I have a few questions for you, Hans— the philosophical ones I referenced."

I said, "OK. Shoot."

"What is your purpose in life?" she asked. "What is it you want to accomplish? Maybe, on a larger scale, what are human beings here to accomplish?"

She gave me an intense look, which I interpreted to mean she expected a serious answer.

"You're going to have to give me a minute to consider this," I replied.

I served myself another piece of Wiener Schnitzel, added a few more dumplings, and covered both with gravy.

As I ate, I pondered her questions. That minute I had asked for turned into more than five. During that time, Anne looked off across the room and didn't push me. We each finished our glass of wine while I was thinking. Anne refilled them.

"Okay," I said. "You asked me three questions. I will make a serious attempt to give you a thoughtful answer to each."

She nodded assent.

"Number one," I started, "what is the purpose of my life? I was tempted to say, *damned if I know*, but I think you would have challenged me on that. So, I am going to take a more constructive approach. My purpose in life is to touch and appreciate the fullness of the world around me— in any way that makes sense at the time— without hurting others— to the degree that's possible."

I looked up at her and waited to see if she was going to give me some sort of response to that.

She just said, "Go ahead. Answer all three. Afterwards, I'll tell you what I think."

"Okay," I said, "Time for number two. *What do I want to accomplish?* I think you asked me that already because my purpose in life and what I want to accomplish are probably the same. I want to accomplish my purpose in life. You probably want me to be more specific. I have the heart of a craftsman, Anne. During my career, people brought me machines— cars, trucks, and, after I entered the military, helicopters. I found satisfaction in doing a good job, in properly repairing and maintaining their transportation machines— doing it with quality and customer service. I enjoyed fixing up my '56 Ford. I may have been the owner, but making it run smoothly, having it look as good as it does— that satisfied me a lot. In fact, each of the projects I've worked on in my home— every single one of them— has given me satisfaction."

I looked up. Anne still gave me no response— positive or negative.

"My goal in life, Anne, was never to be rich," I continued, "and I have achieved that. I mean, I never got rich."

I chuckled. Anne just smirked.

"My goal," I went on, "wasn't to be powerful or popular. I've never defined myself by what other people think of me. I've always wanted to be honest. I won't deceive people, and I don't like seeing people be deceived. Working to pull that off— that has given my life meaning."

I paused. I knew this next question was the tough one.

"OK," I said, "I got this far. At least I have given you answers for your first two questions, more or less. But your third question. It's a humdinger. What are human beings here to accomplish? I don't know, Anne. I think sometimes people spend more time putting together standards for the human race than they do putting together standards for themselves. I use the word *standards* rather than *accomplishments* because an accomplishment is a subjective assessment rather than something that is achieved. I think human beings should define their success by how they behave rather than what they think they accomplish. Forgive me. This answer may contradict my other ones. But hey, I'm not a philosopher and I've just had several glasses of wine."

To prove my point, I drained my glass.

Then I continued. "I don't go to church anymore, Anne. I went to church much of my life, but I don't think it's ever really made a whole hell of a lot of sense to me. That may be a reflection more of how little I think of humanity than any disrespect for Jesus or what he stood for. I believe we should be our brother's keeper. But I'm not sure I've done much for other people. But at least I haven't done a lot *to* them. I've always felt that if everybody did fewer harmful things than they did good things, the world would be a better place."

I laughed and added, "Clearly, I'm in a minority in that regard."

I sighed and said, "So, there are my answers to your questions. They're answers from a person who does not see himself as being bigger than life— but who tries to retain some amount of integrity in his life."

I was sort of taken aback by how seriously and intensely I'd responded to her questions. No one had ever asked me anything like that before. But I could see she had been listening closely. Now that I was done speaking, Anne sat quietly. I began to get a little nervous. Maybe she thought I had either avoided her questions or just given stupid or arrogant answers. I waited for her response.

After sitting silently for a couple of minutes, instead of saying anything, Anne began to clear our dishes. That just made me even more nervous. I figured I must have really screwed up somehow. Except for going over to Jeannie's house, this had been the first time anyone had had me over for dinner in years. I was sitting at the table thinking that the people who hadn't invited me over must have been pretty damn smart.

After the plates were cleared, she brought in two small plates with apple pie and vanilla ice cream. I was stuffed. But who is going to argue with a desert like that!

The pie and ice cream were excellent.

Anne asked me if I wanted a cup of coffee. I told her yes— I would need that as I drove home.

The coffee was a good as everything else had been.

Then Anne responded to my long spiel. "Thank you, Hans, for your thoughtful responses to my questions. I understand why Doc used to say you have so much integrity. I think it is fantastic that you are going to Berlin. It will be meaningful— I'm willing to bet it will go beyond anything you anticipate. However, you shouldn't shut off the possibility of returning to your book. I'm going to go through the draft. As I do, I'll note ideas in the margins that I think you should consider— almost as if you had just told me you were going to go back to work on the project. For me, reviewing and editing your draft is something that can fill my days. I would not be surprised if, after returning from Berlin, you choose to return to the project. I hope so.

Please know that if you do, I would love to work on it with you."

We sat without words for a couple of minutes.

"How would you answer those three questions?" I asked.

"Foiled by my own ruse," she said with a chuckle. "What is my purpose in life? Right now, Hans, I am not so sure. Doc was such a visionary. He was able to create such a positive spin on each and every day. We participated in many community groups working for good causes. But now, the air is out of my tires— to use an auto mechanic's metaphor. I am having difficulty establishing a personal purpose— or, for that matter, identifying anything I want to accomplish. I think that is part of the reason I pushed you to go back to work on *The Weimar Journals*. In that project— and within the nuances of your characters— and I am talking about the characters from your letters and dreams who lived in the Weimar Republic— within the issues that they wrestled with were questions that will drive humanity either to ruin or allow the human race to continue. So, your answers were better than mine, Hans. You had answers that were real— answers with integrity. Right now, I don't have answers to those first two questions."

She paused for a minute. There was a penetrating quiet at the table.

Anne finally broke the silence. "As far as what I think human beings should accomplish? I believe— I know Doc believed— that human beings should work to alleviate the pain in the world— the hunger— and the hate. Right about now, I'm not so confident that human beings are doing so well by that standard. I like what you said about Jesus. I agree. While I was raised as a Jew, it is hard not to respect the statements attributed to Jesus. They get to the heart of the matter a whole lot more than most of the things said by those who claim to represent him."

"And Doc?" she said, "I think Doc would have answered all three questions with similar answers to yours. His purpose, his goal in life, was to assist other human beings."

She looked down at the table for a moment while putting her hands together, almost as if in prayer.

She sighed and continued. "And of that third question? I think Doc would have responded that each human's purpose may be to survive. But collectively, we should be working together— accountable to one another— responsible to improve the lives of less fortunate members of the broader human community."

The silence returned. It was quite comfortable.

I sat for a few more minutes before saying, "I should get going home now. The slush on the roads will have turned to ice. This evening has been wonderful, Anne; the meal fabulous; and I have so enjoyed getting to know you better. I look forward to growing our friendship. I'll get in touch with you in the next few days. We should have coffee again— soon. Thank you for a wonderful dinner and gracious company."

Anne showed me to the door, and I drove home.

3/19/2024— Coffee with Anne

Anne and I got together for a cup of coffee last week and had a pleasant time. We got together again this morning at Electric City for a cup of coffee and some conversation.

When I arrived, Anne was already seated with a cappuccino and chocolate croissant in front of her. After I'd ordered my latte and cinnamon roll and sat down at the table, Anne gave me a big smile and handed me the manuscript I'd given her the evening she fixed dinner. The pages were full of handwritten notes.

I thanked her for her edits and glanced at a couple of pages of her comments.

"I'll read through your edits this week," I said. "I read through the draft as well. It turned out to be more interesting than I anticipated. I was surprised how well the journal entries, notes, and letters fit together. But right now, Anne, I don't have what it would take to get back to work on *The Weimar Journals*. If I ever do, I promise to ask you for help."

"Just let me know," she replied, "when you are ready."

After that, I went over my plans for the trip to Berlin. Anne made a few suggestions of things I might want to see. She also offered to give me a ride to the airport for my departure.

I accepted.

4/22/2024— Exploring Berlin

I have now been in Berlin for three days. I'm pleased with my hotel in the old East Berlin. It is about five miles southeast of the city center.

I've been walking up and down Unter den Linden and becoming familiar with neighborhoods all over the city. Berlin is much more modern than I had imagined. But I realize my image of this city is based on century-old memories shared with me by my grandparents.

When I walk into a shop, people greet me in English. They have somehow figured out I'm from the US. When I respond to them in flawless German, they seem embarrassed and apologize. I don't tell them that they were right about where I'm from.

I wonder if they based their assumption that I'm an American on my bright blue jacket. Most Germans seem to wear dark jackets.

4/25/2024—Putting the Pieces Together

Before I left Great Falls, I created a list of places I wanted to find and things I wanted to learn about Ilse and the people I got to know in my dreams. The list is a little more than a page long, single-spaced. Over the past few days, I've focused on the list, checking off items as I go. What I am doing is a little like a scavenger hunt for places and personal connections. Each time I locate an item from the list, I learn information that affects other places and things I haven't yet found.

Since I organized my list by which person an object or place relates to, rather than by its probable location in Berlin, my list is totally arbitrary from a geographical perspective. As a result, I have been zig-zagging back and forth all over Berlin in a random pattern. Fortunately, I purchased a Berlin transit pass. Otherwise, I'd be worrying about the ticket cost for trams, trains, buses, and subways. With the pass, it all seems to be working out. I can get to any location in Berlin from any other spot in not more than two transit rides and a couple of ten-minute walks.

I am pleased with the progress I've made in putting the pieces of my puzzle together.

4/28/24 — Finding Ilse's Places

Using the return address from Ilse's early letters, I found the apartment in which she and Grandma grew up. It was also where Ilse first lived with Jürgen. The apartment is just a couple of miles toward the city center from my hotel. The plain-looking, five-story, stucco apartment building is in a working-class neighborhood.

A later letter's return address led me to the apartment Ilse and Jürgen moved into after Hitler became chancellor. The building is in the Prenzlauer Berg District. It is an elegant nineteenth-century brick apartment building with tall glass doors that open onto ornate balconies overlooking a quiet residential street. This apartment and its neighborhood obviously were huge improvements from where Ilse and Grandma had grown up.

I discovered that the many strip clubs and raunchy cabarets from a century ago are gone. That risqué area where Ilse was employed and Karl met Greta is now full of cafés, clothing stores, electronics shops, and busy young shoppers.

St. Nicholas Church, where Grandma's family attended mass, was bombed in 1944. After the war, Ilse wrote to Grandma that she worshipped at St. Nicholas until it was heavily damaged by Allied bombs. Ilse wrote that other Berlin Catholic Cathedrals suffered the same fate around the same time. She told Grandma in her letter that with no available options, she had begun to worship at a Protestant Church. Her comment to Grandma was, "I decided my prayers would end up going to the same God anyway."

I have no idea which Protestant Church Ilse attended. As a result, I can't locate any record about the priest who visited Ilse on her deathbed, and am unable to discover the location of the cemetery in which Ilse was buried.

That I can't visit Ilse's grave, say a prayer for her, and leave some flowers— those are the biggest disappointments of this trip.

4/30/2024 — Chasing Ghosts and Dreams

Today, I visited the large public square where, in 1933, Berlin's book burning took place. I imagined the raucous crowd cheering and shouting *Seig Heil* while university students and SS officers threw armfuls of scholarly works— twenty thousand in all— onto the raging bonfire. I read that most of those books had been taken from the shelves of the adjacent university library.

A group of tourists was gazing at a plaque not far from the center of the square. The plaque memorialized the horrid event by quoting the German author Heinrich Heine. In 1821, Heine wrote, "Where they burn books, they will in the end burn human beings."

As I watched tourists snapping photos around the square, it struck me how bizarre it was that a massive book burning had taken place in a square surrounded by Berlin's major Catholic church, its prestigious university library, and its cherished opera.

I tried to find the building in which Klaus' Office might have been located— that is, if Klaus had some basis beyond my dreams. Several nearby university buildings had professors' offices and broad staircases similar to the one in my dream. But no, I didn't locate a probable site for Professor Bauer's office.

Before coming to Berlin, I researched whether a synagogue on Prinzregenten Strasse had been destroyed on Kristallnacht, as I had dreamt. I learned that the Wilmersdorf Synagogue —in that District— was destroyed on that night. I went to the site of the synagogue, knowing that I would not find it but wanting to explore the area. Given my dream, if Karl and Greta were somehow real, their apartment would probably have been in that area. I saw many apartment buildings near there, but nothing struck a chord with my dreams.

So much of Berlin was destroyed by Allied bombing, it is difficult to know whether a building existed before World War II or was built after it. To illustrate, I know that the apartment that was located where the Wilmersdorf Synagogue once stood was built after the war. I learned from a website that the ruins of the synagogue were not removed until the 1950s. If not for that knowledge, I would have guessed that the apartment preceded the Weimar Republic.

After leaving Prinzregenten Strasse, I spent a couple of hours walking through the Tiergarten. As I walked, I imagined Karl and Greta having a happy picnic lunch in one of the beautiful meadows that I passed. The pleasant memory of that dream picnic brightened my day.

I did not know how to search for Klaus and Esther's Apartment. I had no frame of reference for where in Berlin they might have lived— if they really had lived. However, I may have accidentally found what could have been that apartment. While walking around Prenzler Berg, after finding Ilse and Jürgen's apartment, I came across a building that looked awfully similar to the one in which Greta and Karl had gone to see if her mother was alright.

What can I say? The building absolutely looked like the one from my dream. Am I just imagining that? Am I creating new impressions of what things looked like in past dreams? Maybe. Will the answer remain a mystery, one which I never solve? I am convinced I will never know if my dream-friends were real human beings who lived in Weimar Republic Berlin and somehow found a way into my dreams or whether they were just figments of my sleeping imagination.

Now, I can only shrug my shoulders as a response to this special personal mystery.

5/2/2024— A Visit to Sachsenhausen

Yesterday I visited the Sachsenhausen concentration camp. I had read Rick Steve's Guidebook description of the camp on the train. Based upon his advice, I did not sign up for a tour of the camp. That was a good thing.

I walked around the camp, lost in my thoughts, going through replicas of prisoner dormitories, seeing remnants of gas chambers and cremation facilities, reading descriptions and studying pictures of innocent human beings about to die.

Sachsenhausen is a chilling place to visit. Hundreds of thousands of human beings were imprisoned within its barbed-wire-capped walls. Tens of thousands of people died there. A far greater number were sent off from Sachsenhausen to be murdered elsewhere. But I couldn't stop thinking about four people I knew who probably never existed. Klaus, Esther, Karl, and Greta may have been a product of my dreams, but they feel real to me— as if they are my relatives who were murdered, for whom I am grieving.

I couldn't get my dream-friends out of my mind.

I learned that the guards at the camp were treacherous and cruel. One exhibit told how guards brought a few prisoners to the camp gas chambers that had also been fitted with water showers. Inside that chamber, the prisoners received hot showers. Then they were given clean clothes, a good meal, and returned to their barracks. The freshly clothed and fed prisoners told others in their barracks about their positive experience. Later, the others were sent naked into the chambers and told to wash themselves. Instead, they were asphyxiated with poison gas. Afterwards, their bodies were cremated. The Nazis were efficient and kept excellent records. They were also mean.

While walking the grounds of Sachsenhausen, I couldn't stop thinking about Jürgen— in whatever role he had in its development and operation. Jürgen may have died years before I was born. Yet I feel as if he is my personal enemy.

I did not expect to find any record of Karl, Greta, Klaus, or Esther. Before leaving Great Falls, I had searched for information about each of my dream-friends in online holocaust survivor and victim databases. But that didn't stop me from searching at Sachsenhausen.

On the train ride back to Berlin, my feeling at not finding any evidence that they had existed felt like the despair I experienced two months ago after the nightmare in which I searched in vain for Karl and Greta. It could be that I was just responding to all I had learned from the Sachsenhausen exhibits about other innocent people. But I felt lost.

What else should I have expected?

5/3/2024 — Coming to Grips with the Holocaust

During my stay in Berlin, I also played the tourist, visiting a variety of art and history museums. Today, however, was solemn— a response to Sachsenhausen and learning about extreme conditions and Nazi murders.

The day began with visits to several memorials located near the Brandenburg Gate. Two were in the Tiergarten— one was a remembrance of homosexuals persecuted by the Nazis. The second commemorated the hundreds of thousands of Roma peoples— Gypsies— who were murdered by the Nazis. A third memorial, across the street from the Tiergarten, was for the murdered Jews. An entire city block had been turned into a matrix of several thousand black, crypt-sized, concrete cubes.

During the half-hour walk that took me from this Jewish memorial to the Jewish Museum, I thought about how Hitler had led Germany into a world of atrocities. While I have read books about that terror, the facts of history are cold. Seeing a death camp, visiting memorials to millions of murdered people— that is different.

As I walked, I tried to understand people who hated other groups of humans so much that they wanted all of those individuals to be murdered, the groups annihilated.

I appreciate, however, that the German nation has fully accepted the reality of its atrocities, that Germany has memorialized its victims, and elevated its own horrid lessons for the world to absorb.

The Berlin Jewish Museum added to my perspective. It began by summarizing the history of Jews in Berlin. It went on to describe life among the Berlin Jewish community during the late nineteenth century and the first part of the twentieth century. The photos and descriptions told the stories of specific individuals who had made cultural, economic, and social contributions to Berlin, Germany, and the world. The museum then transitioned into telling the story of the growth of antisemitism in Berlin and how it turned into extreme repression. It went on to describe how the Berlin Jewish community was brutally destroyed— its members murdered.

Seeing all of this, after Sachsenhausen and the three memorials for murdered Germans, compounded my sense of horror. As I left the museum, I realized I could not possibly absorb the magnitude of what had been done to those who were not considered to be part of the Aryan race and to others who did not subscribe to the political opinions of the country's fascist dictator.

I thought about how I had once asked Grandpa what his issue was with the Jews. I recalled how angry he became. Grandpa told me that the Jews were devils— that they had backstabbed Germany, and had been part of the group that forced the surrender to the Allies and acceptance of the Treaty of Versailles. Grandpa, in his anger, refused to explain himself further.

I had just seen an exhibit that stated that one hundred thousand German Jews fought in the trenches during the Great War— alongside Grandpa. As I walked away from the Jewish Museum, I wondered what Grandpa's issue really had been. I wondered if maybe the Jews were just some sort of scapegoat— a group to blame for the bad things that had happened in and to Germany. I wondered how many people who participated in those atrocities just needed someone to blame for the pain in their lives. When Hitler offered such a scapegoat, they jumped at the opportunity.

I remembered Anne's comment about her mother. Anne said her mother left Stuttgart in 1932— but that she could tell me that story another time. I assume Anne's mother was Jewish. What is her mother's story? Did she lose loved ones? When I get back from Berlin, I will ask Anne.

All of these things were whirling around in my head this afternoon, as I walked through Berlin. Many questions— and no real answers.

5/3/2024— The Flight Home from Berlin

I'm on the flight home from Berlin. The trip accomplished what I had intended. But I am tired. It will take time to soak it all in.

Yesterday, I went to the largest department store on the European continent. It was big, beautiful, and expensive. I enjoyed walking through the store. But the only thing I purchased was a cappuccino and an almond pastry. Afterwards, as I walked towards the nearby Berlin Zoo, I saw the damaged skeleton of a church tower. I turned and walked toward it.

I learned that the tower was part of the Kaiser Wilhelm Church, which was completed in 1893. The church was heavily damaged fifty years later by Allied bombs. The damaged church tower was left as a monument— a memorial against war and destruction. The recast main bell of the church has an engraved quote from Isaiah— "Your cities are burned with fire: But my salvation shall be forever and my righteousness from generation to generation."

A new Kaiser Wilhelm Church was completed in 1963 next to the original church tower. I entered this modern replacement and took a seat. Music was coming from the church's massive pipe organ. A program told me I was listening to a Bach Cantata.

I hadn't prayed in a church for years. But as I sat listening to the beautiful German music, I said a silent prayer for Karl and Greta, and for her parents, and for Ilse, and for all the victims of Nazi violence. I prayed for Jews, Catholics, Protestants, Gypsies, atheists, Russian Orthodox, and all of the others whose lives had been destroyed. To which God was I praying? What was I praying for? I don't know.

Berlin is my heritage. Grandpa, Grandma, and my father came to America from this city. I realized that while I do want to understand my family's history, I came here to learn about four friends— people who never existed.

I haven't had any more dreams about Greta, Karl, Esther, or Klaus. Now that I have been to Berlin, I don't think I will. Their stories may not have been real. But I have come to understand that these four symbolize people who were real, millions of people who were all murdered.

The Weimar Journals? Am I going to go back to work on the book? Surprisingly, I think I will— if only to digest what I experienced over the past few days.

And America? How has my journey through Berlin affected my perception of the anger that exists between citizens in my own country? Have I learned anything by seeing what happened to the Weimar Republic? Have I seen things that will help me understand what is happening today in the United States?

Only time will tell.

I am tired. I think I will just close my eyes and go to sleep.

5/6/2024— Debrief with Anne

Anne picked me up two days ago at the airport after my return flight from Berlin. She asked how the trip had gone. I told her it had been great, but intense, that I wanted to take some time digesting everything I saw and felt before summarizing it for her. I suggested we get together in a couple of days for coffee. I would tell her more about the trip then.

She said she totally understood. I think she could see how tired I was.

This morning, we got together at the Electric City Coffee shop. It was sunny, but I chose not to walk. I drove over in my cherried-out, '56 Ford Fairlane. After spending two weeks seeing evidence of humanity's inability to be humane, driving my car was a break. It reminded me of how much I enjoy working with my hands.

As we sat sipping our coffee drinks and enjoying our pastries in silence, I thought about how nice it was to be back in Great Falls— to be home again. And it felt good to be able to call Great Falls home.

After a few minutes, Anne asked, "Well, how was it?"

I spent half an hour recapping the details of the trip— day by day. Yesterday, when Jeannie had me over for dinner, I told her about the trip. But I found speaking with Anne to be a great deal more satisfying. She understood what was driving me.

After I had completed telling her about it, she asked, "Was it worth it?"

"Yes, it definitely was," I replied. "I appreciated the food, the architecture, and the mood of the city. I was constantly reminded of things I learned over the past few years about the Weimar Republic. There were so many customs and other nuances that reminded me of my grandparents."

I paused, and I think I smiled a little bit before saying, "I know what you want to hear about. You want me to tell you how the trip impacted my willingness to go back to work on *The Weimar Journals* again."

Anne returned my smile and nodded *yes*.

"On the trip," I said, "I learned how essential the City of Berlin is to who I am. Being there put me in touch with my family's history— and my Berlin dreams, which are, I understand now, a reflection of that history."

"To answer your next question," I said after a pause, "I'm ready to go back to work on the *Weimar Journals*. However, I know I need your assistance. Let's get together next week. By then, I will have gone through your edits. We can talk about next steps. It's time for me to finish this project. It's been fascinating, but I need to complete it. I definitely don't want to drag it into the next election."

Anne replied, "Let's do it."

7/7/2024— Bison Coffee Roundtable Meeting

The Coffee Roundtable had its regular get-together this morning.

Ronnie phoned each of us earlier in the week, letting us know we would share our thoughts about the upcoming presidential election. He suggested we might want to make notes in advance about what we like and don't like about Trump and Biden. His call told me that Ronnie is excited that Donald Trump might be returning to office.

This morning, everyone was there on time except for Jack Riley. We waited to start the discussion until Jack arrived. Jerry updated us on how well the Great Falls Voyagers, our city's minor league baseball team, is doing this season. I can summarize what he told us in five words. They are not doing well.

Lee told us about his softball team, which won a state-wide tournament last weekend. Lee was teased because he is more than a little overweight. Jerry asked him how he could play the game with his girth. Did his teammates move him around the bases in a wheelbarrow? Lee countered that his softball team was doing a hell of a lot better than the Voyagers. There was a lot of laughter.

Jack finally arrived— on crutches. He told us his granddaughter's dog had jumped at him after a firecracker went off on the fourth. Jack tripped, fell, and broke a leg. He was teased about his injury, but took it well.

Ronnie kicked off the political discussion. "It looks like we're going to have a rematch of 2020 in 2024. I'm sure you all watched the debate on June 27th. I don't want to bias anyone's conclusions about who won. So, I'll hold off on stating my thoughts until we've gone around the table. Needless to say, I'm feeling pretty positive. But let's go ahead and hear everyone's perspectives."

Everyone had an opinion. Below is an abbreviated recap of the comments.

Tom spoke first. "You said it all, Ronnie. Trump cleaned Sleepy Joe's clock in that first election. But the Democrats stole it. This one? I don't think it's even going to be close. Biden has screwed up everything in the economy, and he showed up at the debate not knowing who was on first. There is really only one candidate— and one moron. Trump recognizes how hard it is for us with prices up by 22% in the last four years. He has promised to cut inflation and will make groceries affordable. I could go on forever, but I don't want to steal everyone else's thunder."

Steve went next. "The debate was awful. Two old men— a selfish con-artist who may be slightly nuts and an old man who should have retired ten years ago. Given these are the choices, I have to ask myself if we have to pick one, who will do less harm? Do I want the guy who rewarded the wealthy with tax cuts, or is it time to make the wealthy pay their fair share? In spite of the fact that Biden acted older than my great-grandpa, he did get our economy through COVID, and our economy is doing better than any other one in the world. I'm sticking with Biden— even though I agree— his debate performance was a total embarrassment."

"OK, it's my turn in the barrel," said Jerry. "I don't see how we have a choice. Biden created the COVID mess by shutting down the economy. He created the mask mandate and disrupted everything else. Meanwhile, he didn't do a damn thing about the border. Woke Democrats have allowed terrorists and criminals into the country for too long. Meanwhile, inflation's killing us. Trump has promised to deal with all of these things. His tariffs will force China and other countries that have been ripping us off for years to pay the piper, and he'll end the wars in Ukraine and Gaza."

Jack took his turn. "Trump listens to the Christian majority," he said, "and deserves credit for creating a Supreme Court majority that ended Roe versus Wade. Doing that was worth my vote right there. Biden may be a practicing Christian, but he has pushed laws that allow the taking of lives of unborn children. Our pastor told us Biden's administration even allows abortions in the ninth month of a mother's pregnancy! That is murder. I don't see how we Christians have a choice. It has to be Trump."

Lee looked down and slowly shook his head from side to side. "The reason that countries don't respect us is because we are patsies. Trump is tough. The Ukraine war would never have happened if Trump had been president. He and Putin would have worked it out. And even if there was a war, Europe should be footing the bill. If Trump wins, he promises to end the Gaza war immediately. And this Black Lives Matter thing? All of the double standards favor people of color. I believe in equality for all. But the Dems bend over backwards too much to help one group, and they end up screwing the others. We need Trump."

Jim took a big breath before speaking. After slowly letting it out, he said, "I've listened to everyone's comments this morning. Before I speak to the candidates, I just want to make an observation. We've discussed this stuff before, and it always seems like we end up talking past one another. Sure, we respect one another— as old friends. But we don't do a whole lot of listening to one another when we discuss politics. And as a result, I think we don't even think things through. We get lost in slogans. We liken them to facts— or to history. That's just a general comment before I talk about the candidates."

I think that Jim's comments lowered some of the intensity around the table. No one seemed put off by them, and I saw several people nodding in agreement.

Jim continued. "One of the things I liked about Biden was that he always tried to be positive. I think he really cares about people. I agree he is beginning to lose it— I mean, old age has caught up with him. He should've retired. But Trump is so full of anger. That's what drives him. I hope I don't have to put up with four more years of Trump's anger."

Jim paused before saying, "As far as treatment of people of color? It is important to me. Trump gets support from the Proud Boys— and it seems, from all of the other racist groups. You all know I am Chippewa. I don't make a big thing out of that. But some people do make a big thing out of it— often in a manner that is not full of respect. People who tend to have negative attitudes toward Indians— and toward other persons of color— they endorse Trump. I wish all Americans were just more respectful to one another generally, including to members of Tribes. If Trump is elected, I believe we are in trouble."

Jim looked around the table for a second, then said, "That's all I have to say."

It was my turn. I'd given a lot of thought to what I would say. I realized I hadn't told the Coffee Roundtable how I voted in the last election. I'd kept that to myself— partly because I knew how most of the others felt. After

Ronnie gave me a heads-up about today's discussion, I thought about how Doc wasn't going to be there to share his thoughts. I recalled the things Doc had shared with me before the 2020 election.

Before we went to bed last night, I told Anne I wasn't sure what I would say today. She suggested I reread my journal entries from before the 2020 election. I did. I also read my journal entries about the January 6th coup attempt. I considered how coldhearted and dishonest Trump had been leading up to the sixth and how he has acted ever since. I decided I owed it to Doc to be up front with the others in the Roundtable.

I also thought about Karl and Greta. I decided it didn't make any difference whether they were figments of my imagination or real people. Even if they are imaginary, the principles were the same. They represent real people who were murdered because of a megalomaniac's lack of moral compass.

I realized the other members of the Coffee Roundtable would share their honest feelings with me. It was time for me to be that straightforward with them.

So, I went for it.

"This morning, my thoughts are with a person who is not here," I said softly, "someone who has been an important part of our past political discussions. Of course, I'm talking about Doc. I miss him so much. I learned a lot from him. My understanding of politics— and about Trump— has changed over the past decade. I give Doc a bunch of credit for that. I need to start out by saying that in Doc's honor, I am going to be more upfront about my feelings on the election than I was four years ago."

There was silence at the table. I could see that the others were glued to what I was saying.

"My grandparents and father came to Montana in 1922 from Berlin— back when Germany was called the Weimar Republic. I had never really understood what the Weimar Republic was or how Hitler was able to get into power. Doc suggested I study the Weimar Republic. Later, he suggested I work on assembling a book driven by my journal entries about my German roots."

Everyone was paying a lot of attention to my words, and I was a little uncertain about what I was going to say. But I realized, it was now or never.

"During the decade and a half of the Weimar Republic," I continued, "Germany faced huge economic and social challenges— issues that preceded the democratic republic's formation. Germans disagreed on how to approach those challenges. Hitler effectively manipulated one group after another. He used lies, threats, violence, and blamed the problems of Germany on those who were vulnerable. Hitler's propaganda machine was effective. Through it, he made promises to anyone who would listen— often with no intent to follow through on those promises. Hitler told the people of Germany what they wanted to hear— and many thoughtlessly accepted what they heard.

"Once Adolph Hitler became the German chancellor, he used his authority to repress anyone who challenged him. He blamed every problem on whoever was handy— even the problems he had created— sometimes on purpose. Some Germans saw the threat and recognized the lies. But Hitler effectively attacked each person or group that stood in his way. He didn't hesitate to use violence if doing so would increase his power.

"So how does this relate to our upcoming election? In the same breath that I condemn Hitler, I fear Trump. He is dishonest and totally corrupt. He will do whatever he can to pursue power and wealth— and to massage his own fragile ego. When Trump was running his businesses, he cheated his subcontractors and customers all the time— and his businesses still went bankrupt. Everybody knows that. And they know Trump cheated on his income taxes. He refused to accept the results of the election he lost. When his supporters (encouraged by him) stormed the Capitol in an attempted coup, when they threatened his vice president, Trump did nothing to stop them. He cheated on every one of his wives, molested women, and never hesitated to throw his old chums under the bus. In his first term, he showed us how he stood against a free press. If he is elected again, media that don't grovel to him will be repressed, as will anyone who disagrees with him. What I don't understand is how you can trust such a person? Trump's only skill— and he is good at it— is as a master manipulator.

"After all I learned about the Weimar Republic, after watching Trump over the past decade, I will vote for Biden. He did an OK job in his first term— some things he did well, other things not so well. He's definitely too old now and shouldn't be running for president. However, there is no alternative. That's how I see it."

Once I had finished speaking, there was a silence around the table. I was embarrassed. I don't think I had ever spoken about politics that passionately. I'd gone on and on. But I'd meant every word I'd said, and I know Doc would have approved.

It was Ronnie's turn to share his perspectives on the election. He went on for almost as long as I did and spoke just as passionately. I didn't take notes on each thing he said because I was still stunned by how much I had said. However, I can summarize his comments.

Ronnie supports Trump because Trump will help regular guys take on the bureaucrats in Washington. He will stop the criminals from pouring across our borders, and he will end all of the wars. He will reduce the cost of groceries, end inflation, and reduce taxes. Ronnie elaborated on how much Democrats depend on fake news, hoaxes, woke opinions, and political correctness to manipulate honest Americans. He concluded by saying that 2024 was our opportunity to make America great again. He hoped all of us understood that.

And that was it. The conversation transitioned into predictions for the upcoming NFL season. Would the Kansas City Chiefs win it all?

As we made our way out the door, Jim Cooper walked next to me and said quietly, "Thanks, Hans. Doc would have appreciated that."

7/15/2024— A Time for Completion

My father and grandfather taught me skills that allowed me to become a machinist. They always stressed the importance of setting high standards for quality— and for completing a task. I've always taken pride in my ability to embrace those teachings.

After I entered the military, I was often assigned my unit's most complex technical repair challenges. My sergeant had confidence I would do the job well and get it done. When given an unusual challenge, I studied it, researched possible approaches, identified alternative solutions, put together a plan, initiated the repair, and stayed with the project until it was complete.

Completing a project well means walking away from it with confidence that you have done the best you can. After that, you can move on to whatever new challenges emerge.

That was the approach I took during my career in automobile repair, first as a mechanic and later as an owner and operator of the family service station. When I retired, I was proud of how well I had done my job. I have never had to look back in shame.

After I moved to Great Falls, I remodeled and renovated a one-hundred-year-old home, built a garage, and restored a 1956 Ford Fairlane. Each of these projects required planning, thorough execution, and, upon completion, allowed me to walk away with a sense of satisfaction.

Doc encouraged me to combine a series of personal journal entries with a collection of letters from my grandma's sister and to research what happened in and to the Weimar Republic. I dropped the project after Doc passed away. But his widow convinced me I should complete it. She was right to do that. My grandpa and dad would have approved.

I am neither an intellectual nor a writer. But once I take on a project, I try to utilize those same standards for quality and completion that my father and grandfather taught me. With Anne's assistance, significant editing, and encouragement, I have completed *The Weimar Journals* to the best of my ability.

It is now time for conclusion.

This project has been an enormous growing process for me. I have been fascinated by what I have learned about the Weimar Republic in the 1920s and 1930s and surprised by the insight its challenges have given me into the United States.

Whether our country will avoid the sorts of severe outcomes the Weimar Republic encountered is something I cannot predict. I can only hope that the citizens of the United States will select leaders who have the wisdom to focus upon bringing us together rather than separating us and the skills and courage to recognize and take on the major challenges we face.

Notes:

Note 1: Dr. John J. Neumaier delivered this address on November 10, 1993, in remembrance of Kristallnacht. The speech was delivered at the Rockland Center for Holocaust Studies in Suffern, NY. Neumaier was born in Frankfurt, Germany in 1921 and passed away in 2016. Dr. Neumaier is the author's father.

Note 2: Bibliography: The following books were utilized in the research for this book and represent sources of information for anyone wishing to read further about the Weimar Republic.

a. *Before the Deluge, A Portrait of Berlin in the 1920s*; by Otto Freidrich; 1995; Published by Harper Collins

b. *The Rise and Fall of the Third Reich, A History of Nazi Germany* by William L. Shirer; 1959; Published by Simon and Shuster, Inc.

c. *Voluptuous Panic, The Erotic World of Weimar Berlin*; by Mel Gordon; 2008; Published by Feral House

d. *Weimar Germany*; by Eric D. Weitz; 2007; Published by Princeton University Press

e. *The Weimar Republic, The Crisis of Classical Modernity*; by Detlev J. K. Peukert; Translated by Richard Deveson; 1987; Published by Hill and Wang

f. *Life Under Nazi Occupation, The Struggle to Survive During World War II;* by Paul Roland; 1956; Published by Arcturus Holdings, Ltd.

g. *Crooked Cross;* by Sally Carson; 1930; Published by Persephone Books, Ltd.

h. *Weimar Culture, The Outsider as Insider*; by Peter Gay; 1968; Published by W. W. Norton and Company